DARK INTEGERS
AND
OTHER STORIES

DARK INTEGERS
AND
OTHER STORIES

~w~

GREG EGAN

Far Territories 2009

Trade Paperback

ISBN

978-1-59606-219-1

Far Territories
PO Box 190106
Burton, MI 48519

TABLE OF CONTENTS

INTRODUCTION

Two of the stories in this collection, "Luminous" and "Dark Integers", deal with the idea that the mathematics of ordinary numbers might be *malleable*. At first glance this notion seems comically surreal: what could be more solid, timeless and universal than the facts of arithmetic? Human languages and social customs vary from place to place and time to time. Many aspects of biology will probably be radically different on other worlds. The strengths of fundamental forces, the masses of elementary particles, and perhaps even the number of dimensions of space, might turn out to be local quirks of our patch of the universe. But although the particular language, symbols, and medium used to express a simple fact about numbers can vary wildly, it seems inconceivable that in any epoch, or any corner of the universe, the underlying facts could be different from those with which we're familiar.

So, without giving away too much about the stories themselves, I'd like to sketch some of the context for this idea and explain why I believe that it's not quite as crazy as it sounds. There is a sense in which malleable mathematics would slot neatly into a perfectly respectable intellectual lineage, and while that proves nothing whatsoever about reality, I think it lifts the idea above pure whimsy to the point where it merits at least a temporary, science-fictional suspension of disbelief.

We live in an age when Einstein is a far more famous name than Euclid, and people are more likely to have heard of the concept of curved space-time than the axioms of classical geometry, so it's worth recalling that the eighteenth-century philosopher Immanuel Kant could confidently assert that Euclidean geometry — in which a unique straight line joins any two points, and the angles of a triangle always sum to one hundred and eighty degrees — was the only logical possibility for the rules that govern the space we inhabit. Not long afterward, Gauss, Lobachevsky and Riemann demonstrated that other kinds of geometry were conceivable, at least as self-consistent mathematical abstractions, but it was only in the early twentieth century that Einstein realized that the best way to understand gravity was to accept that the geometry of the real world was not only non-Euclidean, it actually varied from place to place and time to time.

Gravity isn't exactly an obscure phenomenon, so how could we have been blind to such an extraordinary fact for so long? The geometry of a small region of mildly curved space is difficult to distinguish from Euclidean geometry, but our everyday experience actually probes some very large regions, not of space, but of *space-time.* If you toss a ball straight up into the air fast enough for it to remain aloft for two seconds, it will rise to a height of just under five meters. In the natural way of comparing spans of time to those of space, two seconds corresponds to a distance of six hundred thousand kilometers; that's how far light would travel in the same period. Over six hundred thousand kilometers, the subtly curved geometry due to the mass of the Earth is enough to ensure that the ball returns to your hand. This is a very small effect — one part in one hundred and twenty million! — but it's easy to observe because everyday objects move so slowly compared to the speed of light.

Of course, the fact that we live in a non-Euclidean universe doesn't render Euclidean geometry meaningless; all the theorems that follow from Euclid's axioms still stand, in the appropriate context. Although these axioms are not obeyed precisely by any real objects, they still serve both as an excellent approximation for many purposes, and as an unblemished abstraction in their own right. Our brains might be immersed in a particular region of mildly curved space-time, but we are still perfectly capable of reasoning about other situations, whether it's the wildly fluctuating geometry around two colliding black holes, or the perfectly flat, homogeneous space envisaged by Euclid.

Quantum mechanics has also changed our view of how certain idealized concepts connect with the real world. A classical logician will tell you that for any meaningful claim you make about the world, either it will be true, or its negation will be: either a spinning ball will have its axis of spin aligned due north, or it won't. But assuming that the same logic holds for the spin of a photon or electron will lead you to make predictions that differ from those of quantum mechanics, and the experimental evidence comes down firmly on the side of QM.

Once again, though, we seem to be able to cope with this divide. Despite being governed at its deepest level by quantum processes, our brain acts as a classical system; Roger Penrose famously disputes this, but most physicists and neuroscientists do not, and in any case nobody doubts that we're capable of understanding both classical and quantum logic.

The third strand in this history is a little more recent, though its most basic insights predate even Euclid. Over the last fifty years, a branch of mathematics that goes by the uninspiring name of "category theory" has emphasized the fact that a mathematical equation is really just shorthand for an entire *process* that establishes the equation's truth.

To take a simple example, when we claim that "two times three equals four plus two", what we really mean is that we can form sets of objects that represent the two sides of our equation, and then match up their contents. If you hand me a set A with two elements, such as {king, queen}, and a set B with three elements, such as {hearts, clubs, diamonds}, then I can "multiply two times three" by forming the set of all ways of pairing elements of A and B: {king of hearts, king of clubs, king of diamonds, queen of hearts, queen of clubs, queen of diamonds}. And if you hand me a set C with four elements, such as {John, Paul, George, Ringo}, and a set D with two elements, such as {Patty, Selma}, I can "add four and two" by forming the set which contains everything from C and everything from D: {John, Paul, George, Ringo, Patty, Selma}. Finally, I can prove the original equation by showing that I can deal all the cards from "A times B" to all the people in "C plus D", so that everybody gets exactly one card, and there are none left over.

Of course, my choice of sets that turn the proof into a kind of English-language story isn't really necessary; sets of nonsense words or abstract symbols would have served just as well. (You might have noticed that our definition of addition would be in trouble if the sets we added had any elements in common, but there are simple formal tricks to get around that.) However, the reason basic arithmetic was invented in the first place is that it *does* work when the sets consist of real, physical objects. "Two times three equals four plus two" is a shorthand description for what we think would happen if we carried out certain physical processes.

Could these processes ever cease behaving in the usual way? It's very hard to imagine them doing so, but then three hundred years ago it was hard to imagine a geometry in which two points could be joined by more than one straight line, or that carrying a direction around a loop could change it so that it no longer agreed with its original orientation.

The geometry of space-time is certainly not determined by some timeless book of geometric rules; it is determined by the geometry of *other space-time* — recent and nearby — just as the shape, at any moment, of a drum head or violin string depends on its shape the moment before. I suspect that all of physics is ultimately like this: there are no rules standing aloof from space, time and matter that dictate what happens across the whole universe; rather, every tiny patch of space-time carries everything it needs within it, and all it can do is listen to its neighbors and pass its own advice on down the line.

Could this ever mean that simple, discrete objects being shuffled from place to place might cease to obey what we've come to think of as the universal rules of arithmetic? And if it did, how would our brains, and our computers, respond to that change? We can contemplate any geometry we like in the mildly curved space-time near the surface of the

Earth, but how much non-standard arithmetic could we tolerate before we stopped thinking about anything at all?

I don't pretend to have certain answers to any of these questions, but I hope you'll suspend your disbelief long enough to enjoy the speculations in "Luminous" and "Dark Integers".

Greg Egan
October 2007

LUMINOUS

woke, disorientated, unsure why. I knew I was lying on the narrow, lumpy single bed in Room 22 of the Hotel Fleapit; after almost a month in Shanghai, the topography of the mattress was depressingly familiar. But there was something wrong with the way I was lying; every muscle in my neck and shoulders was protesting that nobody could end up in this position from natural causes, however badly they'd slept.

And I could smell blood.

I opened my eyes. A woman I'd never seen before was kneeling over me, slicing into my left triceps with a disposable scalpel. I was lying on my side, facing the wall, one hand and one ankle cuffed to the head and foot of the bed.

Something cut short the surge of visceral panic before I could start stupidly thrashing about, instinctively trying to break free. Maybe an even more ancient response—catatonia in the face of danger—took on the adrenaline and won. Or maybe I just decided that I had no right to panic when I'd been expecting something like this for weeks.

I spoke softly, in English. "What you're in the process of hacking out of me is a necrotrap. One heartbeat without oxygenated blood, and the cargo gets fried."

My amateur surgeon was compact, muscular, with short black hair. Not Chinese; Indonesian, maybe. If she was surprised that I'd woken prematurely, she didn't show it. The gene-tailored hepatocytes I'd acquired in Hanoi could degrade almost anything from morphine to curare; it was a good thing the local anesthetic was beyond their reach.

Without taking her eyes off her work, she said, "Look on the table next to the bed."

I twisted my head around. She'd set up a loop of plastic tubing full of blood—mine, presumably—circulated and aerated by a small pump. The stem of a large funnel fed into the loop, the intersection controlled by a valve of some kind. Wires trailed from the pump to a sensor taped to the inside of my elbow, synchronizing the artificial pulse with the real. I had no doubt that she could tear the trap from my vein and insert it into this substitute without missing a beat.

I cleared my throat and swallowed. "Not good enough. The trap knows my blood pressure profile exactly. A generic heartbeat won't fool it."

"You're bluffing." But she hesitated, scalpel raised. The hand-held MRI scanner she'd used to find the trap would have revealed its basic configuration, but few fine details of the engineering—and nothing at all about the software.

"I'm telling you the truth." I looked her squarely in the eye, which wasn't easy given our awkward geometry. "It's new, it's Swedish. You anchor it in a vein forty-eight hours in advance, put yourself through a range of typical activities so it can memorize the rhythms...then you inject the cargo into the trap. Simple, foolproof, effective." Blood trickled down across my chest onto the sheet. I was suddenly very glad that I hadn't buried the thing deeper, after all.

"So how do you retrieve the cargo, yourself?"

"That would be telling."

"Then tell me now, and save yourself some trouble." She rotated the scalpel between thumb and forefinger impatiently. My skin did a cold burn all over, nerve ends jangling, capillaries closing down as blood dived for cover.

I said, "*Trouble* gives me hypertension."

She smiled down at me thinly, conceding the stalemate—then peeled off one stained surgical glove, took out her notepad, and made a call to a medical equipment supplier. She listed some devices which would get around the problem—a blood pressure probe, a more sophisticated pump, a suitable computerized interface—arguing heatedly in fluent Mandarin to extract a promise of a speedy delivery. Then she put down the notepad and placed her ungloved hand on my shoulder.

"You can relax now. We won't have long to wait."

I squirmed, as if angrily shrugging off her hand—and succeeded in getting some blood on her skin. She didn't say a word, but she must have realized at once how careless she'd been; she climbed off the bed and headed for the washbasin, and I heard the water running.

Then she started retching.

I called out cheerfully, "Let me know when you're ready for the antidote."

I heard her approach, and I turned to face her. She was ashen, her face contorted with nausea, eyes and nose streaming mucus and tears.

"Tell me where it is!"

"Uncuff me, and I'll get it for you."

"No! No deals!"

"Fine. Then you'd better start looking, yourself."

She picked up the scalpel and brandished it in my face. "Screw the cargo. *I'll do it!*" She was shivering like a feverish child, uselessly trying to stem the flood from her nostrils with the back of her hand.

I said coldly, "If you cut me again, you'll lose more than the cargo."

She turned away and vomited; it was thin and gray, blood-streaked. The toxin was persuading cells in her stomach lining to commit suicide *en masse.*

"Uncuff me. It'll kill you. It doesn't take long."

She wiped her mouth, steeled herself, made as if to speak—then started puking again. I knew, first-hand, exactly how bad she was feeling. Keeping it down was like trying to swallow a mixture of shit and sulphuric acid. Bringing it up was like evisceration.

I said, "In thirty seconds, you'll be too weak to help yourself—even if I told you where to look. So if I'm not free…"

She produced a gun and a set of keys, uncuffed me, then stood by the foot of the bed, shaking badly but keeping me targeted. I dressed quickly, ignoring her threats, bandaging my arm with a miraculously spare clean sock before putting on a T-shirt and a jacket. She sagged to her knees, still aiming the gun more or less in my direction—but her eyes were swollen half-shut, and brimming with yellow fluid. I thought about trying to disarm her, but it didn't seem worth the risk.

I packed my remaining clothes, then glanced around the room as if I might have left something behind. But everything that really mattered was in my veins; Alison had taught me that that was the only way to travel.

I turned to the burglar. "There is no antidote. But the toxin won't kill you. You'll just wish it would, for the next twelve hours. Goodbye."

As I headed for the door, hairs rose suddenly on the back of my neck. It occurred to me that she might not take me at my word—and might fire a parting shot, believing she had nothing to lose.

Turning the handle, without looking back, I said, "But if you come after me—next time, I'll kill you."

That was a lie, but it seemed to do the trick. As I pulled the door shut behind me, I heard her drop the gun and start vomiting again.

Halfway down the stairs, the euphoria of escape began to give way to a bleaker perspective. If one careless bounty hunter could find me, her more methodical colleagues couldn't be far behind. Industrial Algebra were closing in on us. If Alison didn't gain access to Luminous soon, we'd have no choice but to destroy the map. And even that would only be buying time.

I paid the desk clerk for the room until the next morning, stressing that my companion should not be disturbed, and added a suitable tip to compensate for the mess the cleaners would find. The toxin denatured in air; the bloodstains would be harmless in a matter of hours. The clerk eyed me suspiciously, but said nothing.

Outside, it was a mild, cloudless summer morning. It was barely six o'clock, but Kongjiang Lu was already crowded with pedestrians, cyclists, buses—and a few ostentatious chauffeured limousines, ploughing through the traffic at about ten kph. It looked like the night shift had just emerged from the Intel factory down the road; most of the passing cyclists were wearing the orange, logo-emblazoned overalls.

Two blocks from the hotel I stopped dead, my legs almost giving way beneath me. It wasn't just shock—a delayed reaction, a belated acceptance of how close I'd come to being slaughtered. The burglar's clinical violence was chilling enough—but what it implied was infinitely more disturbing.

Industrial Algebra were paying big money, violating international law, taking serious risks with their corporate and personal futures. The arcane abstraction of the defect was being dragged into the world of blood and dust, boardrooms and assassins, power and pragmatism.

And the closest thing to certainty humanity had ever known was in danger of dissolving into quicksand.

∿

IT HAD all started out as a joke. Argument for argument's sake. Alison and her infuriating heresies.

"A mathematical theorem," she'd proclaimed, "only becomes true when a physical system tests it out: when the system's behavior depends in some way on the theorem being *true* or *false*."

It was June, 1994. We were sitting in a small paved courtyard, having just emerged yawning and blinking into the winter sunlight from the final lecture in a one-semester course on the philosophy of mathematics—a bit of light relief from the hard grind of the real stuff. We had fifteen minutes to kill before meeting some friends for lunch. It was a social conversation—verging on mild flirtation—nothing more. Maybe there were demented academics lurking in dark crypts somewhere, who held views on the nature of mathematical truth which they were willing to die for. But we were twenty years old, and we *knew* it was all angels on the head of a pin.

I said, "Physical systems don't create mathematics. Nothing *creates* mathematics—it's timeless. All of number theory would still be exactly the same, even if the universe contained nothing but a single electron."

Alison snorted. "Yes, because even *one electron*, plus a space-time to put it in, needs all of quantum mechanics and all of general relativity—and all the mathematical infrastructure they entail. One particle floating in a quantum vacuum needs half the major results of group theory, functional analysis, differential geometry—"

"Okay, okay! I get the point. But if that's the case…the events in the first picosecond after the Big Bang would have 'constructed' every last mathematical truth required by *any* physical system, all the way to the Big Crunch. Once you've got the mathematics which underpins the Theory of Everything…that's it, that's all you ever need. End of story."

"But it's not. To *apply* the Theory of Everything to a particular system, you still need all the mathematics for dealing with *that system*—which could include results far beyond the mathematics which the TOE itself requires. I mean, fifteen billion years after the Big Bang, someone can still come along and prove, say…Fermat's Last Theorem." Andrew Wiles at Princeton had recently announced a proof of the famous conjecture, although his work was still being scrutinized by his colleagues, and the final verdict wasn't yet in. "Physics never needed *that* before."

I protested, "What do you mean, 'before'? Fermat's Last Theorem never has—and never will—have anything to do with any branch of physics."

Alison smiled sneakily. "No *branch*—no. But only because the class of physical systems whose behavior depends on it is so ludicrously specific: the brains of mathematicians who are trying to validate the Wiles proof.

"Think about it. Once you start trying to prove a theorem, then even if the mathematics is so 'pure' that it has no relevance to any other object in the universe…you've just made it relevant to *yourself*. You have to choose *some* physical process to test the theorem—whether you use a computer, or a pen and paper…or just close your eyes and shuffle *neurotransmitters*. There's no such thing as a proof which doesn't rely on physical events—and whether they're inside or outside your skull doesn't make them any less real."

"Fair enough," I conceded warily. "But that doesn't mean—"

"And maybe Andrew Wiles's brain—and body, and notepaper—comprised the first physical system whose behavior depended on the theorem being true or false. But I don't think human actions have any special role...and if some swarm of quarks had done the same thing blindly, fifteen billion years before—executed some purely random interaction which just happened to test the conjecture in some way—then *those quarks* would have constructed FLT long before Wiles. We'll never know."

I opened my mouth to complain that no swarm of quarks could have tested the infinite number of cases encompassed by the theorem, but I caught myself just in time. That was true, but it hadn't stopped Wiles. A finite sequence of logical steps linked the axioms of number theory—which included some simple generalities about *all* numbers—to Fermat's own sweeping assertion. And if a mathematician could test those logical steps by manipulating a finite number of physical objects for a finite amount of time—whether they were pencil marks on paper, or neurotransmitters in his or her brain—then all kinds of physical systems could, in theory, mimic the structure of the proof...with or without any awareness of what it was they were "proving."

I leaned back on the bench and mimed tearing out hair. "If I wasn't a die-hard Platonist before, you're forcing me into it! Fermat's Last Theorem didn't *need* to be proved by anyone—or stumbled on by any random swarm of quarks. If it's true, it was always true. Everything implied by a given set of axioms is logically connected to them, timelessly, eternally... even if the links couldn't be traced by people—or quarks—in the lifetime of the universe."

Alison was having none of this; every mention of *timeless and eternal truths* brought a faint smile to the corners of her mouth, as if I was affirming my belief in Santa Claus. She said, "So who, or what, pushed the consequences of 'There exists an entity called zero' and 'Every X has a successor', *et cetera*, all the way to FLT and beyond, before the universe had a chance to test out any of it?"

I stood my ground. "What's joined by logic is just...*joined*. Nothing has to happen—consequences don't have to be 'pushed' into existence by anyone, or anything. Or do you imagine that the first events after the Big Bang, the first wild jitters of the quark-gluon plasma, stopped to fill in all the logical gaps? You think the quarks reasoned: well, so far we've done A and B and C—but now we mustn't do D, because D would be logically inconsistent with the other mathematics we've 'invented' so far…even if it would take a five-hundred-thousand-page proof to spell out the inconsistency?"

Alison thought it over. "No. But what if event D took place, regardless? What if the mathematics it implied *was* logically inconsistent with the rest—but it went ahead and happened anyway…because the universe was too young to have computed the fact that there was any discrepancy?"

I must have sat and stared at her, open-mouthed, for about ten seconds. Given the orthodoxies we'd spent the last two-and-a-half years absorbing, this was a seriously outrageous statement.

"You're claiming that…*mathematics* might be strewn with primordial defects in consistency? Like space might be strewn with cosmic strings?"

"Exactly." She stared back at me, feigning nonchalance. "If space-time doesn't join up with itself smoothly, everywhere…why should mathematical logic?"

I almost choked. "Where do I begin? What happens—now—when some physical system tries to link theorems across the defect? If theorem D has been rendered 'true' by some over-eager quarks, what happens when we program a computer to disprove it? When the software goes through all the logical steps which link A, B and C—which the quarks have also made true—to the contradiction, the dreaded not-D…does it succeed, or doesn't it?"

Alison side-stepped the question. "Suppose they're both true: D and not-D. Sounds like the end of mathematics, doesn't it? The whole system falls apart, instantly. From D and not-D together you can prove anything you like: one equals zero, day equals night. But that's just the boring-old-fart Platonist view—where logic travels faster than light, and computation takes no time at all. People live with omega-inconsistent theories, don't they?"

Omega-inconsistent number theories were non-standard versions of arithmetic, based on axioms which "almost" contradicted each other—their saving grace being that the contradictions could only show up in "infinitely long proofs" (which were formally disallowed, quite apart from being physically impossible). That was perfectly respectable modern mathematics—but Alison seemed prepared to replace "infinitely long" with just plain "long"—as if the difference hardly mattered, in practice.

I said, "Let me get this straight. What you're talking about is taking ordinary arithmetic—no weird counter-intuitive axioms, just the stuff every ten-year-old *knows* is true—and proving that it's inconsistent, in a finite number of steps?"

She nodded blithely. "Finite, but large. So the contradiction would rarely have any physical manifestation—it would be 'computationally distant' from everyday calculations, and everyday physical events. I mean…one cosmic string, somewhere out there, doesn't destroy the universe, does it? It does no harm to anyone."

I laughed dryly. "So long as you don't get too close. So long as you don't tow it back to the solar system and let it twitch around slicing up planets."

"Exactly."

I glanced at my watch. "Time to come down to Earth, I think. You know we're meeting Julia and Ramesh—?"

Alison sighed theatrically. "I know, I know. And this would bore them witless, poor things—so the subject's closed, I promise." She added wickedly, "Humanities students are so *myopic*."

We set off across the tranquil leafy campus. Alison kept her word, and we walked in silence; carrying on the argument up to the last minute would have made it even harder to avoid the topic once we were in polite company.

Half-way to the cafeteria, though, I couldn't help myself.

"If someone ever *did* program a computer to follow a chain of inferences across the defect…what do you claim would actually happen? When the end result of all those simple, trustworthy logical steps finally popped up on the screen—which group of primordial quarks would win the battle? And please don't tell me that the whole computer just conveniently vanishes."

Alison smiled, tongue-in-cheek at last. "Get real, Bruno. How can you expect me to answer that, when the mathematics needed to predict the result doesn't even *exist* yet? Nothing I could say would be true or false—until someone's gone ahead and done the experiment."

⌇

I SPENT most of the day trying to convince myself that I wasn't being followed by some accomplice (or rival) of the surgeon, who might have been lurking outside the hotel. There was something disturbingly Kafkaesque about trying to lose a tail who might or might not have been real: no particular face I could search for in the crowd, just the abstract idea of a pursuer. It was too late to think about plastic surgery to make me look Han Chinese—Alison had raised this as a serious suggestion, back in Vietnam—but Shanghai had over a million foreign residents, so with care even an Anglophone of Italian descent should have been able to vanish.

Whether or not I was up to the task was another matter.

I tried joining the ant-trails of the tourists, following the path of least resistance from the insane crush of the Yuyuan Bazaar (where racks bursting with ten-cent watch-PCs, mood-sensitive contact lenses, and the latest karaoke vocal implants sat beside bamboo cages of live ducks and pigeons) to the one-time residence of Sun Yatsen (whose personality cult was currently undergoing a mini-series-led revival on Phoenix TV, advertised on ten thousand buses and ten times as many T-shirts). From the tomb of the writer Lu Xun ("Always think and study...visit the generals then visit the victims, see the realities of your time with open eyes"—no prime time for *him*) to the Hongkou McDonalds (where they were giving away small plastic Andy Warhol figurines, for reasons I couldn't fathom).

I mimed leisurely window-shopping between the shrines, but kept my body language sufficiently unfriendly to deter even the loneliest

Westerner from attempting to strike up a conversation. If foreigners were unremarkable in most of the city, they were positively eye-glazing here— even to each other—and I did my best to offer no one the slightest reason to remember me.

Along the way I checked for messages from Alison, but there were none. I left five of my own, tiny abstract chalk marks on bus shelters and park benches—all slightly different, but all saying the same thing: CLOSE BRUSH, BUT SAFE NOW. MOVING ON.

By early evening, I'd done all I could to throw off my hypothetical shadow, so I headed for the next hotel on our agreed but unwritten list. The last time we'd met face-to-face, in Hanoi, I'd mocked all of Alison's elaborate preparations. Now I was beginning to wish that I'd begged her to extend our secret language to cover more extreme contingencies. FATALLY WOUNDED. BETRAYED YOU UNDER TORTURE. REALITY DECAYING. OTHERWISE FINE.

The hotel on Huaihai Zhonglu was a step up from the last one, but not quite classy enough to refuse payment in cash. The desk clerk made polite small-talk, and I lied as smoothly as I could about my plans to spend a week sight-seeing before heading for Beijing. The bellperson smirked when I tipped him too much—and I sat on my bed for five minutes afterward, wondering what significance to read into *that*.

I struggled to regain a sense of proportion. Industrial Algebra *could* have bribed every single hotel employee in Shanghai to be on the look-out for us—but that was a bit like saying that, in theory, they could have duplicated our entire twelve-year search for defects, and not bothered to pursue us at all. There was no question that they wanted what we had, badly—but what could they actually do about it? Go to a merchant bank (or the Mafia, or a Triad) for finance? That might have worked if the cargo had been a stray kilogram of plutonium, or a valuable gene sequence—but only a few hundred thousand people on the planet would be capable of understanding what the defect *was*, even in theory. Only a fraction of that number would believe that such a thing could really exist...and even fewer would be both wealthy and immoral enough to invest in the business of exploiting it.

The stakes appeared to be infinitely high—but that didn't make the players omnipotent.

Not yet.

I changed the dressing on my arm, from sock to handkerchief, but the incision was deeper than I'd realized, and it was still bleeding thinly. I left the hotel—and found exactly what I needed in a twenty-four-hour emporium just ten minutes away. Surgical grade tissue repair cream: a mixture of collagen-based adhesive, antiseptic, and growth factors. The emporium wasn't even a pharmaceuticals outlet—it just had aisle after aisle packed with all kinds of unrelated odds and ends, laid out beneath the unblinking blue-white ceiling panels. Canned food, PVC plumbing fixtures, traditional medicines, rat contraceptives, video ROMS. It was a random cornucopia, an almost organic diversity—as if the products had all just grown on the shelves from whatever spores the wind had happened to blow in.

I headed back to the hotel, pushing my way through the relentless crowds, half seduced and half sickened by the odors of cooking, dazed by the endless vista of holograms and neon in a language I barely understood. Fifteen minutes later, reeling from the noise and humidity, I realized that I was lost.

I stopped on a street corner and tried to get my bearings. Shanghai stretched out around me, dense and lavish, sensual and ruthless—a Darwinian economic simulation self-organized to the brink of catastrophe. The Amazon of commerce: this city of sixteen million had more industry of every kind, more exporters and importers, more wholesalers and retailers, traders and resellers and recyclers and scavengers, more billionaires and more beggars, than most nations on the planet.

Not to mention more computing power.

China itself was reaching the cusp of its decades-long transition from brutal totalitarian communism to brutal totalitarian capitalism: a slow seamless morph from Mao to Pinochet set to the enthusiastic applause of its trading partners and the international financial agencies. There'd been no need for a counter-revolution—just layer after layer of carefully reasoned Newspeak to pave the way from previous doctrine to the stunningly obvious conclusion that private property, a thriving middle class, and a few trillion dollars worth of foreign investment were exactly what the Party had been aiming for all along.

The apparatus of the police state remained as essential as ever. Trade unionists with decadent bourgeois ideas about uncompetitive wages, journalists with counter-revolutionary notions of exposing corruption and nepotism, and any number of subversive political activists spreading destabilizing propaganda about the fantasy of free elections, all needed to be kept in check.

In a way, Luminous was a product of this strange transition from communism to not-communism in a thousand tiny steps. No one else, not even the US defense research establishment, possessed a single machine with so much power. The rest of the world had succumbed long ago to networking, giving up their imposing supercomputers with their difficult architecture and customized chips for a few hundred of the latest mass-produced work stations. In fact, the biggest computing feats of the twenty-first century had all been farmed out over the Internet to thousands of volunteers, to run on their machines whenever the processors would otherwise be idle. That was how Alison and I had mapped the defect in the first place: seven thousand amateur mathematicians had shared the joke, for twelve years.

But now the net was the very opposite of what we needed—and only Luminous could take its place. And though only the People's Republic could have paid for it, and only the People's Institute for Advanced Optical Engineering could have built it…only Shanghai's QIPS Corporation could have sold time on it to the world—while it was still being used to model hydrogen bomb shock waves, pilotless fighter jets, and exotic anti-satellite weapons.

I finally decoded the street signs, and realized what I'd done: I'd turned the wrong way coming out of the emporium, it was as simple as that.

I retraced my steps, and I was soon back on familiar territory.

~w~

WHEN I opened the door of my room, Alison was sitting on the bed.

I said, "What is it with locks in this city?"

We embraced, briefly. We'd been lovers, once—but that was long over. And we'd been friends for years afterward—but I wasn't sure if that was still the right word. Our whole relationship now was too functional, too spartan. Everything revolved around the defect, now.

She said, "I got your message. What happened?"

I described the morning's events.

"You know what you should have done?"

That stung. "I'm still here, aren't I? The cargo's still safe."

"You should have killed her, Bruno."

I laughed. Alison gazed back at me placidly, and I looked away. I didn't know if she was serious—and I didn't much want to find out.

She helped me apply the repair cream. My toxin was no threat to her—we'd both installed exactly the same symbionts, the same genotype from the same unique batch in Hanoi. But it was strange to feel her bare fingers on my broken skin, knowing that no one else on the planet could touch me like this, with impunity.

Ditto for sex, but I didn't want to dwell on that.

As I slipped on my jacket, she said, "So guess what we're doing at five am tomorrow?"

"Don't tell me: I fly to Helsinki, and you fly to Cape Town. Just to throw them off the scent."

That got a faint smile. "Wrong. We're meeting Yuen at the Institute—and spending half an hour on Luminous."

"*You* are brilliant." I bent over and kissed her on the forehead. "But I always knew you'd pull it off."

And I should have been delirious—but the truth was, my guts were churning; I felt almost as trapped as I had upon waking cuffed to the bed. If Luminous had remained beyond our reach (as it should have, since we couldn't afford to hire it for a microsecond at the going rate) we would have had no choice but to destroy all the data, and hope for the best. Industrial Algebra had no doubt dredged up a few thousand fragments of the original Internet calculations—but it was clear that, although they knew exactly what we'd found, they still had no idea where we'd found it. If they'd been forced to start their own random search—constrained by the need for secrecy to their own private hardware—it might have taken them centuries.

There was no question now, though, of backing away and leaving everything to chance. We were going to have to confront the defect in person.

"How much did you have to tell him?"

"Everything." She walked over to the washbasin, removed her shirt, and began wiping the sweat from her neck and torso with a flannel. "Short of handing over the map. I showed him the search algorithms and their results, and all the programs we'll need to run on Luminous—all stripped of specific parameter values, but enough for him to validate the techniques. He wanted to see direct evidence of the defect, of course, but I held out on that."

"And how much did he believe?"

"He's reserved judgment. The deal is, we get half an hour's unimpeded access—but he gets to observe everything we do."

I nodded, as if my opinion made any difference, as if we had any choice. Yuen Ting-fu had been Alison's supervisor for her PhD on advanced applications of ring theory, when she'd studied at Fu-tan University in the late nineties. Now he was one of the world's leading cryptographers, working as a consultant to the military, the security services, and a dozen international corporations. Alison had once told me that she'd heard he'd found a polynomial-time algorithm for factoring the product of two primes; that had never been officially confirmed... but such was the power of his reputation that almost everyone on the planet had stopped using the old RSA encryption method as the rumor had spread. No doubt time on Luminous was his for the asking—but that didn't mean he couldn't still be imprisoned for twenty years for giving it away to the wrong people, for the wrong reasons.

I said, "And you trust him? He may not believe in the defect now, but once he's convinced—"

"He'll want exactly what *we* want. I'm sure of that."

"Okay. But are you sure IA won't be watching, too? If they've worked out why we're here, and they've bribed someone—"

Alison cut me off impatiently. "There are still a few things you can't buy in this city. Spying on a military machine like Luminous would be suicidal. No one would risk it."

"What about spying on unauthorized projects being run on a military machine? Maybe the crimes cancel out, and you end up a hero."

She approached me, half naked, drying her face on my towel. "We'd better hope not."

I laughed suddenly. "You know what I like most about Luminous? They're not really letting Exxon and McDonnell-Douglas use the same machine as the People's Liberation Army. Because the whole computer vanishes every time they pull the plug. There's no paradox at all, if you look at it that way."

～〰〰

ALISON INSISTED that we stand guard in shifts. Twenty-four hours earlier, I might have made a joke of it; now I reluctantly accepted the revolver she offered me, and sat watching the door in the neon-tinged darkness while she went out like a light.

The hotel had been quiet for most of the evening—but now it came to life. There were footsteps in the corridor every five minutes—and rats in the walls, foraging and screwing and probably giving birth. Police sirens wailed in the distance; a couple screamed at each other in the street below. I'd read somewhere that Shanghai was now the murder capital of the world—but was that *per capita*, or in absolute numbers?

After an hour, I was so jumpy that it was a miracle I hadn't blown my foot off. I unloaded the gun, then sat playing Russian roulette with the empty barrel. In spite of everything, I still wasn't ready to put a bullet in anyone's brain for the sake of defending the axioms of number theory.

～〰〰

INDUSTRIAL ALGEBRA had approached us in a perfectly civilized fashion, at first. They were a small but aggressive UK-based company, designing specialized high-performance computing hardware for industrial and military applications. That they'd heard about the search was no great surprise—it had been openly discussed on the Internet for years, and even joked about in serious mathematical journals—but it seemed an odd coincidence when they made contact with us just days after Alison had sent me a private message from Zürich mentioning the latest "promising" result. After half a dozen false alarms—all due to bugs and glitches—we'd stopped broadcasting the news of every unconfirmed find to the people who were donating runtime to the project, let alone any wider circle. We were afraid that if we cried wolf one more time, half our collaborators would get so annoyed that they'd withdraw their support.

IA had offered us a generous slab of computing power on the company's private network—several orders of magnitude more than we received from any other donor. *Why?* The answer kept changing. Their deep respect for pure mathematics…their wide-eyed fun-loving attitude to life…their desire to be seen to be sponsoring a project so wild and hip and unlikely to succeed that it made SETI look like a staid blue-chip investment. It was—they'd finally "conceded"—a desperate bid to soften their corporate image, after years of bad press for what certain unsavoury governments did with their really rather nice smart bombs.

We'd politely declined. They'd offered us highly paid consulting jobs. Bemused, we'd suspended all net-based calculations—and started encrypting our mail with a simple but highly effective algorithm Alison had picked up from Yuen.

Alison had been collating the results of the search on her own work station at her current home in Zürich, while I'd helped coordinate things from Sydney. No doubt IA had been eavesdropping on the incoming data, but they'd clearly started too late to gather the information needed to create their own map; each fragment of the calculations meant little in isolation. But when the work station was stolen (all the files were encrypted, it would have told them nothing) we'd finally been forced to ask ourselves: *If the defect turns out to be genuine, if the joke is no joke...* *then exactly what's at stake? How much money? How much power?*

On June 7, 2006, we met in a sweltering, crowded square in Hanoi. Alison wasted no time. She was carrying a backup of the data from the stolen work station in her notepad—and she solemnly proclaimed that, this time, the defect was real.

The notepad's tiny processor would have taken centuries to repeat the long random trawling of the space of arithmetic statements which had been carried out on the net—but, led straight to the relevant computations, it could confirm the existence of the defect in a matter of minutes.

The process began with Statement S. Statement S was an assertion about some ludicrously huge numbers—but it wasn't mathematically sophisticated or contentious in any way. There were no claims here about infinite sets, no propositions concerning "every integer." It merely stated that a certain (elaborate) calculation performed on certain (very large) whole numbers led to a certain result—in essence, it was no different from something like "5+3 = 4x2." It might have taken me ten years to check it with a pen and paper—but I could have carried out the task with nothing but primary school mathematics and a great deal of patience. A statement like this could not be undecidable; it had to be either true or false.

The notepad decided it was true.

Then the notepad took statement S...and in four hundred and twenty-three simple, impeccably logical steps, used it to prove not-S.

I repeated the calculations on my own notepad—using a different software package. The result was exactly the same. I gazed at the screen, trying to concoct a plausible reason why two different machines running two different programs could have failed in identical ways. There'd certainly been cases in the past of a single misprinted algorithm in a computing textbook spawning a thousand dud programs. But the operations here were too simple, too basic.

Which left only two possibilities. Either conventional arithmetic was intrinsically flawed, and the whole Platonic ideal of the natural numbers was ultimately self-contradictory...or Alison was right, and an alternative arithmetic had come to hold sway in a "computationally remote" region, billions of years ago.

I was badly shaken—but my first reaction was to try to play down the significance of the result. "The numbers being manipulated here are greater than the volume of the observable universe, measured in cubic Planck lengths. If IA were hoping to use this on their foreign exchange transactions, I think they've made a slight error of scale." Even as I spoke, though, I knew it wasn't that simple. The raw numbers might have been trans-astronomical—but it was the mere 1024 bits of the notepad's binary representations which had actually, physically misbehaved. Every truth in mathematics was encoded, reflected, in countless other forms. If a paradox like this—which at first glance sounded like a dispute about numbers too large to apply even to the most grandiose cosmological discussions—could affect the behavior of a five-gram silicon chip, then there could easily be a billion other systems on the planet at risk of being touched by the very same flaw.

But there was worse to come.

The theory was, we'd located part of the boundary between two incompatible systems of mathematics—both of which were *physically true*, in their respective domains. Any sequence of deductions which stayed entirely on one side of the defect—whether it was the "near side", where conventional arithmetic applied, or the "far side", where the alternative took over—would be free from contradictions. But any sequence which crossed the border would give rise to absurdities—hence S could lead to not-S.

So, by examining a large number of chains of inference, some of which turned out to be self-contradictory and some not, it should have been possible to map the area around the defect precisely—to assign every statement to one system or the other.

Alison displayed the first map she'd made. It portrayed an elaborately crenelated fractal border, rather like the boundary between two microscopic ice crystals—as if the two systems had been diffusing out at random from different starting points, and then collided, blocking each other's way. By now, I was almost prepared to believe that I really was staring at a snapshot of the creation of mathematics—a fossil of primordial attempts to define the difference between truth and falsehood.

Then she produced a second map of the same set of statements, and overlaid the two. The defect, the border, had shifted—advancing in some places, retreating in others.

My blood went cold. "*That* has got to be a bug in the software."

"It's not."

I inhaled deeply, looking around the square—as if the heedless crowd of tourists and hawkers, shoppers and executives, might offer some simple "human" truth more resilient than mere arithmetic. But all I could think of was *1984*: Winston Smith, finally beaten into submission, abandoning every touchstone of reason by conceding that *two and two make five*.

I said, "Okay. Go on."

"In the early universe, some physical system must have tested out mathematics which was isolated, cut off from all the established results—leaving it free to decide the outcome at random. That's how the defect arose. But by now, *all* the mathematics in this region has been tested, all the gaps have been filled in. When a physical system tests a theorem on the near side, not only has it been tested a billion times before—but all the *logically adjacent* statements around it have been decided, and they imply the correct result in a single step."

"You mean…peer pressure from the neighbors? No inconsistencies allowed, you have to conform? If x-1 = y-1, and x+1 = y+1, then x is left with no choice but to equal y…because there's nothing 'nearby' to support the alternative?"

"Exactly. Truth is determined locally. And it's the same, deep into the far side. The alternative mathematics has dominated there, and every test takes place surrounded by established theorems which reinforce each other, and the 'correct'—non-standard—result."

"At the border, though—"

"At the border, every theorem you test is getting contradictory advice. From one neighbor, x-1 = y-1…but from another, x+1 = y+2. And the topology of the border is so complex that a near-side theorem can have more far-side neighbors than near-side ones—and vice versa.

"So the truth at the border isn't fixed, even now. Both regions can still advance or retreat—*it all depends on the order in which the theorems are tested*. If a solidly near-side theorem is tested first, and it lends support to a more vulnerable neighbor, that can guarantee that they both stay near-side." She ran a brief animation which demonstrated the effect. "But if the order is reversed, the weaker one *will* fall."

I watched, light-headed. Obscure—but supposedly eternal—truths were tumbling like chess pieces. "And…you think that physical processes going on *right now*—chance molecular events which keep inadvertently testing and retesting different theories along the border—cause each side to gain and lose territory?"

"Yes."

"So there's been a kind of…random tide washing back and forth between the two kinds of mathematics, for the past few billion years?" I laughed uneasily, and did some rough calculations in my head. "The expectation value for a random walk is the square root of N. I don't think we have anything to worry about. The tide isn't going to wash over any useful arithmetic in the lifetime of the universe."

Alison smiled humorlessly, and held up the notepad again. "The tide? No. But it's the easiest thing in the world to dig a channel. To bias the random flow." She ran an animation of a sequence of tests which forced the far-side system to retreat across a small front—exploiting a "beach-head" formed by chance, and then pushing on to undermine a succession of theorems. "Industrial Algebra, though—I imagine—would be more interested in the reverse. Establishing a whole network of narrow channels of non-standard mathematics running deep into the realm of conventional arithmetic—which they could then deploy against theorems with practical consequences."

I fell silent, trying to imagine tendrils of contradictory arithmetic reaching down into the everyday world. No doubt IA would aim for surgical precision—hoping to earn themselves a few billion dollars by corrupting the specific mathematics underlying certain financial transactions. But the ramifications would be impossible to predict—or control. There'd be no way to limit the effect, spatially—they could target certain mathematical truths, but they couldn't confine the change to any one location. *A few billion dollars, a few billion neurons, a few billion stars…a few billion people.* Once the basic rules of counting were undermined, the most solid and distinct objects could be rendered as uncertain as swirls of fog. This was not a power I would have entrusted to a cross between Mother Theresa and Carl Friedrich Gauss.

"So what do we do? Erase the map—and just hope that IA never find the defect for themselves?"

"No." Alison seemed remarkably calm—but then, her own long-cherished philosophy had just been confirmed, not razed to the ground—and she'd had time on the flight from Zürich to think through all the *Realmathematik.* "There's only one way to be sure that they can never use this. We have to strike first. We have to get hold of enough computing power to map the entire defect. And then we either iron the border flat, so it *can't* move—if you amputate all the pincers, there can be no pincer movements. Or—better yet, if we can get the resources—we push the border in, from all directions, and shrink the far-side system down to nothing."

I hesitated. "All we've mapped so far is a tiny fragment of the defect. We don't know how large the far side could be. Except that it can't be small—or the random fluctuations would have swallowed it long ago. And it *could* go on forever; it could be infinite, for all we know."

Alison gave me a strange look. "You still don't get it, do you, Bruno? You're still thinking like a Platonist. The universe has only been around for fifteen billion years. It hasn't had time to create infinities. The far side *can't* go on forever—because somewhere beyond the defect, there are theorems which don't belong to <u>any</u> system. Theorems which have never been touched, never been tested, never been rendered true or false.

"And if we have to reach beyond the existing mathematics of the universe in order to surround the far side…then that's what we'll do. There's no reason why it shouldn't be possible—just so long as we get there first."

〰〰

WHEN ALISON took my place, at one in the morning, I was certain I wouldn't get any sleep. When she shook me awake three hours later, I still felt like I hadn't.

I used my notepad to send a priming code to the data caches buried in our veins, and then we stood together side-by-side, left-shoulder-to-right-shoulder. The two chips recognized each other's magnetic and electrical signatures, interrogated each other to be sure—and then began radiating low power microwaves. Alison's notepad picked up the transmission, and merged the two complementary data streams. The result was still heavily encrypted—but after all the precautions we'd taken so far, shifting the map into a hand-held computer felt about as secure as tattooing it onto our foreheads.

A taxi was waiting for us downstairs. The People's Institute for Advanced Optical Engineering was in Minhang, a sprawling technology park some thirty kilometers south of the city center. We rode in silence through the gray predawn light, past the giant ugly tower blocks thrown up by the landlords of the new millennium, riding out the fever as the necrotraps and their cargo dissolved into our blood.

As the taxi turned into an avenue lined with biotech and aerospace companies, Alison said, "If anyone asks, we're PhD students of Yuen's, testing a conjecture in algebraic topology."

"Now you tell me. I don't suppose you have any specific conjecture in mind? What if they ask us to elaborate?"

"On *algebraic topology?* At five o'clock in the morning?"

The Institute building was unimposing—sprawling black ceramic, three storeys high—but there was a five-meter electrified fence, and the entrance was guarded by two armed soldiers. We paid the taxi driver and approached on foot. Yuen had supplied us with visitor's passes—complete with photographs and fingerprints. The names were our own; there was no point indulging in unnecessary deception. If we were caught out, pseudonyms would only make things worse.

The soldiers checked the passes, then led us through an MRI scanner. I forced myself to breathe calmly as we waited for the results; in theory, the scanner could have picked up our symbionts' foreign proteins, lingering breakdown products from the necrotraps, and a dozen other suspicious trace chemicals. But it all came down to a question of what they were looking for; magnetic resonance spectra for billions of molecules had been catalogued—but no machine could hunt for all of them at once.

One of the soldiers took me aside and asked me to remove my jacket. I fought down a wave of panic—and then struggled not to overcompensate: if I'd had nothing to hide, I would still have been nervous. He prodded the bandage on my upper arm; the surrounding skin was still red and inflamed.

"What's this?"

"I had a cyst there. My doctor cut it out, this morning."

He eyed me suspiciously, and peeled back the adhesive bandage—with ungloved hands. I couldn't bring myself to look; the repair cream should have sealed the wound completely—at worst there should have been old, dried blood—but I could *feel* a faint liquid warmth along the line of the incision.

The soldier laughed at my gritted teeth, and waved me away with an expression of distaste. I had no idea what he thought I might have been hiding—but I saw fresh red droplets beading the skin before I closed the bandage.

Yuen Ting-fu was waiting for us in the lobby. He was a slender, fit-looking man in his late sixties, casually dressed in denim. I let Alison do all the talking: apologizing for our lack of punctuality (although we weren't actually late), and thanking him effusively for granting us this precious opportunity to pursue our unworthy research. I stood back and tried to appear suitably deferential. Four soldiers looked on impassively; they didn't seem to find all this grovelling excessive. And no doubt I would have been giddy with awe, if I really had been a student granted time here for some run-of-the-mill thesis.

We followed Yuen as he strode briskly through a second checkpoint and scanner (this time, no one stopped us) then down a long corridor with a soft gray vinyl floor. We passed a couple of white-coated technicians, but they barely gave us a second glance. I'd had visions of a pair of obvious foreigners attracting as much attention here as we would have wandering through a military base—but that was absurd. Half the runtime on Luminous was sold to foreign corporations—and because the machine was most definitely *not* linked to any communications network, commercial users had to come here in person. Just how often Yuen wangled free time for his students—whatever their nationality—was another question, but if he believed it was the best cover for us, I was in no position to argue. I only hoped he'd planted a seamless trail of reassuring lies in the university records and beyond, in case the Institute administration decided to check up on us in any detail.

We stopped in at the operations room, and Yuen chatted with the technicians. Banks of flatscreens covered one wall, displaying status histograms and engineering schematics. It looked like the control center for a small particle accelerator—which wasn't far from the truth.

Luminous was, literally, a computer made of light. It came into existence when a vacuum chamber, a cube five meters wide, was filled with an elaborate standing wave created by three vast arrays of high-powered lasers. A coherent electron beam was fed into the chamber—and just as a finely machined grating built of solid matter could diffract a beam of light, a sufficiently ordered (and sufficiently intense) configuration of light could diffract a beam of matter.

The electrons were redirected from layer to layer of the light cube, recombining and interfering at each stage, every change in their phase and intensity performing an appropriate computation—and the whole system could be reconfigured, nanosecond by nanosecond, into complex new "hardware" optimized for the calculations at hand. The auxiliary supercomputers controlling the laser arrays could design, and then instantly build, the perfect machine of light to carry out each particular stage of any program.

It was, of course, fiendishly difficult technology, incredibly expensive and temperamental. The chance of ever putting it on the desktops of Tetris-playing accountants was zero, so nobody in the West had bothered to pursue it.

And this cumbersome, unwieldy, impractical machine ran faster than all the pieces of silicon hanging off the Internet, combined.

We continued on to the programming room. At first glance, it might have been the computing center in a small primary school, with half a dozen perfectly ordinary work stations sitting on white formica tables. They just happened to be the only six in the world which were hooked up to Luminous.

We were alone with Yuen now—and Alison cut the protocol and just glanced briefly in his direction for approval, before hurriedly linking her notepad to one of the work stations and uploading the encrypted map. As she typed in the instructions to decode the file, all the images running through my head of what would have happened if I'd poisoned the soldier at the gate receded into insignificance. We now had half an hour to banish the defect—and we still had no idea how far it extended.

Yuen turned to me; the tension on his face betrayed his own anxieties, but he mused philosophically, "If our arithmetic seems to fail for these large numbers—does it mean the mathematics, the ideal, is really flawed and mutable—or only that the behavior of matter always falls short of the ideal?"

I replied, "If every class of physical objects 'falls short' in exactly the same way—whether it's boulders or electrons or abacus beads…what is it that their common behavior is obeying—or defining—if not the mathematics?"

He smiled, puzzled. "Alison seemed to think you were a Platonist."

"Lapsed. Or…defeated. I don't see what it can *mean* to talk about standard number theory still being true for these statements—in some vague Platonic sense—if no real objects can ever reflect that truth."

"We can still imagine it. We can still contemplate the abstraction. It's only the physical act of validation that must fall through. Think of transfinite arithmetic: no one can physically test the properties of Cantor's infinities, can they? We can only reason about them from afar."

I didn't reply. Since the revelations in Hanoi, I'd pretty much lost faith in my power to "reason from afar" about anything I couldn't personally describe with Arabic numerals on a single sheet of paper. Maybe Alison's idea of "local truth" was the most we could hope for; anything more ambitious was beginning to seem like the comic-book "physics" of swinging a rigid beam ten billion kilometers long around your head, and predicting that the far end would exceed the speed of light.

An image blossomed on the work station screen: it began as the familiar map of the defect—but Luminous was already extending it at a mind-boggling rate. Billions of inferential loops were being spun around the margins: some confirming their own premises, and thus delineating regions where a single, consistent mathematics held sway...others skewing into self-contradiction, betraying a border crossing. I tried to imagine what it would have been like to follow one of those Möbius-strips of deductive logic in my head; there were no difficult concepts involved, it was only the sheer size of the statements which made that impossible. But would the contradictions have driven me into gibbering insanity—or would I have found every step perfectly reasonable, and the conclusion simply unavoidable? Would I have ended up calmly, happily conceding: *Two and two make five?*

As the map grew—smoothly rescaled to keep it fitting on the screen, giving the unsettling impression that we were retreating from the alien mathematics as fast as we could, and only just avoiding being swallowed—Alison sat hunched forward, waiting for the big picture to be revealed. The map portrayed the network of statements as an intricate lattice in three dimensions (a crude representational convention, but it was as good as any other). So far, the border between the regions showed no sign of overall curvature—just variously sized random incursions in both directions. For all we knew, it was possible that the far-side mathematics enclosed the near side completely—that the arithmetic we'd once believed stretched out to infinity was really no more than a tiny island in an ocean of contradictory truths.

I glanced at Yuen; he was watching the screen with undisguised pain. He said, "I read your software, and I thought: sure, this looks fine—but some glitch on your machines is the real explanation. Luminous will soon put you right."

Alison broke in jubilantly, "Look, it's turning!"

She was right. As the scale continued to shrink, the random fractal meanderings of the border were finally being subsumed by an overall convexity—a convexity of the far side. It was as if the viewpoint was backing away from a giant spiked sea-urchin. Within minutes, the map showed a crude hemisphere, decorated with elaborate crystalline extrusions at every scale. The sense of observing some palaeomathematical remnant was stronger than ever, now: this bizarre cluster of theorems really did look as if it had exploded out from some central premise into the vacuum of unclaimed truths, perhaps a billionth of a second after the Big Bang— only to be checked by an encounter with our own mathematics.

The hemisphere slowly extended into a three-quarters sphere…and then a spiked whole. The far side was bounded, finite. It was the island, not us.

Alison laughed uneasily. "Was that true before we started—or did we just make it true?" *Had the near side enclosed the far side for billions of years—or had Luminous broken new ground, actively extending the near side into mathematical territory which had never been tested by any physical system before?*

We'd never know. We'd designed the software to advance the mapping along a front in such a way that any unclaimed statements would be instantly recruited into the near side. If we'd reached out blindly, far into the void, we might have tested an isolated statement—and inadvertently spawned a whole new alternative mathematics to deal with.

Alison said, "Okay—now we have to decide. Do we try to seal the border—or do we take on the whole structure?" The software, I knew, was busy assessing the relative difficulty of the tasks.

Yuen replied at once, "Seal the border, nothing more. You mustn't destroy this." He turned to me, imploringly. "Would you smash up a fossil of *Australopithecus*? Would you wipe the cosmic background radiation out of the sky? This may shake the foundations of all my beliefs—but it encodes the truth about our history. We have no right to obliterate it, like vandals."

Alison eyed me nervously. *What was this—majority rule?* Yuen was the only one with any power here; he could pull the plug in an instant. And yet it was clear from his demeanor that he wanted a consensus—he wanted our moral support for any decision.

I said cautiously, "If we smooth the border, that'll make it literally impossible for IA to exploit the defect, won't it?"

Alison shook her head. "We don't know that. There may be a quantum-like component of spontaneous defections, even for statements which appear to be in perfect equilibrium."

Yuen countered, "Then there could be spontaneous defections *anywhere*—even far from any border. Erasing the whole structure will guarantee nothing."

"It will guarantee that IA won't find it! Maybe pin-point defections *do* occur, all the time—but the next time they're tested, they'll always revert. They're surrounded by explicit contradictions, they have no chance of getting a foothold. You can't compare a few transient glitches with this…*armory* of counter-mathematics!"

The defect bristled on the screen like a giant caltrap. Alison and Yuen both turned to me expectantly. As I opened my mouth, the work station chimed. The software had examined the alternatives in detail: destroying the entire far side would take Luminous twenty-three minutes and seventeen seconds—about a minute less than the time we had left. Sealing the border would take more than an hour.

I said, "That can't be right."

Alison groaned. "But it is! There's random interference going on at the border from other systems all the time—and doing anything finicky there means coping with that noise, fighting it. Charging ahead and pushing the border inward is different: you can exploit the noise to speed the advance. It's not a question of *dealing with a mere surface* versus *dealing with a whole volume*. It's more like…trying to carve an island into an absolutely perfect circle, while waves are constantly crashing on the beach—versus bulldozing the whole thing into the ocean."

We had thirty seconds to decide—or we'd be doing neither today. And maybe Yuen had the resources to keep the map safe from IA, while we waited a month or more for another session on Luminous—but I wasn't prepared to live with that kind of uncertainty.

"I say we get rid of the whole thing. Anything less is too dangerous. Future mathematicians will still be able to study the map—and if no one believes that the defect itself ever really existed, that's just too bad. IA are too close. We can't risk it."

Alison had one hand poised above the keyboard. I turned to Yuen; he was staring at the floor with an anguished expression. He'd let us state our views—but in the end, it was his decision.

He looked up, and spoke sadly but decisively.

"Okay. Do it."

Alison hit the key—with about three seconds to spare. I sagged into my chair, light-headed with relief.

~~~

WE WATCHED the far side shrinking. The process didn't look quite as crass as *bulldozing an island*—more like dissolving some quirkily beautiful crystal in acid. Now that the danger was receding before our eyes, though, I was beginning to suffer faint pangs of regret. Our mathematics had coexisted with this strange anomaly for fifteen billion years, and it shamed me to think that within months of its discovery, we'd backed ourselves into a corner where we'd had no choice but to destroy it.

Yuen seemed transfixed by the process. "So are we breaking the laws of physics—or enforcing them?"

Alison said, "Neither. We're merely changing what the laws imply."

He laughed softly. "'Merely.' For some esoteric set of complex systems, we're rewriting the high-level rules of their behavior. Not including the human brain, I hope."

My skin crawled. "Don't you think that's…unlikely?"

"I was joking." He hesitated, then added soberly, "Unlikely for humans—but *someone* could be relying on this, somewhere. We might be destroying the whole basis of their existence: certainties as fundamental to them as a child's multiplication tables are to us."

Alison could barely conceal her scorn. "This is junk mathematics—a relic of a pointless accident. Any kind of life which evolved from simple to complex forms would have no use for it. Our mathematics works for…rocks, seeds, animals in the herd, members of the tribe. *This* only kicks in beyond the number of particles in the universe—"

"Or smaller systems which represent those numbers," I reminded her.

"And you think life somewhere might have a burning need to do *non-standard trans-astronomical arithmetic*, in order to survive? I doubt that very much."

We fell silent. Guilt and relief could fight it out later, but no one suggested halting the program. In the end, maybe nothing could outweigh the havoc the defect would have caused if it had ever been harnessed as a weapon—and I was looking forward to composing a long message to Industrial Algebra, informing them of precisely what we'd done to the object of their ambitions.

Alison pointed to a corner of the screen. "What's that?" A narrow dark spike protruded from the shrinking cluster of statements. For a moment I thought it was merely avoiding the near side's assault—but it wasn't. It was slowly, steadily growing longer.

"Could be a bug in the mapping algorithm." I reached for the keyboard and zoomed in on the structure. In close-up, it was several thousand statements wide. At its border, Alison's program could be seen in action, testing statements in an order designed to force tendrils of the near side ever deeper into the interior. This slender extrusion, ringed by contradictory mathematics, should have been corroded out of existence in a fraction of a second. Something was actively countering the assault, though—repairing every trace of damage before it could spread.

"If IA have a bug here—" I turned to Yuen. "They couldn't take on Luminous directly, so they couldn't stop the whole far side shrinking—but a tiny structure like this...what do you think? Could they stabilize it?"

"Perhaps," he conceded. "Four or five hundred top-speed work stations could do it."

Alison was typing frantically on her notepad. She said, "I'm writing a patch to identify any systematic interference—and divert all our resources against it." She brushed her hair out of her eyes. "Look over my shoulder will you, Bruno? Check me as I go."

"Okay." I read through what she'd written so far. "You're doing fine. Stay calm." Her hands were trembling.

The spike continued to grow steadily. By the time the patch was ready, the map was rescaling constantly to fit it on the screen.

Alison triggered the patch. An overlay of electric blue appeared along the spike, flagging the concentration of computing power—and the spike abruptly froze.

I held my breath, waiting for IA to notice what we'd done—and switch their resources elsewhere? If they did, no second spike would appear—they'd never get that far—but the blue marker on the screen would shift to the site where they'd regrouped and tried to make it happen.

But the blue glow didn't move from the existing spike. And the spike didn't vanish under the weight of Luminous's undivided efforts.

Instead, it began to grow again, slowly.

Yuen looked ill. "This is *not* Industrial Algebra. There's no computer on the planet—"

Alison laughed derisively. "What are you saying now? Aliens who need the far side are defending it? Aliens *where?* Nothing we've done has had time to reach even…Jupiter." There was an edge of hysteria in her voice.

"Have you measured how fast the changes propagate? Do you know, for certain, that they can't travel faster than light—with the far-side mathematics undermining the logic of relativity?"

I said, "Whoever it is, they're not defending all their borders. They're putting everything they've got into the spike."

"They're aiming at something. A specific target." Yuen reached over Alison's shoulder for the keyboard. "We're shutting this down. Right now."

She turned on him, blocking his way. "Are you crazy? We're almost holding them off! I'll rewrite the program, fine-tune it, get an edge in efficiency—"

"No! We stop threatening them, then see how they react. We don't know what harm we're doing—"

He reached for the keyboard again.

Alison jabbed him in the throat with her elbow, hard. He staggered backward, gasping for breath, then crashed to the floor, bringing a chair down on top of him. She hissed at me, "Quick—shut him up!"

I hesitated, loyalties fracturing; his idea had sounded perfectly sane to me. But if he started yelling for security—

I crouched down over him, pushed the chair aside, then clasped my hand over his mouth, forcing his head back with pressure on the lower jaw. We'd have to tie him up—and then try brazenly marching out of the building without him. But he'd be found in a matter of minutes. Even if we made it past the gate, we were screwed.

Yuen caught his breath and started struggling; I clumsily pinned his arms with my knees. I could hear Alison typing, a ragged staccato; I tried to get a glimpse of the work station screen, but I couldn't turn that far without taking my weight off Yuen.

I said, "Maybe he's right—maybe we should pull back, and see what happens." *If the alterations could propagate faster than light...how many distant civilizations might have felt the effects of what we'd done?* Our first contact with extraterrestrial life could turn out to be an attempt to obliterate mathematics which they viewed as...what? A precious resource? A sacred relic? An essential component of their entire world view?

The sound of typing stopped abruptly. "Bruno? Do you feel—?"

"What?"

Silence.

"*What?*"

Yuen seemed to have given up the fight. I risked turning around.

Alison was hunched forward, her face in her hands. On the screen, the spike had ceased its relentless linear growth—but now an elaborate dendritic structure had blossomed at its tip. I glanced down at Yuen; he seemed dazed, oblivious to my presence. I took my hand from his mouth, warily. He lay there placidly, smiling faintly, eyes scanning something I couldn't see.

I climbed to my feet. I took Alison by the shoulders and shook her gently; her only response was to press her face harder into her hands. The spike's strange flower was still growing—but it wasn't spreading out into new territory; it was sending narrow shoots back in on itself, crisscrossing the same region again and again with ever finer structures.

Weaving a net? Searching for something?

It hit me with a jolt of clarity more intense than anything I'd felt since childhood. It was like reliving the moment when the whole concept of *numbers* had finally snapped into place—but with an adult's understanding of everything it opened up, everything it implied. It was a lightning-bolt revelation—but there was no taint of mystical confusion: no opiate haze of euphoria, no pseudo-sexual rush. In the clean-lined logic of the simplest concepts, I saw and understood exactly how the world worked—

—except that it was all wrong, it was all false, it was all impossible. *Quicksand.*

Assailed by vertigo, I swept my gaze around the room—counting frantically: *Six work stations. Two people. Six chairs.* I grouped the work stations: three sets of two, two sets of three. One and five, two and four; four and two, five and one.

I weaved a dozen cross-checks for consistency—*for sanity*...but everything added up.

They hadn't stolen the old arithmetic; they'd merely blasted the new one into my head, on top of it.

Whoever had resisted our assault with Luminous had reached down with the spike and rewritten our neural metamathematics—the arithmetic which underlay our own reasoning *about* arithmetic—enough to let us glimpse what we'd been trying to destroy.

Alison was still uncommunicative, but she was breathing slowly and steadily. Yuen seemed fine, lost in a happy reverie. I relaxed slightly, and began trying to make sense of the flood of far-side arithmetic surging through my brain.

On their own terms, the axioms were...trivial, obvious. I could see that they corresponded to elaborate statements about trans-astronomical integers, but performing an exact translation was far beyond me—and thinking about the entities they described in terms of the huge integers they represented was a bit like thinking about *pi* or *the square root of two* in terms of the first ten thousand digits of their decimal expansion: it would be missing the point entirely. These alien "numbers"—the basic objects of the alternative arithmetic—had found a way to embed themselves in the integers, and to relate to each other in a simple, elegant way—and if the messy corollaries they implied upon translation contradicted the rules integers were supposed to obey…well, only a small, remote patch of obscure truths had been subverted.

Someone touched me on the shoulder. I started—but Yuen was beaming amiably, all arguments and violence forgotten.

He said, "Lightspeed is *not* violated. All the logic which requires that remains intact." I could only take him at his word; the result would have taken me hours to prove. Maybe the aliens had done a better job on him—or maybe he was just a superior mathematician in either system.

"Then…where are they?" At lightspeed, our attack on the far side could not have been felt any further away than Mars—and the strategy used to block the corrosion of the spike would have been impossible with even a few seconds' time lag.

"The atmosphere?"

"You mean—*Earth's?*"

"Where else? Or maybe the oceans."

I sat down heavily. Maybe it was no stranger than any conceivable alternative, but I still balked at the implications.

Yuen said, "To us, their structure wouldn't look like 'structure' at all. The simplest unit might involve a group of thousands of atoms—representing a trans-astronomical number—not necessarily even *bonded together* in any conventional way, but breaking the normal consequences of the laws of physics, obeying a different set of high-level rules which arise from the alternative mathematics. People have often mused about the chances of intelligence being coded into long-lived vortices on distant gas giants…but *these* creatures won't be in hurricanes or tornadoes. They'll be drifting in the most innocuous puffs of air—invisible as neutrinos."

"Unstable—"

"Only according to our mathematics. Which does not apply."

Alison broke in suddenly, angrily. "Even if all of this is true—where does it get us? Whether the defect supports a whole invisible ecosystem or not—IA will still find it, and use it, in exactly the same way."

For a moment I was dumbstruck. *We were facing the prospect of sharing the planet with an undiscovered civilization—and all she could think about was IA's grubby machinations?*

She was absolutely right, though. Long before any of these extravagant fantasies could be proved or disproved, IA could still do untold harm.

I said, "Leave the mapping software running—but shut down the shrinker."

She glanced at the screen. "No need. They've overpowered it—or undermined its mathematics." The far side was back to its original size.

"Then there's nothing to lose. Shut it down."

She did. No longer under attack, the spike began to reverse its growth. I felt a pang of loss as my limited grasp of the far-side mathematics suddenly evaporated; I tried to hold on, but it was like clutching at air.

When the spike had retracted completely, I said, "Now we try doing an Industrial Algebra. We try bringing the defect closer."

We were almost out of time, but it was easy enough—in thirty seconds, we rewrote the shrinking algorithm to function in reverse.

Alison programmed a function key with the commands to revert to the original version—so that if the experiment backfired, one keystroke would throw the full weight of Luminous behind a defense of the near side again.

Yuen and I exchanged nervous glances. I said, "Maybe this wasn't such a good idea."

Alison disagreed. "We need to know how they'll react to this. Better we find out now than leave it to IA."

She started the program running.

The sea-urchin began to swell, slowly. I broke out in a sweat. The farsiders hadn't harmed us, so far—but this felt like tugging hard at a door which you really, badly, didn't want to see thrown open.

A technician poked her head into the room and announced cheerfully, "Down for maintenance in two minutes!"

Yuen said, "I'm sorry, there's nothing—"

The whole far side turned electric blue. Alison's original patch had detected a systematic intervention.

We zoomed in. Luminous was picking off vulnerable statements of the near side—but something else was repairing the damage.

I let out a strangled noise that might have been a cheer. Alison smiled serenely. She said, "I'm satisfied. IA don't stand a chance."

Yuen mused, "Maybe they have a reason to defend the status quo—maybe they rely on the border itself, as much as the far side."

Alison shut down our reversed shrinker. The blue glow vanished; both sides were leaving the defect alone. And there were a thousand questions we all wanted answered—but the technicians had thrown the master switch, and Luminous itself had ceased to exist.

THE SUN was breaking through the skyline as we rode back into the city. As we pulled up outside the hotel, Alison started shaking and sobbing. I sat beside her, squeezing her hand. I knew she'd felt the weight of what might have happened, all along, far more than I had.

I paid the driver, and then we stood on the street for a while, silently watching the cyclists go by, trying to imagine how the world would change as it endeavored to embrace this new contradiction between the exotic and the mundane, the pragmatic and the Platonic, the visible and the invisible.

RIDING THE CROCODILE

n their ten-thousand, three hundred and ninth year of marriage, Leila and Jasim began contemplating death. They had known love, raised children, and witnessed the flourishing generations of their offspring. They had traveled to a dozen worlds and lived among a thousand cultures. They had educated themselves many times over, proved theorems, and acquired and abandoned artistic sensibilities and skills. They had not lived in every conceivable manner, far from it, but what room would there be for the multitude if each individual tried to exhaust the permutations of existence? There were some experiences, they agreed, that everyone should try, and others that only a handful of people in all of time need bother with. They had no wish to give up their idiosyncrasies, no wish to uproot their personalities from the niches they had settled in long ago, let alone start cranking mechanically through some tedious enumeration of all the other people they might have been. They had been themselves, and for that they had done, more or less, enough.

Before dying, though, they wanted to attempt something grand and audacious. It was not that their lives were incomplete, in need of some final flourish of affirmation. If some unlikely calamity had robbed them of the chance to orchestrate this finale, the closest of their friends would never have remarked upon, let alone mourned, its absence. There was no esthetic compulsion to be satisfied, no aching existential void to be filled. Nevertheless, it was what they both wanted, and once they had acknowledged this to each other their hearts were set on it.

Choosing the project was not a great burden; that task required nothing but patience. They knew they'd recognize it when it came to them. Every night before sleeping, Jasim would ask Leila, "Did you see it yet?"

"No. Did you?"

"Not yet."

Sometimes Leila would dream that she'd found it in her dreams, but the transcripts proved otherwise. Sometimes Jasim felt sure that it was lurking just below the surface of his thoughts, but when he dived down to check it was nothing but a trick of the light.

Years passed. They occupied themselves with simple pleasures: gardening, swimming in the surf, talking with their friends, catching up with their descendants. They had grown skilled at finding pastimes that could bear repetition. Still, were it not for the nameless adventure that awaited them they would have thrown a pair of dice each evening and agreed that two sixes would end it all.

One night, Leila stood alone in the garden, watching the sky. From their home world, Najib, they had traveled only to the nearest stars with inhabited worlds, each time losing just a few decades to the journey. They had chosen those limits so as not to alienate themselves from friends and family, and it had never felt like much of a constraint. True, the civilization of the Amalgam wrapped the galaxy, and a committed traveler could spend two hundred thousand years circling back home, but what was to be gained by such an overblown odyssey? The dozen worlds of their neighborhood held enough variety for any traveler, and whether more distant realms were filled with fresh novelties or endless repetition hardly seemed to matter. To have a goal, a destination, would be one thing, but to drown in the sheer plenitude of worlds for its own sake seemed utterly pointless.

A destination? Leila overlaid the sky with information, most of it by necessity millennia out of date. There were worlds with spectacular views of nebulas and star clusters, views that could be guaranteed still to be in existence if they traveled to see them, but would taking in such sights firsthand be so much better than immersion in the flawless images already available in Najib's library? To blink away ten thousand years just to wake beneath a cloud of green and violet gas, however lovely, seemed like a terrible anticlimax.

The stars tingled with self-aggrandisement, plaintively tugging at her attention. The architecture here, the rivers, the festivals! Even if these tourist attractions could survive the millennia, even if some were literally unique, there was nothing that struck her as a fitting prelude to death. If she and Jasim had formed some whimsical attachment, centuries before, to a world on the other side of the galaxy rumoured to hold great beauty or interest, and if they had talked long enough about chasing it down when they had nothing better to do, then keeping that promise might have been worth it, even if the journey led them to a world in ruins. They had no such cherished destination, though, and it was too late to cultivate one now.

Leila's gaze followed a thinning in the advertising, taking her to the bulge of stars surrounding the galaxy's center. The disk of the Milky Way belonged to the Amalgam, whose various ancestral species had effectively merged into a single civilization, but the central bulge was inhabited by beings who had declined to do so much as communicate with those around them. All attempts to send probes into the bulge—let alone the kind of engineering spores needed to create the infrastructure for travel—had been gently but firmly rebuffed, with the intruders swatted straight back out again. The Aloof had maintained their silence and isolation since before the Amalgam itself had even existed.

The latest news on this subject was twenty thousand years old, but the status quo had held for close to a million years. If she and Jasim traveled to the innermost edge of the Amalgam's domain, the chances were exceptionally good that the Aloof would not have changed their ways in the meantime. In fact, it would be no disappointment at all if the Aloof had suddenly thrown open their borders: that unheralded thaw would itself be an extraordinary thing to witness. If the challenge remained, though, all the better.

She called Jasim to the garden and pointed out the richness of stars, unadorned with potted histories.

"We go where?" he asked.

"As close to the Aloof as we're able."

"And do what?"

"Try to observe them," she said. "Try to learn something about them. Try to make contact, in whatever way we can."

"You don't think that's been tried before?"

"A million times. Not so much lately, though. Maybe while the interest on our side has ebbed, they've been changing, growing more receptive."

"Or maybe not." Jasim smiled. He had appeared a little stunned by her proposal at first, but the idea seemed to be growing on him. "It's a hard, hard problem to throw ourselves against. But it's not futile. Not quite." He wrapped her hands in his. "Let's see how we feel in the morning."

In the morning, they were both convinced. They would camp at the gates of these elusive strangers, and try to rouse them from their indifference.

They summoned the family from every corner of Najib. There were some grandchildren and more distant descendants who had settled in other star systems, decades away at lightspeed, but they chose not to wait to call them home for this final farewell.

Two hundred people crowded the physical house and garden, while two hundred more confined themselves to the virtual wing. There was talk and food and music, like any other celebration, and Leila tried to undercut any edge of solemnity that she felt creeping in. As the night wore on, though, each time she kissed a child or grandchild, each time she embraced an old friend, she thought: this could be the last time, ever. There had to be a last time, she couldn't face ten thousand more years, but a part of her spat and struggled like a cornered animal at the thought of each warm touch fading to nothing.

As dawn approached, the party shifted entirely into the acorporeal. People took on fancy dress from myth or xenology, or just joked and played with their illusory bodies. It was all very calm and gentle, nothing like the surreal excesses she remembered from her youth, but

Leila still felt a tinge of vertigo. When her son Khalid made his ears grow and spin, this amiable silliness carried a hard message: the machinery of the house had ripped her mind from her body, as seamlessly as ever, but this time she would never be returning to the same flesh.

Sunrise brought the first of the goodbyes. Leila forced herself to release each proffered hand, to unwrap her arms from around each non-existent body. She whispered to Jasim, "Are you going mad, too?"

"Of course."

Gradually the crowd thinned out. The wing grew quiet. Leila found herself pacing from room to room, as if she might yet chance upon someone who'd stayed behind, then she remembered urging the last of them to go, her children and friends tearfully retreating down the hall. She skirted inconsolable sadness, then lifted herself above it and went looking for Jasim.

He was waiting for her outside their room.

"Are you ready to sleep?" he asked her gently.

She said, "For an eon."

2

LEILA WOKE in the same bed as she'd lain down in. Jasim was still sleeping beside her. The window showed dawn, but it was not the usual view of the cliffs and the ocean.

Leila had the house brief her. After twenty thousand years—traveling more or less at lightspeed, pausing only for a microsecond or two at various way-stations to be cleaned up and amplified—the package of information bearing the two of them had arrived safely at Nazdeek-be-Beegane. This world was not crowded, and it had been tweaked to render it compatible with a range of metabolic styles. The house had negotiated a site where they could live embodied in comfort if they wished.

Jasim stirred and opened his eyes. "Good morning. How are you feeling?"

"Older."

"Really?"

Leila paused to consider this seriously. "No. Not even slightly. How about you?"

"I'm fine. I'm just wondering what's out there." He raised himself up to peer through the window. The house had been instantiated on a wide, empty plain, covered with low stalks of green and yellow vegetation. They could eat these plants, and the house had already started a spice garden while they slept. He stretched his shoulders. "Let's go and make breakfast."

They went downstairs, stepping into freshly minted bodies, then out into the garden. The air was still, the sun already warm. The house had tools prepared to help them with the harvest. It was the nature of travel that they had come empty-handed, and they had no relatives here, no fifteenth cousins, no friends of friends. It was the nature of the Amalgam that they were welcome nonetheless, and the machines that supervised this world on behalf of its inhabitants had done their best to provide for them.

"So this is the afterlife," Jasim mused, scything the yellow stalks. "Very rustic."

"Speak for yourself," Leila retorted. "I'm not dead yet." She put down her own scythe and bent to pluck one of the plants out by its roots.

The meal they made was filling but bland. Leila resisted the urge to tweak her perceptions of it; she preferred to face the challenge of working out decent recipes, which would make a useful counterpoint to the more daunting task they'd come here to attempt.

They spent the rest of the day just tramping around, exploring their immediate surroundings. The house had tapped into a nearby stream for water, and sunlight, stored, would provide all the power they needed. From some hills about an hour's walk away they could see into a field with another building, but they decided to wait a little longer before introducing themselves to their neighbors. The air had a slightly odd smell, due to the range of components needed to support other metabolic styles, but it wasn't too intrusive.

The onset of night took them by surprise. Even before the sun had set a smattering of stars began appearing in the east, and for a moment

Leila thought that these white specks against the fading blue were some kind of exotic atmospheric phenomenon, perhaps small clouds forming in the stratosphere as the temperature dropped. When it became clear what was happening, she beckoned to Jasim to sit beside her on the bank of the stream and watch the stars of the bulge come out.

They'd come at a time when Nazdeek lay between its sun and the galactic center. At dusk one half of the Aloof's dazzling territory stretched from the eastern horizon to the zenith, with the stars' slow march westward against a darkening sky only revealing more of their splendor.

"You think that was to die for?" Jasim joked as they walked back to the house.

"We could end this now, if you're feeling unambitious."

He squeezed her hand. "If this takes ten thousand years, I'm ready."

It was a mild night, they could have slept outdoors, but the spectacle was too distracting. They stayed downstairs, in the physical wing. Leila watched the strange thicket of shadows cast by the furniture sliding across the walls. These neighbors never sleep, she thought. When we come knocking, they'll ask what took us so long.

3

HUNDREDS OF observatories circled Nazdeek, built then abandoned by others who'd come on the same quest. When Leila saw the band of pristine space junk mapped out before her—orbits scrupulously maintained and swept clean by robot sentinels for eons—she felt as if she'd found the graves of their predecessors, stretching out in the field behind the house as far as the eye could see.

Nazdeek was prepared to offer them the resources to loft another package of instruments into the vacuum if they wished, but many of the abandoned observatories were perfectly functional, and most had been left in a compliant state, willing to take instructions from anyone.

Leila and Jasim sat in their living room and woke machine after machine from millennia of hibernation. Some, it turned out, had not been sleeping at all, but had been carrying on systematic observations, accumulating data long after their owners had lost interest.

In the crowded stellar precincts of the bulge, disruptive gravitational effects made planet formation rarer than it was in the disk, and orbits less stable. Nevertheless, planets had been found. A few thousand could be tracked from Nazdeek, and one observatory had been monitoring their atmospheric spectra for the last twelve millennia. In all of those worlds for all of those years, there were no signs of atmospheric composition departing from plausible, purely geochemical models. That meant no wild life, and no crude industries. It didn't prove that these worlds were uninhabited, but it suggested either that the Aloof went to great lengths to avoid leaving chemical fingerprints, or they lived in an entirely different fashion to any of the civilizations that had formed the Amalgam.

Of the eleven forms of biochemistry that had been found scattered around the galactic disk, all had given rise eventually to hundreds of species with general intelligence. Of the multitude of civilizations that had emerged from those roots, all contained cultures that had granted themselves the flexibility of living as software, but they also all contained cultures that persisted with corporeal existence. Leila would never have willingly given up either mode, herself, but while it was easy to imagine a subculture doing so, for a whole species it seemed extraordinary. In a sense, the intertwined civilization of the Amalgam owed its existence to the fact that there was as much cultural variation within every species as there was between one species and another. In that explosion of diversity, overlapping interests were inevitable.

If the Aloof were the exception, and their material culture had shrunk to nothing but a few discreet processors—each with the energy needs of a gnat, scattered throughout a trillion cubic light years of dust and blazing stars—then finding them would be impossible.

Of course, that worst-case scenario couldn't quite be true. The sole reason the Aloof were assumed to exist at all was the fact that some component of their material culture was tossing back every probe that was sent into the bulge. However discreet that machinery was, it certainly couldn't be sparse: given that it had managed to track, intercept and reverse the trajectories of billions of individual probes that had been sent in along thousands of different routes, relativistic constraints on the information flow implied that the Aloof had some kind of presence at more or less every star at the edge of the bulge.

Leila and Jasim had Nazdeek brief them on the most recent attempts to enter the bulge, but even after forty thousand years the basic facts hadn't changed. There was no crisply delineated barrier marking the Aloof's territory, but at some point within a border region about fifty light years wide, every single probe that was sent in ceased to function. The signals from those carrying in-flight beacons or transmitters went dead without warning. A century or so later, they would appear again at almost the same point, traveling in the opposite direction: back to where they'd come from. Those that were retrieved and examined were found to be unharmed, but their data logs contained nothing from the missing decades.

Jasim said, "The Aloof could be dead and gone. They built the perfect fence, but now it's outlasted them. It's just guarding their ruins."

Leila rejected this emphatically. "No civilization that's spread to more than one star system has ever vanished completely. Sometimes they've changed beyond recognition, but not one has ever died without descendants."

"That's a fact of history, but it's not a universal law," Jasim persisted. "If we're going to argue from the Amalgam all the time, we'll get nowhere. If the Aloof weren't exceptional, we wouldn't be here."

"That's true. But I won't accept that they're dead until I see some evidence."

"What would count as evidence? Apart from a million years of silence?"

Leila said, "Silence could mean anything. If they're really dead, we'll find something more, something definite."

"Such as?"

"If we see it, we'll know."

They began the project in earnest, reviewing data from the ancient observatories, stopping only to gather food, eat and sleep. They had resisted making detailed plans back on Najib, reasoning that any approach they mapped out in advance was likely to be rendered obsolete once they learned about the latest investigations. Now that they'd arrived and found the state of play utterly unchanged, Leila wished that they'd come armed with some clear options for dealing with the one situation they could have prepared for before they'd left.

In fact, though they might have felt like out-of-touch amateurs back on Najib, now that the Aloof had become their entire *raison d'être* it was far harder to relax and indulge in the kind of speculation that might actually bear fruit, given that every systematic approach had failed. Having come twenty thousand light years for this, they couldn't spend their time day-dreaming, turning the problem over in the backs of their minds while they surrendered to the rhythms of Nazdeek's rural idyll. So they studied everything that had been tried before, searching methodically for a new approach, hoping to see the old ideas with fresh eyes, hoping that—by chance if for no other reason—they might lack some crucial blind spot that had afflicted all of their predecessors.

After seven months without results or inspiration, it was Jasim who finally dragged them out of the rut. "We're getting nowhere," he said. "It's time to accept that, put all this aside, and go visit the neighbors."

Leila stared at him as if he'd lost his mind. "Go visit them? How? What makes you think that they're suddenly going to let us in?"

He said, "The neighbors. Remember? Over the hill. The ones who might actually want to talk to us."

4

THEIR NEIGHBORS had published a précis stating that they welcomed social contact in principle, but might take a while to respond. Jasim sent them an invitation, asking if they'd like to join them in their house, and waited.

After just three days, a reply came back. The neighbors did not want to put them to the trouble of altering their own house physically, and preferred not to become acorporeal at present. Given the less stringent requirements of Leila and Jasim's own species when embodied, might they wish to come instead to the neighbors' house?

Leila said, "Why not?" They set a date and time.

The neighbors' précis included all the biological and sociological details needed to prepare for the encounter. Their biochemistry was carbon-based and oxygen-breathing, but employed a different replicator to Leila and Jasim's DNA. Their ancestral phenotype resembled a large furred snake, and when embodied they generally lived in nests of a hundred or so. The minds of the individuals were perfectly autonomous, but solitude was an alien and unsettling concept for them.

Leila and Jasim set out late in the morning, in order to arrive early in the afternoon. There were some low, heavy clouds in the sky, but it was not completely overcast, and Leila noticed that when the sun passed behind the clouds, she could discern some of the brightest stars from the edge of the bulge.

Jasim admonished her sternly, "Stop looking. This is our day off."

The Snakes' building was a large squat cylinder resembling a water tank, which turned out to be packed with something mossy and pungent. When they arrived at the entrance, three of their hosts were waiting to greet them, coiled on the ground near the mouth of a large tunnel emerging from the moss. Their bodies were almost as wide as their guests', and some eight or ten meters long. Their heads bore two front-facing eyes, but their other sense organs were not prominent. Leila could make out their mouths, and knew from the briefing how many rows of teeth lay behind them, but the wide pink gashes stayed closed, almost lost in the gray fur.

The Snakes communicated with a low-frequency thumping, and their system of nomenclature was complex, so Leila just mentally tagged the three of them with randomly chosen, slightly exotic names—Tim, John and Sarah—and tweaked her translator so she'd recognize intuitively who was who, who was addressing her, and the significance of their gestures.

"Welcome to our home," said Tim enthusiastically.

"Thank you for inviting us," Jasim replied.

"We've had no visitors for quite some time," explained Sarah. "So we really are delighted to meet you."

"How long has it been?" Leila asked.

"Twenty years," said Sarah.

"But we came here for the quiet life," John added. "So we expected it would be a while."

Leila pondered the idea of a clan of a hundred ever finding a quiet life, but then, perhaps unwelcome intrusions from outsiders were of a different nature to family dramas.

"Will you come into the nest?" Tim asked. "If you don't wish to enter we won't take offense, but everyone would like to see you, and some of us aren't comfortable coming out into the open."

Leila glanced at Jasim. He said privately, "We can push our vision to IR. And tweak ourselves to tolerate the smell."

Leila agreed.

"Okay," Jasim told Tim.

Tim slithered into the tunnel and vanished in a quick, elegant motion, then John motioned with his head for the guests to follow. Leila went first, propelling herself up the gentle slope with her knees and elbows. The plant the Snakes cultivated for the nest formed a cool, dry, resilient surface. She could see Tim ten meters or so ahead, like a giant glow-worm shining with body heat, slowing down now to let her catch up. She glanced back at Jasim, who looked even weirder than the Snakes now, his face and arms blotched with strange bands of radiance from the exertion.

After a few minutes, they came to a large chamber. The air was humid, but after the confines of the tunnel it felt cool and fresh. Tim led them toward the center, where about a dozen other Snakes were already waiting to greet them. They circled the guests excitedly, thumping out a delighted welcome. Leila felt a surge of adrenaline; she knew that she and Jasim were in no danger, but the sheer size and energy of the creatures was overwhelming.

"Can you tell us why you've come to Nazdeek?" asked Sarah.

"Of course." For a second or two Leila tried to maintain eye contact with her, but like all the other Snakes she kept moving restlessly, a gesture that Leila's translator imbued with a sense of warmth and enthusiasm. As for lack of eye contact, the Snakes' own translators would understand perfectly that some aspects of ordinary, polite human behavior became impractical under the circumstances, and would not mislabel her actions. "We're here to learn about the Aloof," she said.

"The Aloof?" At first Sarah just seemed perplexed, then Leila's translator hinted at a touch of irony. "But they offer us nothing."

Leila was tongue-tied for a moment. The implication was subtle but unmistakable. Citizens of the Amalgam had a protocol for dealing with each other's curiosity: they published a précis, which spelled out clearly any information that they wished people in general to know about them, and also specified what, if any, further inquiries would be welcome. However, a citizen was perfectly entitled to publish no précis at all and have that decision respected. When no information was published, and no invitation offered, you simply had no choice but to mind your own business.

"They offer us nothing as far as we can tell," she said, "but that might be a misunderstanding, a failure to communicate."

"They send back all the probes," Tim replied. "Do you really think we've misunderstood what that means?"

Jasim said, "It means that they don't want us physically intruding on their territory, putting our machines right next to their homes, but I'm not convinced that it proves that they have no desire to communicate whatsoever."

"We should leave them in peace," Tim insisted. "They've seen the probes, so they know we're here. If they want to make contact, they'll do it in their own time."

"Leave them in peace," echoed another Snake. A chorus of affirmation followed from others in the chamber.

Leila stood her ground. "We have no idea how many different species and cultures might be living in the bulge. *One of them* sends back the probes, but for all we know there could be a thousand others who don't yet even know that the Amalgam has tried to make contact."

This suggestion set off a series of arguments, some between guests and hosts, some between the Snakes themselves. All the while, the Snakes kept circling excitedly, while new ones entered the chamber to witness the novel sight of these strangers.

When the clamor about the Aloof had quietened down enough for her to change the subject, Leila asked Sarah, "Why have you come to Nazdeek yourself?"

"It's out of the way, off the main routes. We can think things over here, undisturbed."

"But you could have the same amount of privacy anywhere. It's all a matter of what you put in your précis."

Sarah's response was imbued with a tinge of amusement. "For us, it would be unimaginably rude to cut off all contact explicitly, by decree. Especially with others from our own ancestral species. To live a quiet life, we had to reduce the likelihood of encountering anyone who would seek us out. We had to make the effort of rendering ourselves physically remote, in order to reap the benefits."

"Yet you've made Jasim and myself very welcome."

"Of course. But that will be enough for the next twenty years."

So much for resurrecting their social life. "What exactly is it that you're pondering in this state of solitude?"

"The nature of reality. The uses of existence. The reasons to live, and the reasons not to."

Leila felt the skin on her forearms tingle. She'd almost forgotten that she'd made an appointment with death, however uncertain the timing.

She explained how she and Jasim had made their decision to embark on a grand project before dying.

"That's an interesting approach," Sarah said. "I'll have to give it some thought." She paused, then added, "Though I'm not sure that you've solved the problem."

"What do you mean?"

"Will it really be easier now to choose the right moment to give up your life? Haven't you merely replaced one delicate judgment with an even more difficult one: deciding when you've exhausted the possibilities for contacting the Aloof?"

"You make it sound as if we have no chance of succeeding." Leila was not afraid of the prospect of failure, but the suggestion that it was inevitable was something else entirely.

Sarah said, "We've been here on Nazdeek for fifteen thousand years. We don't pay much attention to the world outside the nest, but even from this cloistered state we've seen many people break their backs against this rock."

"So when will you accept that your own project is finished?" Leila countered. "If you still don't have what you're looking for after fifteen thousand years, when will you admit defeat?"

"I have no idea," Sarah confessed. "I have no idea, any more than you do."

5

WHEN THE way forward first appeared, there was nothing to set it apart from a thousand false alarms that had come before it.

It was their seventeenth year on Nazdeek. They had launched their own observatory—armed with the latest refinements culled from around the galaxy—fifteen years before, and it had been confirming the null results of its predecessors ever since.

They had settled into an unhurried routine, systematically exploring the possibilities that observation hadn't yet ruled out. Between the scenarios that were obviously stone cold dead—the presence of an energy-rich, risk-taking, extroverted civilization in the bulge actively seeking contact by every means at its disposal—and the infinite number of possibilities that could never be distinguished at this distance from the absence of all life, and the absence of all machinery save one dumb but efficient gatekeeper, tantalizing clues would bubble up out of the data now and then, only to fade into statistical insignificance in the face of continued scrutiny.

Tens of billions of stars lying within the Aloof's territory could be discerned from Nazdeek, some of them evolving or violently interacting on a time scale of years or months. Black holes were flaying and swallowing their companions. Neutron stars and white dwarfs were stealing fresh fuel and flaring into novas. Star clusters were colliding and tearing each other apart. If you gathered data on this whole menagerie for long enough, you could expect to see almost anything. Leila would not have been surprised to wander into the garden at night and find a great welcome sign spelled out in the sky, before the fortuitous pattern of novas faded and the message dissolved into randomness again.

When their gamma ray telescope caught a glimmer of something odd—the nuclei of a certain isotope of fluorine decaying from an excited state, when there was no nearby source of the kind of radiation that could have put the nuclei into that state in the first place—it might have been just another random, unexplained fact to add to a vast pile. When the same glimmer was seen again, not far away, Leila reasoned that if a gas cloud enriched with fluorine could be affected at one location by an unseen radiation source, it should not be surprising if the same thing happened elsewhere in the same cloud.

It happened again. The three events lined up in space and time in a manner suggesting a short pulse of gamma rays in the form of a tightly focused beam, striking three different points in the gas cloud. Still, in the mountains of data they had acquired from their predecessors, coincidences far more compelling than this had occurred hundreds of thousands of times.

With the fourth flash, the balance of the numbers began to tip. The secondary gamma rays reaching Nazdeek gave only a weak and distorted impression of the original radiation, but all four flashes were consistent with a single, narrow beam. There were thousands of known gamma ray sources in the bulge, but the frequency of the radiation, the direction of the beam, and the time profile of the pulse did not fit with any of them.

The archives revealed a few dozen occasions when the same kind of emissions had been seen from fluorine nuclei under similar conditions.

There had never been more than three connected events before, but one sequence had occurred along a path not far from the present one.

Leila sat by the stream and modeled the possibilities. If the beam was linking two objects in powered flight, prediction was impossible. If receiver and transmitter were mostly in free-fall, though, and only made corrections occasionally, the past and present data combined gave her a plausible forecast for the beam's future orientation.

Jasim looked into her simulation, a thought-bubble of stars and equations hovering above the water. "The whole path will lie out of bounds," he said.

"No kidding." The Aloof's territory was more or less spherical, which made it a convex set: you couldn't get between any two points that lay inside it without entering the territory itself. "But look how much the beam spreads out. From the fluorine data, I'd say it could be tens of kilometers wide by the time it reaches the receiver."

"So they might not catch it all? They might let some of the beam escape into the disk?" He sounded unpersuaded.

Leila said, "Look, if they really were doing everything possible to hide this, we would never have seen these blips in the first place."

"Gas clouds with this much fluorine are extremely rare. They obviously picked a frequency that wouldn't be scattered under ordinary circumstances."

"Yes, but that's just a matter of getting the signal through the local environment. We choose frequencies ourselves that won't interact with any substance that's likely to be present along the route, but no choice is perfect, and we just live with that. It seems to me that they've done the same thing. If they were fanatical purists, they'd communicate by completely different methods."

"All right." Jasim reached into the model. "So where can we go that's in the line of sight?"

The short answer was: nowhere. If the beam was not blocked completely by its intended target it would spread out considerably as it made its way through the galactic disk, but it would not grow so wide that it would sweep across a single point where the Amalgam had any kind of outpost.

Leila said, "This is too good to miss. We need to get a decent observatory into its path."

Jasim agreed. "And we need to do it before these nodes decide they've drifted too close to something dangerous, and switch on their engines for a course correction."

They crunched through the possibilities. Wherever the Amalgam had an established presence, the infrastructure already on the ground could convert data into any kind of material object. Transmitting yourself to such a place, along with whatever you needed, was simplicity itself: lightspeed was the only real constraint. Excessive demands on the local resources might be denied, but modest requests were rarely rejected.

Far more difficult was building something new at a site with raw materials but no existing receiver; in that case, instead of pure data, you needed to send an engineering spore of some kind. If you were in a hurry, not only did you need to spend energy boosting the spore to relativistic velocities—a cost that snowballed due to the mass of protective shielding—you then had to waste much of the time you gained on a lengthy braking phase, or the spore would hit its target with enough energy to turn it into plasma. Interactions with the interstellar medium could be used to slow down the spore, avoiding the need to carry yet more mass to act as a propellant for braking, but the whole business was disgustingly inefficient.

Harder still was getting anything substantial to a given point in the vast empty space between the stars. With no raw materials to hand at the destination, everything had to be moved from somewhere else. The best starting point was usually to send an engineering spore into a cometary cloud, loosely bound gravitationally to its associated star, but not every such cloud was open to plunder, and everything took time, and obscene amounts of energy.

To arrange for an observatory to be delivered to the most accessible point along the beam's line of sight, traveling at the correct velocity, would take about fifteen thousand years all told. That assumed that the local cultures who owned the nearest facilities, and who had a right to veto the use of the raw materials, acceded immediately to their request.

"How long between course corrections?" Leila wondered. If the builders of this hypothetical network were efficient, the nodes could drift for a while in interstellar space without any problems, but in the bulge everything happened faster than in the disk, and the need to counter gravitational effects would come much sooner. There was no way to make a firm prediction, but they could easily have as little as eight or ten thousand years.

Leila struggled to reconcile herself to the reality. "We'll try at this location, and if we're lucky we might still catch something. If not, we'll try again after the beam shifts." Sending the first observatory chasing after the beam would be futile; even with the present free-fall motion of the nodes, the observation point would be moving at a substantial fraction of lightspeed relative to the local stars. Magnified by the enormous distances involved, a small change in direction down in the bulge could see the beam lurch thousands of light years sideways by the time it reached the disk.

Jasim said, "Wait." He magnified the region around the projected path of the beam.

"What are you looking for?"

He asked the map, "Are there two outposts of the Amalgam lying on a straight line that intersects the beam?"

The map replied in a tone of mild incredulity. "No."

"That was too much to hope for. Are there three lying on a plane that intersects the beam?"

The map said, "There are about ten-to-the-eighteen triples that meet that condition."

Leila suddenly realized what it was he had in mind. She laughed and squeezed his arm. "You are completely insane!"

Jasim said, "Let me get the numbers right first, then you can mock me." He rephrased his question to the map. "For how many of those triples would the beam pass between them, intersecting the triangle whose vertices they lie on?"

"About ten-to-the-sixth."

"How close to us is the closest point of intersection of the beam with any of those triangles—if the distance in each case is measured via the worst of the three outposts, the one that makes the total path longest."

"Seven thousand four hundred and twenty-six light years."

Leila said, "Collision braking. With three components?"

"Do you have a better idea?"

Better than twice as fast as the fastest conventional method? "Nothing comes to mind. Let me think about it."

Braking against the flimsy interstellar medium was a slow process. If you wanted to deliver a payload rapidly to a point that fortuitously lay somewhere on a straight line between two existing outposts, you could fire two separate packages from the two locations and let them "collide" when they met—or rather, let them brake against each other magnetically. If you arranged for the packages to have equal and opposite momenta, they would come to a halt without any need to throw away reaction mass or clutch at passing molecules, and some of their kinetic energy could be recovered as electricity and stored for later use.

The aim and the timing had to be perfect. Relativistic packages did not make in-flight course corrections, and the data available at each launch site about the other's precise location was always a potentially imperfect prediction, not a rock-solid statement of fact. Even with the Amalgam's prodigious astrometric and computing resources, achieving millimeter alignments at thousand-light-year distances could not be guaranteed.

Now Jasim wanted to make three of these bullets meet, perform an elaborate electromagnetic dance, and end up with just the right velocity needed to keep tracking the moving target of the beam.

In the evening, back in the house, they sat together working through simulations. It was easy to find designs that would work if everything went perfectly, but they kept hunting for the most robust variation, the one that was most tolerant of small misalignments. With standard two-body collision braking, the usual solution was to have the first package, shaped like a cylinder, pass right through a hole in the second package. As it emerged from the other side and the two moved apart again, the magnetic fields were switched from repulsive to attractive. Several "bounces" followed, and in the process as much of the kinetic energy as possible was gradually converted into superconducting currents for storage, while the rest was dissipated as electromagnetic radiation. Having three objects meeting at an angle would not only make the timing and positioning more critical, it would destroy the simple, axial symmetry and introduce a greater risk of instability.

It was dawn before they settled on the optimal design, which effectively split the problem in two. First, package one, a sphere, would meet package two, a torus, threading the gap in the middle, then bouncing back and forth through it seventeen times. The plane of the torus would lie at an angle to its direction of flight, allowing the sphere to approach it head-on. When the two finally came to rest with respect to each other, they would still have a component of their velocity carrying them straight toward package three, a cylinder with an axial borehole.

Because the electromagnetic interactions were the same as the two-body case—self-centring, intrinsically stable—a small amount of misalignment at each of these encounters would not be fatal. The usual two-body case, though, didn't require the combined package, after all the bouncing and energy dissipation was completed, to be moving on a path so precisely determined that it could pass through yet another narrow hoop.

There were no guarantees, and in the end the result would be in other people's hands. They could send requests to the three outposts, asking for these objects to be launched at the necessary times on the necessary trajectories. The energy needs hovered on the edge of politeness, though, and it was possible that one or more of the requests would simply be refused.

Jasim waved the models away, and they stretched out on the carpet, side by side.

He said, "I never thought we'd get this far. Even if this is only a mirage, I never thought we'd find one worth chasing."

Leila said, "I don't know what I expected. Some kind of great folly: some long, exhausting, exhilarating struggle that felt like wandering through a jungle for years and ending up utterly lost."

"And then what?"

"Surrender."

Jasim was silent for a while. Leila could sense that he was brooding over something, but she didn't press him.

He said, "Should we travel to this observatory ourselves, or wait here for the results?"

"We should go. Definitely! I don't want to hang around here for fifteen thousand years, waiting. We can leave the Nazdeek observatories hunting for more beam fluorescence and broadcasting the results, so we'll hear about them wherever we end up."

"That makes sense." Jasim hesitated, then added, "When we go, I don't want to leave a back-up."

"Ah." They'd traveled from Najib leaving nothing of themselves behind: if their transmission had somehow failed to make it to Nazdeek, no stored copy of the data would ever have woken to resume their truncated lives. Travel within the Amalgam's established network carried negligible risks, though. If they flung themselves toward the hypothetical location of this yet-to-be-assembled station in the middle of nowhere, it was entirely possible that they'd sail off to infinity without ever being instantiated again.

Leila said, "Are you tired of what we're doing? Of what we've become?"

"It's not that."

"This one chance isn't the be-all and end-all. Now that we know how to hunt for the beams, I'm sure we'll find this one again after its shifts. We could find a thousand others, if we're persistent."

"I know that," he said. "I don't want to stop, I don't want to end this. But I want to *risk* ending it. Just once. While that still means something."

Leila sat up and rested her head on her knees. She could understand what he was feeling, but it still disturbed her.

Jasim said, "We've already achieved something extraordinary. No one's found a clue like this in a million years. If we leave that to posterity, it will be pursued to the end, we can be sure of that. But I desperately want to pursue it myself. With you."

"And because you want that so badly, you need to face the chance of losing it?"

"Yes."

It was one thing they had never tried. In their youth, they would never have knowingly risked death. They'd been too much in love, too eager for the life they'd yet to live; the stakes would have been unbearably high. In the twilight years, back on Najib, it would have been an easy thing to do, but an utterly insipid pleasure.

Jasim sat up and took her hand. "Have I hurt you with this?"

"No, no." She shook her head pensively, trying to gather her thoughts. She didn't want to hide her feelings, but she wanted to express them precisely, not blurt them out in a confusing rush. "I always thought we'd reach the end together, though. We'd come to some point in the jungle, look around, exchange a glance, and know that we'd arrived. Without even needing to say it aloud."

Jasim drew her to him and held her. "All right, I'm sorry. Forget everything I said."

Leila pushed him away, annoyed. "This isn't something you can take back. If it's the truth, it's the truth. Just give me some time to decide what I want."

They put it aside, and buried themselves in work: polishing the design for the new observatory, preparing the requests to send to the three outposts. One of the planets they would be petitioning belonged to the Snakes, so Leila and Jasim went to visit the nest for a second time, to seek advice on the best way to beg for this favor. Their neighbors seemed more excited just to see them again than they were at the news that a tiny rent had appeared in the Aloof's million-year-old cloak of discretion. When Leila gently pushed her on this point, Sarah said, "You're here, here and now, our guests in flesh and blood. I'm sure I'll be dead long before the Aloof are willing to do the same."

Leila thought: What kind of strange greed is it that I'm suffering from? I can be feted by creatures who rose up from the dust through a completely different molecule than my own ancestors. I can sit among them and discuss the philosophy of life and death. The Amalgam has already joined every willing participant in the galaxy into one vast conversation. And I want to go and eavesdrop on the Aloof? Just because they've played hard-to-get for a million years?

They dispatched requests for the three modules to be built and launched by their three as-yet unwitting collaborators, specifying the final countdown to the nanosecond but providing a ten-year period for the project to be debated. Leila felt optimistic; however blasé the Nazdeek nest had been, she suspected that no space-faring culture really could resist the chance to peek behind the veil.

They had thirty-six years to wait before they followed in the wake of their petitions; on top of the ten-year delay, the new observatory's modules would be traveling at a fraction of a percent below lightspeed, so they needed a head start.

No more tell-tale gamma ray flashes appeared from the bulge, but Leila hadn't expected any so soon. They had sent the news of their discovery to other worlds close to the Aloof's territory, so eventually a thousand other groups with different vantage points would be searching for the same kind of evidence and finding their own ways to interpret and exploit it. It hurt a little, scattering their hard-won revelation to the wind for anyone to use—perhaps even to beat them to some far greater prize—but they'd relied on the generosity of their predecessors from the moment they'd arrived on Nazdeek, and the sheer scale of the overall problem made it utterly perverse to cling selfishly to their own small triumph.

As the day of their departure finally arrived, Leila came to a decision. She understood Jasim's need to put everything at risk, and in a sense she shared it. If she had always imagined the two of them ending this together—struggling on, side by side, until the way forward was lost and the undergrowth closed in on them—then *that* was what she'd risk. She would take the flip side to his own wager.

When the house took their minds apart and sent them off to chase the beam, Leila left a copy of herself frozen on Nazdeek. If no word of their safe arrival reached it by the expected time, it would wake and carry on the search.

Alone.

6

"WELCOME TO Trident. We're honored by the presence of our most distinguished guest."

Jasim stood beside the bed, waving a triangular flag. Red, green and blue in the corners merged to white in the center.

"How long have you been up?"

"About an hour," he said. Leila frowned, and he added apologetically, "You were sleeping very deeply, I didn't want to disturb you."

"I should be the one giving the welcome," she said. "You're the one who might never have woken."

The bedroom window looked out into a dazzling field of stars. It was not a view facing the bulge—by now Leila could recognize the distinctive spectra of the region's stars with ease—but even these disk stars were so crisp and bright that this was like no sky she had ever seen.

"Have you been downstairs?" she said.

"Not yet. I wanted us to decide on that together." The house had no physical wing here; the tiny observatory had no spare mass for such frivolities as embodying them, let alone constructing architectural follies in the middle of interstellar space. "Downstairs" would be nothing but a scape that they were free to design at will.

"Everything worked," she said, not quite believing it.

Jasim spread his arms. "We're here, aren't we?"

They watched a reconstruction of the first two modules coming together. The timing and the trajectories were as near to perfect as they could have hoped for, and the superconducting magnets had been constructed to a standard of purity and homogeneity that made the magnetic embrace look like an idealized simulation. By the time the two had locked together, the third module was just minutes away. Some untraceable discrepancy between reality and prediction in the transfer of momentum to radiation had the composite moving at a tiny angle away from its expected course, but when it met the third module the magnetic fields still meshed in a stable configuration, and there was energy to spare to nudge the final assembly precisely into step with the predicted swinging of the Aloof's beam.

The Amalgam had lived up to its promise: three worlds full of beings they had never met, who owed them nothing, who did not even share their molecular ancestry, had each diverted enough energy to light up all their cities for a decade, and followed the instructions of strangers down to the atom, down to the nanosecond, in order to make this work.

What happened now was entirely in the hands of the Aloof.

Trident had been functioning for about a month before its designers had arrived to take up occupancy. So far, it had not yet observed any gamma ray signals spilling out of the bulge. The particular pulse that Leila and Jasim had seen triggering fluorescence would be long gone, of course, but the usefulness of their present location was predicated on three assumptions: the Aloof would use the same route for many other bursts of data; some of the radiation carrying that data would slip past the intended receiver; and the two nodes of the network would have continued in free fall long enough for the spilt data to be arriving here still, along the same predictable path.

Without those three extra components, delivered by their least reliable partners, Trident would be worthless.

"Downstairs," Leila said. "Maybe a kind of porch with glass walls?"

"Sounds fine to me."

She conjured up a plan of the house and sketched some ideas, then they went down to try them out at full scale.

THEY HAD been into orbit around Najib, and they had traveled embodied to its three beautiful, barren sibling worlds, but they had never been in interstellar space before. Or at least, they had never been conscious of it.

They were still not truly embodied, but you didn't need flesh and blood to feel the vacuum around you; to be awake and plugged-in to an honest depiction of your surroundings was enough. The nearest of Trident's contributor worlds was six hundred light years away. The distance to Najib was unthinkable. Leila paced around the porch, looking out at the stars, vertiginous in her virtual body, unsteady in the phoney gravity.

It had been twenty-eight thousand years since they'd left Najib. All her children and grandchildren had almost certainly chosen death, long ago. No messages had been sent after them to Nazdeek; Leila had asked for that silence, fearing that it would be unbearably painful to hear news, day after day, to which she could give no meaningful reply, about events in which she could never participate. Now she regretted that. She wanted to read the lives of her grandchildren, as she might the biography of an ancestor. She wanted to know how things had ended up, like the time traveler she was.

A second month of observation passed, with nothing. A data feed reaching them from Nazdeek was equally silent. For any new hint of the beam's location to reach Nazdeek, and then the report of that to reach Trident, would take thousands of years longer than the direct passage of the beam itself, so if Nazdeek saw evidence that the beam was "still" on course, that would be old news about a pulse they had not been here to intercept. However, if Nazdeek reported that the beam had shifted, at least that would put them out of their misery immediately, and tell them that Trident had been built too late.

Jasim made a vegetable garden on the porch and grew exotic food in the starlight. Leila played along, and ate beside him; it was a harmless game. They could have painted anything at all around the house: any planet they'd visited, drawn from their memories, any imaginary world. If this small pretense was enough to keep them sane and anchored to reality, so be it.

Now and then, Leila felt the strangest of the many pangs of isolation Trident induced: here, the knowledge of the galaxy was no longer at her fingertips. Their descriptions as travelers had encoded their vast personal memories, declarative and episodic, and their luggage had included prodigious libraries, but she was used to having so much more. Every civilized planet held a storehouse of information that was simply too bulky to fit into Trident, along with a constant feed of exabytes of news flooding in from other worlds. Wherever you were in the galaxy, some news was old news, some cherished theories long discredited, some facts hopelessly out of date. Here, though, Leila knew, there were billions of rigourously established truths—the results of hundreds of millennia of thought, experiment, and observation—that had slipped out of her reach. Questions that any other child of the Amalgam could expect to have answered instantly would take twelve hundred years to receive a reply.

No such questions actually came into her mind, but there were still moments when the mere fact of it was enough to make her feel unbearably rootless, cut adrift not only from her past and her people, but from civilization itself.

∿

TRIDENT SHOUTED: "Data!"

Leila was half-way through recording a postcard to the Nazdeek Snakes. Jasim was on the porch watering his plants. Leila turned to see him walking through the wall, commanding the bricks to part like a gauze curtain.

They stood side by side, watching the analysis emerge.

A pulse of gamma rays of the expected frequency, from precisely the right location, had just washed over Trident. The beam was greatly attenuated by distance, not to mention having had most of its energy intercepted by its rightful owner, but more than enough had slipped past and reached them for Trident to make sense of the nature of the pulse.

It was, unmistakably, modulated with information. There were precisely repeated phase shifts in the radiation that were unimaginable in any natural gamma ray source, and which would have been pointless in any artificial beam produced for any purpose besides communication.

The pulse had been three seconds long, carrying about ten-to-the-twenty-fourth bits of data. The bulk of this appeared to be random, but that did not rule out meaningful content, it simply implied efficient encryption. The Amalgam's network sent encrypted data via robust classical channels like this, while sending the keys needed to decode it by a second, quantum channel. Leila had never expected to get hold of unencrypted data, laying bare the secrets of the Aloof in an instant. To have clear evidence that someone in the bulge was talking to someone else, and to have pinned down part of the pathway connecting them, was vindication enough.

There was more, though. Between the messages themselves, Trident had identified brief, orderly, unencrypted sequences. Everything was guesswork to a degree, but with such a huge slab of data statistical measures were powerful indicators. Part of the data looked like routing information, addresses for the messages as they were carried through the network. Another part looked like information about the nodes' current and future trajectories. If Trident really had cracked that, they could work out where to position its successor. In fact, if they placed the successor close enough to the bulge, they could probably keep that one observatory constantly inside the spill from the beam.

Jasim couldn't resist playing devil's advocate. "You know, this could just be one part of whatever throws the probes back in our faces, talking to another part. The Aloof themselves could still be dead, while their security system keeps humming with paranoid gossip."

Leila said blithely, "Hypothesize away. I'm not taking the bait."

She turned to embrace him, and they kissed. She said, "I've forgotten how to celebrate. What happens now?"

He moved his fingertips gently along her arm. Leila opened up the scape, creating a fourth spatial dimension. She took his hand, kissed it, and placed it against her beating heart. Their bodies reconfigured, nerve-endings crowding every surface, inside and out.

Jasim climbed inside her, and she inside him, the topology of the scape changing to wrap them together in a mutual embrace. Everything vanished from their lives but pleasure, triumph, and each other's presence, as close as it could ever be.

7

"ARE YOU here for the Listening Party?"

The chitinous heptapod, who'd been wandering the crowded street with a food cart dispensing largesse at random, offered Leila a plate of snacks tailored to her and Jasim's preferences. She accepted it, then paused to let Tassef, the planet they'd just set foot on, brief her as to the meaning of this phrase. People, Tassef explained, had traveled to this world from throughout the region in order to witness a special event. Some fifteen thousand years before, a burst of data from the Aloof's network had been picked up by a nearby observatory. In isolation, these bursts meant very little; however, the locals were hopeful that at least one of several proposed observatories near Massa, on the opposite side of the bulge, would have seen spillage including many of the same data packets, forty thousand years before. If any such observations had in fact taken place, news of their precise contents should now, finally, be about to reach Tassef by the longer, disk-based routes of the Amalgam's own network. Once the two observations could be compared, it would become clear which messages from the earlier Eavesdropping session had made their way to the part of the Aloof's network that could be sampled from Tassef. The comparison would advance the project of mapping all the symbolic addresses seen in the data onto actual physical locations.

Leila said, "That's not why we came, but now we know, we're even more pleased to be here."

The heptapod emitted a chirp that Leila understood as a gracious welcome, then pushed its way back into the throng.

Jasim said, "Remember when you told me that everyone would get bored with the Aloof while we were still in transit?"

"I said that would happen eventually. If not this trip, the next one."

"Yes, but you said it five journeys ago."

Leila scowled, preparing to correct him, but then she checked and he was right.

They hadn't expected Tassef to be so crowded when they'd chosen it as their destination, some ten thousand years before. The planet had given them a small room in this city, Shalouf, and imposed a thousand-year limit on their presence if they wished to remain embodied without adopting local citizenship. More than a billion visitors had arrived over the last fifty years, anticipating the news of the observations from Massa, but unable to predict the precise time it would reach Tassef because the details of the observatories' trajectories had still been in transit.

She confessed, "I never thought a billion people would arrange their travel plans around this jigsaw puzzle."

"Travel plans?" Jasim laughed. "We chose to have our own deaths revolve around the very same thing."

"Yes, but we're just weird."

Jasim gestured at the crowded street. "I don't think we can compete on that score."

They wandered through the city, drinking in the decades-long-carnival atmosphere. There were people of every phenotype Leila had encountered before, and more: bipeds, quadrupeds, hexapods, heptapods, walking, shuffling, crawling, scuttling, or soaring high above the street on feathered, scaled or membranous wings. Some were encased in their preferred atmospheres; others, like Leila and Jasim, had chosen instead to be embodied in ersatz flesh that didn't follow every ancestral chemical dictate. Physics and geometry tied evolution's hands, and many attempts to solve the same problems had converged on similar answers, but the galaxy's different replicators still managed their idiosyncratic twists. When Leila let her translator sample the cacophony of voices and signals at random, she felt as if the whole disk, the whole Amalgam, had converged on this tiny metropolis.

In fact, most of the travelers had come just a few hundred light years to be here. She and Jasim had chosen to keep their role in the history of Eavesdropping out of their précis, and Leila caught herself with a rather smug sense of walking among the crowd like some unacknowledged sage, bemused by the late-blooming, and no doubt superficial, interest of the masses. On reflection, though, any sense of superior knowledge was hard to justify, when most of these people would have grown up steeped in developments that she was only belatedly catching up with. A new generation of observatories had been designed while she and Jasim were in transit, based on "strong bullets": specially designed femtomachines, clusters of protons and neutrons stable only for trillionths of a second, launched at ultra-relativistic speeds so great that time dilation enabled them to survive long enough to collide with other components and merge into tiny, short-lived gamma-ray observatories. The basic trick that had built Trident had gone from a one-off gamble into a miniaturized, mass-produced phenomenon, with literally billions of strong bullets being fired continuously from thousands of planets around the inner disk.

Femtomachines themselves were old hat, but it had taken the technical challenges of Eavesdropping to motivate someone into squeezing a few more tricks out of them. Historians had always understood that in the long run, technological progress was a horizontal asymptote: once people had more or less everything they wanted that was physically possible, every incremental change would take exponentially longer to achieve, with diminishing returns and ever less reason to bother. The Amalgam would probably spend an eon inching its way closer to the flatline, but this was proof that shifts of circumstance alone could still trigger a modest renaissance or two, without the need for any radical scientific discovery or even a genuinely new technology.

They stopped to rest in a square, beside a small fountain gushing aromatic hydrocarbons. The Tassef locals, quadrupeds with slick, rubbery hides, played in the sticky black spray then licked each other clean.

Jasim shaded his eyes from the sun. He said, "We've had our autumn child, and we've seen its grandchildren prosper. I'm not sure what's left."

"No." Leila was in no rush to die, but they'd sampled fifty thousand years of their discovery's consequences. They'd followed in the wake of the news of the gamma ray signals as it circled the inner disk, spending less than a century conscious as they sped from world to world. At first they'd been hunting for some vital new role to play, but they'd slowly come to accept that the avalanche they'd triggered had out-raced them. Physical and logical maps of the Aloof's network were being constructed, as fast as the laws of physics allowed. Billions of people on thousands of planets, scattered around the inner rim of the Amalgam's territory, were sharing their observations to help piece together the living skeleton of their elusive neighbors. When that project was complete it would not be the end of anything, but it could mark the start of a long hiatus. The encrypted, classical data would never yield anything more than traffic routes; no amount of ingenuity could extract its content. The quantum keys that could unlock it, assuming the Aloof even used such things, would be absolutely immune to theft, duplication, or surreptitious sampling. One day, there would be another breakthrough, and everything would change again, but did they want to wait a hundred thousand years, a million, just to see what came next?

The solicitous heptapods—not locals, but visitors from a world thirty light years away who had nonetheless taken on some kind of innate duty of hospitality—seemed to show up whenever anyone was hungry. Leila tried to draw this second one into conversation, but it politely excused itself to rush off and feed someone else.

Leila said, "Maybe this is it. We'll wait for the news from Massa, then celebrate for a while, then finish it."

Jasim took her hand. "That feels right to me. I'm not certain, but I don't think I'll ever be."

"Are you tired?" she said. "Bored?"

"Not at all," he replied. "I feel *satisfied*. With what we've done, what we've seen. And I don't want to dilute that. I don't want to hang around forever, watching it fade, until we start to feel the way we did on Najib all over again."

"No."

They sat in the square until dusk, and watched the stars of the bulge come out. They'd seen this dazzling jewelled hub from every possible angle now, but Leila never grew tired of the sight.

Jasim gave an amused, exasperated sigh. "That beautiful, maddening, unreachable place. I think the whole Amalgam will be dead and gone without anyone setting foot inside it."

Leila felt a sudden surge of irritation, which deepened into a sense of revulsion. "It's a place, like any other place! Stars, gas, dust, planets. It's not some metaphysical realm. It's not even far away. Our own home world is twenty times more distant."

"Our own home world doesn't have an impregnable fence around it. If we really wanted to, we could go back there."

Leila was defiant. "If we really wanted to, we could enter the bulge."

Jasim laughed. "Have you read something in those messages that you didn't tell me about? How to say 'open sesame' to the gatekeepers?"

Leila stood, and summoned a map of the Aloof's network to superimpose across their vision, criss-crossing the sky with slender cones of violet light. One cone appeared head-on, as a tiny circle: the beam whose spillage came close to Tassef. She put her hand on Jasim's shoulder, and zoomed in on that circle. It opened up before them like a beckoning tunnel.

She said, "We know where this beam is coming from. We don't know for certain that the traffic between these particular nodes runs in both directions, but we've found plenty of examples where it does. If we aim a signal from here, back along the path of the spillage, and we make it wide enough, then we won't just hit the sending node. We'll hit the receiver as well."

Jasim was silent.

"We know the data format," she continued. "We know the routing information. We can address the data packets to a node on the other side of the bulge, one where the spillage comes out at Massa."

Jasim said, "What makes you think they'll accept the packets?"

"There's nothing in the format we don't understand, nothing we can't write for ourselves."

"Nothing in the unencrypted part. If there's an authorization, even a checksum, in the encrypted part, then any packet without that will be tossed away as noise."

"That's true," she conceded.

"Do you really want to do this?" he said. Her hand was still on his shoulder, she could feel his body growing tense.

"Absolutely."

"We mail ourselves from here to Massa, as unencrypted, classical data that anyone can read, anyone can copy, anyone can alter or corrupt?"

"A moment ago you said they'd throw us away as noise."

"That's the least of our worries."

"Maybe."

Jasim shuddered, his body almost convulsing. He let out a string of obscenities, then made a choking sound. "What's wrong with you? Is this some kind of test? If I call your bluff, will you admit that you're joking?"

Leila shook her head. "And no, it's not revenge for what you did on the way to Trident. This is our chance. *This* is what we were waiting to do—not the Eavesdropping, that's nothing! The bulge is right here in front of us. The Aloof are in there, somewhere. We can't force them to engage with us, but we can get closer to them than anyone has ever been before."

"If we go in this way, they could do anything to us."

"They're not barbarians. They haven't made war on us. Even the engineering spores come back unharmed."

"If we infest their network, that's worse than an engineering spore."

"'Infest'! None of these routes are crowded. A few exabytes passing through is nothing."

"You have no idea how they'll react."

"No," she confessed. "I don't. But I'm ready to find out."

Jasim stood. "We could send a test message first. Then go to Massa and see if it arrived safely."

"We could do that," Leila conceded. "That would be a sensible plan."

"So you agree?" Jasim gave her a wary, frozen smile. "We'll send a test message. Send an encyclopedia. Send greetings in some universal language."

"Fine. We'll send all of those things first. But I'm not waiting more than one day after that. I'm not going to Massa the long way. I'm taking the short-cut; I'm going through the bulge."

8

THE AMALGAM had been so generous to Leila, and local interest in the Aloof so intense, that she had almost forgotten that she was not, in fact, entitled to a limitless and unconditional flow of resources, to be employed to any end that involved her obsession.

When she asked Tassef for the means to build a high-powered gamma-ray transmitter to aim into the bulge, it interrogated her for an hour, then replied that the matter would require a prolonged and extensive consultation. It was, she realized, no use protesting that compared to hosting a billion guests for a couple of centuries, the cost of this was nothing. The sticking point was not the energy use, or any other equally microscopic consequence for the comfort and amenity of the Tassef locals. The issue was whether her proposed actions might be seen as unwelcome and offensive by the Aloof, and whether that affront might in turn provoke some kind of retribution.

Countless probes and spores had been gently and patiently returned from the bulge unharmed, but they'd come blundering in at less than lightspeed. A flash of gamma rays could not be intercepted and returned before it struck its chosen target. Though it seemed to Leila that it would be a trivial matter for the network to choose to reject the data, it was not unreasonable to suppose that the Aloof's sensibilities might differ on this point from her own.

Jasim had left Shalouf for a city on the other side of the planet. Leila's feelings about this were mixed; it was always painful when they separated, but the reminder that they were not irrevocably welded together also brought an undeniable sense of space and freedom. She loved him beyond measure, but that was not the final word on every question. She was not certain that she would not relent in the end, and die quietly beside him when the news came through from Massa; there were moments when it seemed utterly perverse, masochistic and self-aggrandising to flee from that calm, dignified end for the sake of trying to cap their modest revolution with a new and spectacularly dangerous folly. Nor though, was she certain that Jasim would not change his own mind, and take her hand while they plunged off this cliff together.

When the months dragged on with no decision on her request, no news from Massa and no overtures from her husband, Leila became an orator, traveling from city to city promoting her scheme to blaze a trail through the heart of the bulge. Her words and image were conveyed into virtual fora, but her physical presence was a way to draw attention to her cause, and Listening Party pilgrims and Tassefi alike packed the meeting places when she came. She mastered the locals' language and style, but left it inflected with some suitably alien mannerisms. The fact that a rumor had arisen that she was one of the First Eavesdroppers did no harm to her attendance figures.

When she reached the city of Jasim's self-imposed exile, she searched the audience for him in vain. As she walked out into the night a sense of panic gripped her. She felt no fear for herself, but the thought of him dying here alone was unbearable.

She sat in the street, weeping. How had it come to this? They had been prepared for a glorious failure, prepared to be broken by the Aloof's unyielding silence, and instead the fruits of their labor had swept through the disk, reinvigorating a thousand cultures. How could the taste of success be so bitter?

Leila imagined calling out to Jasim, finding him, holding him again, repairing their wounds.

A splinter of steel remained inside her, though. She looked up into the blazing sky. The Aloof were there, waiting, daring her to stand before them. To come this far, then step back from the edge for the comfort of a familiar embrace, would diminish her. She would not retreat.

~w~

THE NEWS arrived from Massa: forty thousand years before, the spillage from the far side of the bulge had been caught in time. Vast swathes of the data matched the observations that Tassef had been holding in anticipation of this moment, for the last fifteen thousand years.

There was more: reports of other correlations from other observatories followed within minutes. As the message from Massa had been relayed around the inner disk, a cascade of similar matches with other stores of data had been found.

By seeing where packets dropped out of the stream, their abstract addresses became concrete, physical locations within the bulge. As Leila stood in Shalouf's main square in the dusk, absorbing the reports, the Aloof's network was growing more solid, less ethereal, by the minute.

The streets around her were erupting with signs of elation: polyglot shouts, chirps and buzzes, celebratory scents and vivid pigmentation changes. Bursts of luminescence spread across the square. Even the relentlessly sober heptapods had abandoned their food carts to lie on their backs, spinning with delight. Leila wheeled around, drinking it in, commanding her translator to punch the meaning of every disparate gesture and sound deep into her brain, unifying the kaleidoscope into a single emotional charge.

As the stars of the bulge came out, Tassef offered an overlay for everyone to share, with the newly mapped routes shining like golden highways. From all around her, Leila picked up the signals of those who were joining the view: people of every civilization, every species, every replicator were seeing the Aloof's secret roads painted across the sky.

Leila walked through the streets of Shalouf, feeling Jasim's absence sharply, but too familiar with that pain to be overcome by it. If the joy of this moment was muted, every celebration would be blighted in the same way, now. She could not expect anything else. She would grow inured to it.

Tassef spoke to her.

"The citizens have reached a decision. They will grant your request."

"I'm grateful."

"There is a condition. The transmitter must be built at least twenty light-years away, either in interstellar space, or in the circumstellar region of an uninhabited system."

"I understand." This way, in the event that the Aloof felt threatened to the point of provoking destructive retribution, Tassef would survive an act of violence, at least on a stellar scale, directed against the transmitter itself.

"We advise you to prepare your final plans for the hardware, and submit them when you're sure they will fulfill your purpose."

"Of course."

Leila went back to her room, and reviewed the plans she had already drafted. She had anticipated the Tassefi wanting a considerable safety margin, so she had worked out the energy budgets for detailed scenarios involving engineering spores and forty-seven different cometary clouds that fell within Tassef's jurisdiction. It took just seconds to identify the best one that met the required conditions, and she lodged it without hesitation.

Out on the streets, the Listening Party continued. For the billion pilgrims, this was enough: they would go home, return to their grandchildren, and die happy in the knowledge that they had finally seen something new in the world. Leila envied them; there'd been a time when that would have been enough for her, too.

She left her room and rejoined the celebration, talking, laughing, dancing with strangers, letting herself grow giddy with the moment. When the sun came up, she made her way home, stepping lightly over the sleeping bodies that filled the street.

ᵐᵥᵥᵥ

THE ENGINEERING spores were the latest generation: strong bullets launched at close to lightspeed that shed their momentum by diving through the heart of a star, and then rebuilding themselves at atomic density as they decayed in the stellar atmosphere. In effect, the dying femtomachines constructed nanomachines bearing the same blueprints as they'd carried within themselves at nuclear densities, and which then continued out to the cometary cloud to replicate and commence the real work of mining raw materials and building the gamma ray transmitter.

Leila contemplated following in their wake, sending herself as a signal to be picked up by the as-yet-unbuilt transmitter. It would not have been as big a gamble as Jasim's with Trident; the strong bullets had already been used successfully this way in hundreds of similar stars.

In the end, she chose to wait on Tassef for a signal that the transmitter had been successfully constructed, and had tested, aligned and calibrated itself. If she was going to march blindly into the bulge, it would be absurd to stumble and fall prematurely, before she even reached the precipice.

When the day came, some ten thousand people gathered in the center of Shalouf to bid the traveler a safe journey. Leila would have preferred to slip away quietly, but after all her lobbying she had surrendered her privacy, and the Tassefi seemed to feel that she owed them this last splash of color and ceremony.

Forty-six years after the Listening Party, most of the pilgrims had returned to their homes, but of the few hundred who had lingered in Shalouf nearly all had showed up for this curious footnote to the main event. Leila wasn't sure that anyone here believed the Aloof's network would do more than bounce her straight back into the disk, but the affection these well-wishers expressed seemed genuine. Someone had even gone to the trouble of digging up a phrase in the oldest known surviving language of her ancestral species: *safar bekheyr*, may your journey be blessed. They had written it across the sky in an ancient script that she'd last seen eighty thousand years before, and it had been spread among the crowd phonetically so that everyone she met could offer her this hopeful farewell as she passed.

Tassef, the insentient delegate of all the planet's citizens, addressed the crowd with some somber ceremonial blather. Leila's mind wandered, settling on the observation that she was probably partaking in a public execution. No matter. She had said goodbye to her friends and family long ago. When she stepped through the ceremonial gate, which had been smeared with a tarry mess that the Tassefi considered the height of beauty, she would close her eyes and recall her last night on Najib, letting the intervening millennia collapse into a dream. Everyone chose death in the end, and no one's exit was perfect. Better to rely on your own flawed judgments, better to make your own ungainly mess of it, than live in the days when nature would simply take you at random.

As Tassef fell silent, a familiar voice rose up from the crowd.

"Are you still resolved to do this foolish thing?"

Leila glared down at her husband. "Yes, I am."

"You won't reconsider?"

"No."

"Then I'm coming with you."

Jasim pushed his way through the startled audience, and climbed onto the stage.

Leila spoke to him privately. "You're embarrassing us both."

He replied the same way. "Don't be petty. I know I've hurt you, but the blame lies with both of us."

"Why are you doing this? You've made your own wishes very plain."

"Do you think I can watch you walk into danger, and not walk beside you?"

"You were ready to die if Trident failed. You were ready to leave me behind then."

"Once I spoke my mind on that you gave me no choice. You insisted." He took her hand. "You know I only stayed away from you all this time because I hoped it would dissuade you. I failed. So now I'm here."

Leila's heart softened. "You're serious? You'll come with me?"

Jasim said, "Whatever they do to you, let them do it to us both."

Leila had no argument to make against this, no residue of anger, no false solicitousness. She had always wanted him beside her at the end, and she would not refuse him now.

She spoke to Tassef. "One more passenger. Is that acceptable?" The energy budget allowed for a thousand years of test transmissions to follow in her wake; Jasim would just be a minor blip of extra data.

"It's acceptable." Tassef proceeded to explain the change to the assembled crowd, and to the onlookers scattered across the planet.

Jasim said, "We'll interweave the data from both of us into a single packet. I don't want to end up at Massa and find they've sent you to Jahnom by mistake."

"All right." Leila arranged the necessary changes. None of the Eavesdroppers yet knew that they were coming, and no message sent the long way could warn them in time, but the data they sent into the bulge would be prefaced by instructions that anyone in the Amalgam would find clear and unambiguous, asking that their descriptions only be embodied if they were picked up at Massa. If they were found in other spillage along the way, they didn't want to be embodied multiple times. And if they did not emerge at Massa at all, so be it.

Tassef's second speech came to an end. Leila looked down at the crowd one last time, and let her irritation with the whole bombastic ceremony dissipate into amusement. If she had been among the sane, she might easily have turned up herself to watch a couple of ancient fools try to step onto the imaginary road in the sky, and wish them *safar bekheyr*.

She squeezed Jasim's hand, and they walked toward the gate.

9

Leila's fingers came together, her hand empty. She felt as if she was falling, but nothing in sight appeared to be moving. Then again, all she could see was a distant backdrop, its scale and proximity impossible to judge: thousands of fierce blue stars against the blackness of space.

She looked around for Jasim, but she was utterly alone. She could see no vehicle or other machine that might have disgorged her into this emptiness. There was not even a planet below her, or a single brightest star to which she might be bound. Absurdly, she was breathing. Every other cue told her that she was drifting through vacuum, probably through interstellar space. Her lungs kept filling and emptying, though. The air, and her skin, felt neither hot nor cold.

Someone or something had embodied her, or was running her as software. She was not on Massa, she was sure of that; she had never visited that world, but nowhere in the Amalgam would a guest be treated like this. Not even one who arrived unannounced in data spilling out from the bulge.

Leila said, "Are you listening to me? Do you understand me?" She could hear her own voice, flat and without resonance. The acoustics made perfect sense in a vast, empty, windless place, if not an airless one.

Anywhere in the Amalgam, you *knew* whether you were embodied or not; it was the nature of all bodies, real or virtual, that declarative knowledge of every detail was there for the asking. Here, when Leila tried to summon the same information, her mind remained blank. It was like the strange absence she'd felt on Trident, when she'd been cut off from the repositories of civilization, but here the amputation had reached all the way inside her.

She inhaled deeply, but there was no noticeable scent at all, not even the whiff of her own body odor that she would have expected, whether she was wearing her ancestral phenotype or any of the forms of ersatz flesh that she adopted when the environment demanded it. She pinched the skin of her forearm; it felt more like her original skin than any of the substitutes she'd ever worn. They might have fashioned this body out of something both remarkably lifelike and chemically inert, and placed her in a vast, transparent container of air, but she was beginning to pick up a strong stench of ersatz physics. Air and skin alike, she suspected, were made of bits, not atoms.

So where was Jasim? Were they running him too, in a separate scape? She called out his name, trying not to make the exploratory cry sound plaintive. She understood all too well now why he'd tried so hard to keep her from this place, and why he'd been unable to face staying behind: the thought that the Aloof might be doing something unspeakable to his defenseless consciousness, in some place she couldn't hope to reach or see, was like a white hot blade pressed to her heart. All she could do was try to shut off the panic and talk down the possibility. *All right, he's alone here, but so am I, and it's not that bad.* She would put her faith in symmetry; if they had not abused her, why would they have harmed Jasim?

She forced herself to be calm. The Aloof had taken the trouble to grant her consciousness, but she couldn't expect the level of amenity she was accustomed to. For a start, it would be perfectly reasonable if her hosts were unable or unwilling to plug her into any data source equivalent to the Amalgam's libraries, and perhaps the absence of somatic knowledge was not much different. Rather than deliberately fooling her about her body, maybe they had looked at the relevant data channels and decided that *anything* they fed into them would be misleading. Understanding her transmitted description well enough to bring her to consciousness was one thing, but it didn't guarantee that they knew how to translate the technical details of their instantiation of her into her own language.

And if this ignorance-plus-honesty excuse was too sanguine to swallow, it wasn't hard to think of the Aloof as being pathologically secretive without actually being malicious. If they wanted to keep quiet about the way they'd brought her to life lest it reveal something about themselves, that too was understandable. They need not be doing it for the sake of tormenting her.

Leila surveyed the sky around her, and felt a jolt of recognition. She'd memorized the positions of the nearest stars to the target node where her transmission would first be sent, and now a matching pattern stood out against the background in a collection of distinctive constellations. She was being shown the sky from that node. This didn't prove anything about her actual location, but the simplest explanation was that the Aloof had instantiated her here, rather than sending her on through the network. The stars were in the positions she'd predicted for her time of arrival, so if this was the reality, there had been little delay in choosing how to deal with the intruder. No thousand-year-long deliberations, no passing of the news to a distant decision-maker. Either the Aloof themselves were present here, or the machinery of the node was so sophisticated that they might as well have been. She could not have been woken by accident; it had to have been a deliberate act. It made her wonder if the Aloof had been expecting something like this for millennia.

"What now?" she asked. Her hosts remained silent. "Toss me back to Tassef?" The probes with their reversed trajectories bore no record of their experience; perhaps the Aloof wouldn't incorporate these new memories into her description before returning her. She spread her arms imploringly. "If you're going to erase this memory, why not speak to me first? I'm in your hands completely, you can send me to the grave with your secrets. Why wake me at all, if you don't want to talk?"

In the silence that followed, Leila had no trouble imagining one answer: to study her. It was a mathematical certainty that some questions about her behavior could never be answered simply by examining her static description; the only reliable way to predict what she'd do in any given scenario was to wake her and confront her with it. They might, of course, have chosen to wake her any number of times before, without granting her memories of the previous instantiations. She experienced a moment of sheer existential vertigo: this could be the thousandth, the billionth, in a vast series of experiments, as her captors permuted dozens of variables to catalog her responses.

The vertigo passed. Anything was possible, but she preferred to entertain more pleasant hypotheses.

"I came here to talk," she said. "I understand that you don't want us sending in machinery, but there must be something we can discuss, something we can learn from each other. In the disk, every time two space-faring civilizations met, they found they had something in common. Some mutual interests, some mutual benefits."

At the sound of her own earnest speech dissipating into the virtual air around her, Leila started laughing. The arguments she'd been putting for centuries to Jasim, to her friends on Najib, to the Snakes on Nazdeek, seemed ridiculous now, embarrassing. How could she face the Aloof and claim that she had anything to offer them that they had not considered, and rejected, hundreds of thousands of years before? The Amalgam had never tried to keep its nature hidden. The Aloof would have watched them, studied them from afar, and consciously chosen isolation. To come here and list the advantages of contact as if they'd never crossed her hosts' minds was simply insulting.

Leila fell silent. If she had lost faith in her role as cultural envoy, at least she'd proved to her own satisfaction that there was something in here smarter than the sling-shot fence the probes had encountered. The Aloof had not embraced her, but the whole endeavor had not been in vain. To wake in the bulge, even to silence, was far more than she'd ever had the right to hope for.

She said, "Please, just bring me my husband now, then we'll leave you in peace."

This entreaty was met in the same way as all the others. Leila resisted speculating again about experimental variables. She did not believe that a million-year-old civilization was interested in testing her tolerance to isolation, robbing her of her companion and seeing how long she took to attempt suicide. The Aloof did not take orders from her; fine. If she was neither an experimental subject to be robbed of her sanity, nor a valued guest whose every wish was granted, there had to be some other relationship between them that she had yet to fathom. She had to be conscious for a reason.

She searched the sky for a hint of the node itself, or any other feature she might have missed, but she might as well have been living inside a star map, albeit one shorn of the usual annotations. The Milky Way, the plane of stars that bisected the sky, was hidden by the thicker clouds of gas and dust here, but Leila had her bearings; she knew which way led deeper into the bulge, and which way led back out to the disk.

She contemplated Tassef's distant sun with mixed emotions, as a sailor might look back on the last sight of land. As the yearning for that familiar place welled up, a cylinder of violet light appeared around her, encircling the direction of her gaze. For the first time, Leila felt her weightlessness interrupted: a gentle acceleration was carrying her forward along the imaginary beam.

"No! Wait!" She closed her eyes and curled into a ball. The acceleration halted, and when she opened her eyes the tunnel of light was gone.

She let herself float limply, paying no attention to anything in the sky, waiting to see what happened if she kept her mind free of any desire for travel.

After an hour like this, the phenomenon had not recurred. Leila turned her gaze in the opposite direction, into the bulge. She cleared her mind of all timidity and nostalgia, and imagined the thrill of rushing deeper into this violent, spectacular, alien territory. At first there was no response from the scape, but then she focused her attention sharply in the direction of a second node, the one she'd hoped her transmission would be forwarded to from the first, on its way through the galactic core.

The same violet light, the same motion. This time, Leila waited a few heartbeats longer before she broke the spell.

Unless this was some pointlessly sadistic game, the Aloof were offering her a clear choice. She could return to Tassef, return to the Amalgam. She could announce that she'd put a toe in these mysterious waters, and lived to tell the tale. Or she could dive into the bulge, as deep as she'd ever imagined, and see where the network took her.

"No promises?" she asked. "No guarantee I'll come out the other side? No intimations of contact, to tempt me further?" She was thinking aloud, she did not expect answers. Her hosts, she was beginning to conclude, viewed strangers through the prism of a strong, but very sharply delineated, sense of obligation. They sent back the insentient probes to their owners, scrupulously intact. They had woken this intruder to give her the choice: did she really want to go where her transmission suggested, or had she wandered in here like a lost child who just needed to find the way home? They would do her no harm, and send her on no journey without her consent, but those were the limits of their duty of care. They did not owe her any account of themselves. She would get no greeting, no hospitality, no conversation.

"What about Jasim? Will you give me a chance to consult with him?" She waited, picturing his face, willing his presence, hoping they might read her mind if her words were beyond them. If they could decode a yearning toward a point in the sky, surely this wish for companionship was not too difficult to comprehend? She tried variations, dwelling on the abstract structure of their intertwined data in the transmission, hoping this might clarify the object of her desire if his physical appearance meant nothing to them.

She remained alone.

The stars that surrounded her spelt out the only choices on offer. If she wanted to be with Jasim once more before she died, she had to make the same decision as he did.

Symmetry demanded that he faced the same dilemma.

How would he be thinking? He might be tempted to retreat back to the safety of Tassef, but he'd reconciled with her in Shalouf for the sole purpose of following her into danger. He would understand that she'd want to go deeper, would want to push all the way through to Massa, opening up the short-cut through the core, proving it safe for future travelers.

Would he understand, too, that she'd feel a pang of guilt at this presumptuous line of thought, and that she'd contemplate making a sacrifice of her own? He had braved the unknown for her, and they had reaped the reward already: they had come closer to the Aloof than any-one in history. Why couldn't that be enough? For all Leila knew, her hosts might not even wake her again before Massa. What would she be giving up if she turned back now?

More to the point, what would Jasim expect of her? That she'd march on relentlessly, following her obsession to the end, or that she'd put her love for him first?

The possibilities multiplied in an infinite regress. They knew each other as well as two people could, but they didn't carry each other's minds inside them.

Leila drifted through the limbo of stars, wondering if Jasim had already made his decision. Having seen that the Aloof were not the tor-turers he'd feared, had he already set out for Tassef, satisfied that she faced no real peril at their hands? Or had he reasoned that their experi-ence at this single node meant nothing? This was not the Amalgam, the culture could be a thousand times more fractured.

This cycle of guesses and doubts led nowhere. If she tried to pursue it to the end she'd be paralyzed. There were no guarantees; she could only choose the least worst case. If she returned to Tassef, only to find that Jasim had gone on alone through the bulge, it would be unbearable: she would have lost him for nothing. If that happened, she could try to fol-low him, returning to the bulge immediately, but she would already be centuries behind him.

If she went on to Massa, and it was Jasim who retreated, at least she'd know that he'd ended up in safety. She'd know, too, that he had not been desperately afraid for her, that the Aloof's benign indifference at this first node had been enough to persuade him that they'd do her no harm.

That was her answer: she had to continue, all the way to Massa. With the hope, but no promise, that Jasim would have thought the same way.

The decision made, she lingered in the scape. Not from any second thoughts, but from a reluctance to give up lightly the opportunity she'd fought so hard to attain. She didn't know if any member of the Aloof was watching and listening to her, reading her thoughts, examining her desires. Perhaps they were so indifferent and incurious that they'd delegated everything to insentient software, and merely instructed their machines to baby-sit her while she made up her mind where she wanted to go. She still had to make one last attempt to reach them, or she would never die in peace.

"Maybe you're right," she said. "Maybe you've watched us for the last million years, and seen that we have nothing to offer you. Maybe our technology is backward, our philosophy naive, our customs bizarre, our manners appalling. If that's true, though, if we're so far beneath you, you could at least point us in the right direction. Offer us some kind of argument as to why we should change."

Silence.

Leila said, "All right. Forgive my impertinence. I have to tell you honestly, though, that we won't be the last to bother you. The Amalgam is full of people who will keep trying to find ways to reach you. This is going to go on for another million years, until we believe that we understand you. If that offends you, don't judge us too harshly. We can't help it. It's who we are."

She closed her eyes, trying to assure herself that there was nothing she'd regret having left unsaid.

"Thank you for granting us safe passage," she added, "if that's what you're offering. I hope my people can return the favor one day, if there's anywhere you want to go."

She opened her eyes and sought out her destination: deeper into the network, on toward the core.

10

THE MOUNTAINS outside the town of Astraahat started with a gentle slope that promised an easy journey, but gradually grew steeper. Similarly, the vegetation was low and sparse in the foothills, but became steadily thicker and taller the higher up the slope you went.

Jasim said, "Enough." He stopped and leaned on his climbing stick.

"One more hour?" Leila pleaded.

He considered this. "Half an hour resting, then half an hour walking?"

"One hour resting, then one hour walking."

He laughed wearily. "All right. One of each."

The two of them hacked away at the undergrowth until there was a place to sit.

Jasim poured water from the canteen into her hands, and she splashed her face clean.

They sat in silence for a while, listening to the sounds of the unfamiliar wildlife. Under the forest canopy it was almost twilight, and when Leila looked up into the small patch of sky above them she could see the stars of the bulge, like tiny, pale, translucent beads.

At times it felt like a dream, but the experience never really left her. The Aloof had woken her at every node, shown her the view, given her a choice. She had seen a thousand spectacles, from one side of the core to the other: cannibalistic novas, dazzling clusters of newborn stars, twin white dwarfs on the verge of collision. She had seen the black hole at the galaxy's center, its accretion disk glowing with X-rays, slowly tearing stars apart.

It might have been an elaborate lie, a plausible simulation, but every detail accessible from disk-based observatories confirmed what she had witnessed. If anything had been changed, or hidden from her, it must have been small. Perhaps the artifacts of the Aloof themselves had been painted out of the view, though Leila thought it was just as likely that the marks they'd left on their territory were so subtle, anyway, that there'd been nothing to conceal.

Jasim said sharply, "Where are you?"

She lowered her gaze and replied mildly, "I'm here, with you. I'm just remembering."

When they'd woken on Massa, surrounded by delirious, cheering Eavesdroppers, they'd been asked: *What happened in there? What did you see?* Leila didn't know why she'd kept her mouth shut and turned to her husband before replying, instead of letting every detail come tumbling out immediately. Perhaps she just hadn't known where to begin.

For whatever reason, it was Jasim who had answered first. "Nothing. We stepped through the gate on Tassef, and now here we are. On the other side of the bulge."

For almost a month, she'd flatly refused to believe him. *Nothing? You saw nothing?* It had to be a lie, a joke. It had to be some kind of revenge.

That was not in his nature, and she knew it. Still, she'd clung to that explanation for as long as she could, until it became impossible to believe any longer, and she'd asked for his forgiveness.

Six months later, another traveler had spilled out of the bulge. One of the die-hard Listening Party pilgrims had followed in their wake and taken the short cut. Like Jasim, this heptapod had seen nothing, experienced nothing.

Leila had struggled to imagine why she might have been singled out. So much for her theory that the Aloof felt morally obliged to check that each passenger on their network knew what they were doing, unless they'd decided that her actions were enough to demonstrate that intruders from the disk, considered generically, were making an informed choice. Could just one sample of a working, conscious version of their neighbors really be enough for them to conclude that they understood everything they needed to know? Could this capriciousness, instead, have been part of a strategy to lure in more visitors, with the enticing possibility that each one might, with luck, witness something far beyond all those who'd preceded them? Or had it been part of a scheme to discourage intruders by clouding the experience with uncertainty? The simplest act of discouragement would have been to discard all unwelcome transmissions, and the most effective incentive would have been to offer a few plain words of welcome, but then, the Aloof would not have been the Aloof if they'd followed such reasonable dictates.

Jasim said, "You know what I think. You wanted to wake so badly, they couldn't refuse you. They could tell I didn't care as much. It was as simple as that."

"What about the heptapod? It went in alone. It wasn't just tagging along to watch over someone else."

He shrugged. "Maybe it acted on the spur of the moment. They all seem unhealthily keen to me, whatever they're doing. Maybe the Aloof could discern its mood more clearly."

Leila said, "I don't believe a word of that."

Jasim spread his hands in a gesture of acceptance. "I'm sure you could change my mind in five minutes, if I let you. But if we walked back down this hill and waited for the next traveler from the bulge, and the next, until the reason some of them received the grand tour and some didn't finally became plain, there would still be another question, and another. Even if I wanted to live for ten thousand years more, I'd rather move on to something else. And in this last hour..." He trailed off.

Leila said, "I know. You're right."

She sat, listening to the strange chirps and buzzes emitted by creatures she knew nothing about. She could have absorbed every recorded fact about them in an instant, but she didn't care, she didn't need to know.

Someone else would come after them, to understand the Aloof, or advance that great, unruly, frustrating endeavor by the next increment. She and Jasim had made a start, that was enough. What they'd done was more than she could ever have imagined, back on Najib. Now, though, was the time to stop, while they were still themselves: enlarged by the experience, but not disfigured beyond recognition.

They finished their water, drinking the last drops. They left the canteen behind. Jasim took her hand and they climbed together, struggling up the slope side by side.

DARK INTEGERS

〰〜〆**"G**ood morning, Bruno. How is the weather there in Sparseland?"

The screen icon for my interlocutor was a three-holed torus tiled with triangles, endlessly turning itself inside out. The polished tones of the male synthetic voice I heard conveyed no specific origin, but gave a sense nonetheless that the speaker's first language was something other than English.

I glanced out the window of my home office, taking in a patch of blue sky and the verdant gardens of a shady West Ryde cul-de-sac. Sam used "good morning" regardless of the hour, but it really was just after ten a.m., and the tranquil Sydney suburb was awash in sunshine and birdsong.

"Perfect," I replied. "I wish I wasn't chained to this desk."

There was a long pause, and I wondered if the translator had mangled the idiom, creating the impression that I had been shackled by ruthless assailants, who had nonetheless left me with easy access to my instant messaging program. Then Sam said, "I'm glad you didn't go for a run today. I've already tried Alison and Yuen, and they were both unavailable. If I hadn't been able to get through to you, it might have been difficult to keep some of my colleagues in check."

I felt a surge of anxiety, mixed with resentment. I refused to wear an iWatch, to make myself reachable twenty-four hours a day. I was a mathematician, not an obstetrician. Perhaps I was an amateur diplomat as well, but even if Alison, Yuen and I didn't quite cover the time zones, it would never be more than a few hours before Sam could get hold of at least one of us.

"I didn't realize you were surrounded by hot-heads," I replied. "What's the great emergency?" I hoped the translator would do justice to the sharpness in my voice. Sam's colleagues were the ones with all the firepower, all the resources; they should not have been jumping at shadows. True, we had once tried to wipe them out, but that had been a perfectly innocent mistake, more than ten years before.

Sam said, "Someone from your side seems to have jumped the border."

"*Jumped* it?"

"As far as we can see, there's no trench cutting through it. But a few hours ago, a cluster of propositions on our side started obeying your axioms."

I was stunned. "An isolated cluster? With no derivation leading back to us?"

"None that we could find."

I thought for a while. "Maybe it was a natural event. A brief surge across the border from the background noise that left a kind of tidal pool behind."

Sam was dismissive. "The cluster was too big for that. The probability would be vanishingly small." Numbers came through on the data channel; he was right.

I rubbed my eyelids with my fingertips; I suddenly felt very tired. I'd thought our old nemesis, Industrial Algebra, had given up the chase long ago. They had stopped offering bribes and sending mercenaries to harass me, so I'd assumed they'd finally written off the defect as a hoax or a mirage, and gone back to their core business of helping the world's military kill and maim people in ever more technologically sophisticated ways.

Maybe this wasn't IA. Alison and I had first located the defect—a set of contradictory results in arithmetic that marked the border between our mathematics and the version underlying Sam's world—by means of a vast set of calculations farmed out over the internet, with thousands of volunteers donating their computers' processing power when the machines would otherwise have been idle. When we'd pulled the plug on that project—keeping our discovery secret, lest IA find a way to weaponize it—a few participants had been resentful, and had talked about continuing the search. It would have been easy enough for them to write their own software, adapting the same open source framework that Alison and I had used, but it was difficult to see how they could have gathered enough supporters without launching some kind of public appeal.

I said, "I can't offer you an immediate explanation for this. All I can do is promise to investigate."

"I understand," Sam replied.

"You have no clues, yourself?" A decade before, in Shanghai, when Alison, Yuen and I had used the supercomputer called Luminous to mount a sustained attack on the defect, the mathematicians of the far side had grasped the details of our unwitting assault clearly enough to send a plume of alternative mathematics back across the border with pinpoint precision, striking at just the three of us.

Sam said, "If the cluster had been connected to something, we could have followed the trail. But in isolation it tells us nothing. That's why my colleagues are so anxious."

"Yeah." I was still hoping that the whole thing might turn out to be a glitch—the mathematical equivalent of a flock of birds with a radar echo that just happened to look like something more sinister—but the full gravity of the situation was finally dawning on me.

The inhabitants of the far side were as peaceable as anyone might reasonably wish their neighbors to be, but if their mathematical infrastructure came under threat they faced the real prospect of annihilation. They had defended themselves from such a threat once before, but because they had been able to trace it to its source and understand its nature, they had shown great forbearance. They had not struck their assailants dead, or wiped out Shanghai, or pulled the ground out from under our universe.

This new assault had not been sustained, but nobody knew its origins, or what it might portend. I believed that our neighbors would do no more than they had to in order to ensure their survival, but if they were forced to strike back blindly, they might find themselves with no path to safety short of turning our world to dust.

~w~

SHANGHAI TIME was only two hours behind Sydney, but Yuen's IM status was still "unavailable". I emailed him, along with Alison, though it was the middle of the night in Zürich and she was unlikely to be awake for another four or five hours. All of us had programs that connected us to Sam by monitoring, and modifying, small portions of the defect: altering a handful of precariously balanced truths of arithmetic, wiggling the border between the two systems back and forth to encode each transmitted bit. The three of us on the near side might have communicated with each other in the same way, but on consideration we'd decided that conventional cryptography was a safer way to conceal our secret. The mere fact that communications data seemed to come from nowhere had the potential to attract suspicion, so we'd gone as far as to write software to send fake packets across the net to cover for our otherwise inexplicable conversations with Sam; anyone but the most diligent and resourceful of eavesdroppers would conclude that he was addressing us from an internet café in Lithuania.

While I was waiting for Yuen to reply, I scoured the logs where my knowledge miner deposited results of marginal relevance, wondering if some flaw in the criteria I'd given it might have left me with a blind spot. If anyone, anywhere had announced their intention to carry out some kind of calculation that might have led them to the defect, the news should have been plastered across my desktop in flashing red letters within seconds. Granted, most organizations with the necessary computing resources were secretive by nature, but they were also unlikely to be motivated to indulge in such a crazy stunt. Luminous itself had been decommissioned in 2012; in principle, various national security agencies, and even a few IT-centric businesses, now had enough silicon to hunt down the defect if they'd really set their sights on it, but as far as I knew Yuen, Alison and I were still the only three people in the world who were certain of its existence. The black budgets of even the most profligate governments, the deep pockets of even the richest tycoons, would not stretch far enough to take on the search as a long shot, or an act of whimsy.

An IM window popped up with Alison's face. She looked ragged. "What time is it there?" I asked.

"Early. Laura's got colic."

"Ah. Are you OK to talk?"

"Yeah, she's asleep now."

My email had been brief, so I filled her in on the details. She pondered the matter in silence for a while, yawning unashamedly.

"The only thing I can think of is some gossip I heard at a conference in Rome a couple of months ago. It was a fourth-hand story about some guy in New Zealand who thinks he's found a way to test fundamental laws of physics by doing computations in number theory."

"Just random crackpot stuff, or…what?"

Alison massaged her temples, as if trying to get more blood flowing to her brain. "I don't know, what I heard was too vague to make a judgment. I gather he hasn't tried to publish this anywhere, or even mentioned it in blogs. I guess he just confided in a few people directly, one of whom must have found it too amusing for them to keep their mouth shut."

"Have you got a name?"

She went off camera and rummaged for a while. "Tim Campbell," she announced. Her notes came through on the data channel. "He's done respectable work in combinatorics, algorithmic complexity, optimization. I scoured the net, and there was no mention of this weird stuff. I was meaning to email him, but I never got around to it."

I could understand why; that would have been about the time Laura was born. I said, "I'm glad you still go to so many conferences in the flesh. It's easier in Europe, everything's so close."

"Ha! Don't count on it continuing, Bruno. You might have to put your fat arse on a plane sometime yourself."

"What about Yuen?"

Alison frowned. "Didn't I tell you? He's been in hospital for a couple of days. Pneumonia. I spoke to his daughter, he's not in great shape."

"I'm sorry." Alison was much closer to him than I was; he'd been her doctoral supervisor, so she'd known him long before the events that had bound the three of us together.

Yuen was almost eighty. That wasn't yet ancient for a middle-class Chinese man who could afford good medical care, but he would not be around forever.

I said, "Are we crazy, trying to do this ourselves?" She knew what I meant: liaising with Sam, managing the border, trying to keep the two worlds talking but the two sides separate, safe and intact.

Alison replied, "Which government would you trust not to screw this up? Not to try to exploit it?"

"None. But what's the alternative? You pass the job on to Laura? Kate's not interested in having kids. So do I pick some young mathematician at random to anoint as my successor?"

"Not at random, I'd hope."

"You want me to advertise? 'Must be proficient in number theory, familiar with Machiavelli, and own the complete boxed set of *The West Wing*?'"

She shrugged. "When the time comes, find someone competent you can trust. It's a balance: the fewer people who know, the better, so long as there are always enough of us that the knowledge doesn't risk getting lost completely."

"And this goes on generation after generation? Like some secret society? The Knights of the Arithmetic Inconsistency?"

"I'll work on the crest."

We needed a better plan, but this wasn't the time to argue about it. I said, "I'll contact this guy Campbell and let you know how it goes."

"OK. Good luck." Her eyelids were starting to droop.

"Take care of yourself."

Alison managed an exhausted smile. "Are you saying that because you give a damn, or because you don't want to end up guarding the Grail all by yourself?"

"Both, of course."

∿

"I HAVE to fly to Wellington tomorrow."

Kate put down the pasta-laden fork she'd raised halfway to her lips and gave me a puzzled frown. "That's short notice."

"Yeah, it's a pain. It's for the Bank of New Zealand. I have to do something on-site with a secure machine, one they won't let anyone access over the net."

Her frown deepened. "When will you be back?"

"I'm not sure. It might not be until Monday. I can probably do most of the work tomorrow, but there are certain things they restrict to the weekends, when the branches are off-line. I don't know if it will come to that."

I hated lying to her, but I'd grown accustomed to it. When we'd met, just a year after Shanghai, I could still feel the scar on my arm where one of Industrial Algebra's hired thugs had tried to carve a data cache out of my body. At some point, as our relationship deepened, I'd made up my mind that however close we became, however much I trusted her, it would be safer for Kate if she never knew anything about the defect.

"They can't hire someone local?" she suggested. I didn't think she was suspicious, but she was definitely annoyed. She worked long hours at the hospital, and she only had every second weekend off; this would be one of them. We'd made no specific plans, but it was part of our routine to spend this time together.

I said, "I'm sure they could, but it'd be hard to find someone at short notice. And I can't tell them to shove it, or I'll lose the whole contract. It's one weekend, it's not the end of the world."

"No, it's not the end of the world." She finally lifted her fork again. "Is the sauce OK?"

"It's delicious, Bruno." Her tone made it clear that no amount of culinary effort would have been enough to compensate, so I might as well not have bothered.

I watched her eat with a strange knot growing in my stomach. Was this how spies felt, when they lied to their families about their work? But my own secret sounded more like something from a psychiatric ward. I was entrusted with the smooth operation of a treaty that I, and two friends, had struck with an invisible ghost world that coexisted with our own. The ghost world was far from hostile, but the treaty was the most important in human history, because either side had the power to annihilate the other so thoroughly that it would make a nuclear holocaust seem like a pin-prick.

VICTORIA UNIVERSITY was in a hilltop suburb overlooking Wellington. I caught a cable car, and arrived just in time for the Friday afternoon seminar. Contriving an invitation to deliver a paper here myself would have been difficult, but wangling permission to sit in as part of the audience was easy; although I hadn't been an academic for almost twenty years, my ancient PhD and a trickle of publications, however tenuously related to the topic of the seminar, were still enough to make me welcome.

I'd taken a gamble that Campbell would attend—the topic was peripheral to his own research, official or otherwise—so I was relieved to spot him in the audience, recognizing him from a photo on the faculty web site. I'd emailed him straight after I'd spoken to Alison, but his reply had been a polite brush-off: he acknowledged that the work I'd heard about on the grapevine owed something to the infamous search that Alison and I had launched, but he wasn't ready to make his own approach public.

I sat through an hour on "Monoids and Control Theory", trying to pay enough attention that I wouldn't make a fool of myself if the seminar organizer quizzed me later on why I'd been sufficiently attracted to the topic to interrupt my "sightseeing holiday" in order to attend. When the seminar ended, the audience split into two streams: one heading out of the building, the other moving into an adjoining room where refreshments were on offer. I saw Campbell making for the open air, and it was all I could do to contrive to get close enough to call out to him without making a spectacle.

"Dr Campbell?"

He turned and scanned the room, probably expecting to see one of his students wanting to beg for an extension on an assignment. I raised a hand and approached him.

"Bruno Costanzo. I emailed you yesterday."

"Of course." Campbell was a thin, pale man in his early thirties. He shook my hand, but he was obviously taken aback. "You didn't mention that you were in Wellington."

I made a dismissive gesture. "I was going to, but then it seemed a bit presumptuous." I didn't spell it out, I just left him to conclude that I was as ambivalent about this whole inconsistency nonsense as he was.

If fate had brought us together, though, wouldn't it be absurd not to make the most of it?

"I was going to grab some of those famous scones," I said; the seminar announcement on the web had made big promises for them. "Are you busy?"

"Umm. Just paperwork. I suppose I can put it off."

As we made our way into the tea room, I waffled on airily about my holiday plans. I'd never actually been to New Zealand before, so I made it clear that most of my itinerary still lay in the future. Campbell was no more interested in the local geography and wildlife than I was; the more I enthused, the more distant his gaze became. Once it was apparent that he wasn't going to cross-examine me on the finer points of various hiking trails, I grabbed a buttered scone and switched subject abruptly.

"The thing is, I heard you'd devised a more efficient strategy for searching for a defect." I only just managed to stop myself from using the definite article; it was a while since I'd spoken about it as if it were still hypothetical. "You know the kind of computing power that Dr Tierney and I had to scrounge up?"

"Of course. I was just an undergraduate, but I heard about the search."

"Were you one of our volunteers?" I'd checked the records, and he wasn't listed, but people had had the option of registering anonymously.

"No. The idea didn't really grab me, at the time." As he spoke, he seemed more discomfited than the failure to donate his own resources twelve years ago really warranted. I was beginning to suspect that he'd actually been one of the people who'd found the whole tongue-in-cheek conjecture that Alison and I had put forward to be unforgivably foolish. We had never asked to be taken seriously—and we had even put prominent links to all the worthy biomedical computing projects on our web page, so that people knew there were far better ways to spend their spare megaflops—but nonetheless, some mathematical/philosophical stuffed shirts had spluttered with rage at the sheer impertinence and naivety of our hypothesis. Before things turned serious, it was the entertainment value of that backlash that had made our efforts worthwhile.

"But now you've refined it somehow?" I prompted him, doing my best to let him see that I felt no resentment at the prospect of being outdone. In fact, the hypothesis itself had been Alison's, so even if there hadn't been more important things than my ego at stake, that really wasn't a factor. As for the search algorithm, I'd cobbled it together on a Sunday afternoon, as a joke, to call Alison's bluff. Instead, she'd called mine, and insisted that we release it to the world.

Campbell glanced around to see who was in earshot, but then perhaps it dawned on him that if the news of his ideas had already reached Sydney via Rome and Zürich, the battle to keep his reputation pristine in Wellington was probably lost.

He said, "What you and Dr Tierney suggested was that random processes in the early universe might have included proofs of mutually contradictory theorems about the integers, the idea being that no computation to expose the inconsistency had yet had time to occur. Is that a fair summary?"

"Sure."

"One problem I have with that is, I don't see how it could lead to an inconsistency that could be detected here and now. If the physical system A proved theorem A, and the physical system B proved theorem B, then you might have different regions of the universe obeying different axioms, but it's not as if there's some universal mathematics textbook hovering around outside spacetime, listing every theorem that's ever been proved, which our computers then consult in order to decide how to behave. The behavior of a classical system is determined by its own particular causal past. If we're the descendants of a patch of the universe that proved theorem A, our computers should be perfectly capable of *disproving* theorem B, whatever happened somewhere else 14 billion years ago."

I nodded thoughtfully. "I can see what you're getting at." If you weren't going to accept full-blooded Platonism, in which there *was* a kind of ghostly textbook listing the eternal truths of mathematics, then a half-baked version where the book started out empty and was only filled in line-by-line as various theorems were tested seemed like the worst kind of compromise. In fact, when the far side had granted Yuen, Alison and I insight into their mathematics for a few minutes in Shanghai, Yuen had proclaimed that the flow of mathematical information *did* obey Einstein locality; there was no universal book of truths, just records of the past sloshing around at lightspeed or less, intermingling and competing.

I could hardly tell Campbell, though, that not only did I know for a fact that a single computer could prove both a theorem and its negation, but depending on the order in which it attacked the calculations it could sometimes even shift the boundary where one set of axioms failed and the other took over.

I said, "And yet you still believe it's worth searching for an inconsistency?"

"I do," he conceded. "Though I came to the idea from a very different approach." He hesitated, then picked up a scone from the table beside us.

"One rock, one apple, one scone. We have a clear idea of what we mean by those phrases, though each one might encompass ten-to-the-ten-to-the-thirty-something slightly different configurations of matter. My 'one scone' is not the same as your 'one scone'."

"Right."

"You know how banks count large quantities of cash?"

"By weighing them?" In fact there were several other cross-checks as well, but I could see where he was heading and I didn't want to distract him with nit-picking.

"Exactly. Suppose we tried to count scones the same way: weigh the batch, divide by some nominal value, then round to the nearest integer. The weight of any individual scone varies so much that you could easily end up with a version of arithmetic different from our own. If you 'counted' two separate batches, then merged them and 'counted' them together, there's no guarantee that the result would agree with the ordinary process of integer addition."

I said, "Clearly not. But digital computers don't run on scones, and they don't count bits by weighing them."

"Bear with me," Campbell replied. "It isn't a perfect analogy, but I'm not as crazy as I sound. Suppose, now, that *everything* we talk about as 'one thing' has a vast number of possible configurations that we're either ignoring deliberately, or are literally incapable of distinguishing. Even something as simple as an electron prepared in a certain quantum state."

I said, "You're talking about hidden variables now?"

"Of a kind, yes. Do you know about Gerard 't Hooft's models for deterministic quantum mechanics?"

"Only vaguely," I admitted.

"He postulated fully deterministic degrees of freedom at the Planck scale, with quantum states corresponding to equivalence classes containing many different possible configurations. What's more, all the ordinary quantum states we prepare at an atomic level would be complex superpositions of those primordial states, which allows him to get around the Bell inequalities." I frowned slightly; I more-or-less got the picture, but I'd need to go away and read 't Hooft's papers.

Campbell said, "In a sense, the detailed physics isn't all that important, so long as you accept that 'one thing' might not *ever* be exactly the same as another 'one thing', regardless of the kind of objects we're talking about. Given that supposition, physical processes that *seem* to be rigorously equivalent to various arithmetic operations can turn out not to be as reliable as you'd think. With scone-weighing, the flaws are obvious, but I'm talking about the potentially subtler results of misunderstanding the fundamental nature of matter."

"Hmm." Though it was unlikely that anyone else Campbell had confided in had taken these speculations as seriously as I did, not only did I not want to seem a pushover, I honestly had no idea whether anything he was saying bore the slightest connection to reality.

I said, "It's an interesting idea, but I still don't see how it could speed up the hunt for inconsistencies."

"I have a set of models," he said, "which are constrained by the need to agree with some of 't Hooft's ideas about the physics, and also by the need to make arithmetic *almost* consistent for a very large range of objects. From neutrinos to clusters of galaxies, basic arithmetic involving the kinds of numbers we might encounter in ordinary situations should work out in the usual way." He laughed. "I mean, that's the world we're living in, right?"

Some of us. "Yeah."

"But the interesting thing is, I can't make the physics work at all if the arithmetic doesn't run askew eventually—if there aren't trans-astronomical numbers where the physical representations no longer capture the arithmetic perfectly. And each of my models lets me predict, more or less, where those effects should begin to show up. By starting with the fundamental physical laws, I can deduce a sequence of calculations with large integers that ought to reveal an inconsistency, when performed with pretty much any computer."

"Taking you straight to the defect, with no need to search at all." I'd let the definite article slip out, but it hardly seemed to matter anymore.

"That's the theory." Campbell actually blushed slightly. "Well, when you say 'no search', what's involved really is a much smaller search. There are still free parameters in my models; there are potentially billions of possibilities to test."

I grinned broadly, wondering if my expression looked as fake as it felt. "But no luck yet?"

"No." He was beginning to become self-conscious again, glancing around to see who might be listening.

Was he lying to me? Keeping his results secret until he could verify them a million more times, and then decide how best to explain them to incredulous colleagues and an uncomprehending world? Or had whatever he'd done that had lobbed a small grenade into Sam's universe somehow registered in Campbell's own computer as arithmetic as usual, betraying no evidence of the boundary he'd crossed? After all, the offending cluster of propositions had obeyed *our* axioms, so perhaps Campbell had managed to force them to do so without ever realizing that they hadn't in the past. His ideas were obviously close to the mark—and I could no longer believe this was just a coincidence—but he seemed to have no room in his theory for something that I knew for a fact: arithmetic wasn't merely inconsistent, it was *dynamic*. You could take its contradictions and slide them around like bumps in a carpet.

Campbell said, "Parts of the process aren't easy to automate; there's some manual work to be done setting up the search for each broad class of models. I've only been doing this in my spare time, so it could be a while before I get around to examining all the possibilities."

"I see." If all of his calculations so far had produced just one hit on the far side, it was conceivable that the rest would pass without incident. He would publish a negative result ruling out an obscure class of physical theories, and life would go on as normal on both sides of the inconsistency.

What kind of weapons inspector would I be, though, to put my faith in that rosy supposition?

Campbell was looking fidgety, as if his administrative obligations were beckoning. I said, "It'd be great to talk about this a bit more while we've got the chance. Are you busy tonight? I'm staying at a backpacker's down in the city, but maybe you could recommend a restaurant around here somewhere?"

He looked dubious for a moment, but then an instinctive sense of hospitality seemed to overcome his reservations. He said, "Let me check with my wife. We're not really into restaurants, but I was cooking tonight anyway, and you'd be welcome to join us."

CAMPBELL'S HOUSE was a fifteen minute walk from the campus; at my request, we detoured to a liquor store so I could buy a couple of bottles of wine to accompany the meal. As I entered the house, my hand lingered on the doorframe, depositing a small device that would assist me if I needed to make an uninvited entry in the future.

Campbell's wife, Bridget, was an organic chemist, who also taught at Victoria University. The conversation over dinner was all about department heads, budgets, and grant applications, and despite having left academia long ago, I had no trouble relating sympathetically to the couple's gripes. My hosts ensured that my wine glass never stayed empty for long.

When we'd finished eating, Bridget excused herself to make a call to her mother, who lived in a small town on the south island. Campbell led me into his study and switched on a laptop with fading keys that must have been twenty years old. Many households had a computer like this: the machine that could no longer run the latest trendy bloatware, but which still worked perfectly with its original OS.

Campbell turned his back to me as he typed his password, and I was careful not to be seen even trying to look. Then he opened some C++ files in an editor, and scrolled over parts of his search algorithm.

I felt giddy, and it wasn't the wine; I'd filled my stomach with an over-the-counter sobriety aid that turned ethanol into glucose and water faster than any human being could imbibe it. I fervently hoped that Industrial Algebra really had given up their pursuit; if I could get this close to Campbell's secrets in half a day, IA could be playing the stockmarket with alternative arithmetic before the month was out, and peddling inconsistency weapons to the Pentagon soon after.

I did not have a photographic memory, and Campbell was just showing me fragments anyway. I didn't think he was deliberately taunting me; he just wanted me to see that he had something concrete, that all his claims about Planck scale physics and directed search strategies had been more than hot air.

I said, "Wait! What's that?" He stopped hitting the PAGE DOWN key, and I pointed at a list of variable declarations in the middle of the screen:

```
long int i1, i2, i3;
dark d1, d2, d3;
```

A "long int" was a long integer, a quantity represented by twice as many bits as usual. On this vintage machine, that was likely to be a total of just sixty-four bits. "What the fuck is a 'dark'?" I demanded. It wasn't how I'd normally speak to someone I'd only just met, but then, I wasn't meant to be sober.

Campbell laughed. "A dark integer. It's a type I defined. It holds four thousand and ninety-six bits."

"But why the name?"

"Dark matter, dark energy…dark integers. They're all around us, but we don't usually see them, because they don't quite play by the rules."

Hairs rose on the back of my neck. I could not have described the infrastructure of Sam's world more concisely myself.

Campbell shut down the laptop. I'd been looking for an opportunity to handle the machine, however briefly, without arousing his suspicion, but that clearly wasn't going to happen, so as we walked out of the study I went for plan B.

"I'm feeling kind of…" I sat down abruptly on the floor of the hallway. After a moment, I fished my phone out of my pocket and held it up to him. "Would you mind calling me a taxi?"

"Yeah, sure." He accepted the phone, and I cradled my head in my arms. Before he could dial the number, I started moaning softly. There was a long pause; he was probably weighing up the embarrassment factor of various alternatives.

Finally he said, "You can sleep here on the couch if you like." I felt a genuine pang of sympathy for him; if some clown I barely knew had pulled a stunt like this on me, I would at least have made him promise to foot the cleaning bills if he threw up in the middle of the night.

In the middle of the night, I did make a trip to the bathroom, but I kept the sound effects restrained. Halfway through, I walked quietly to the study, crossed the room in the dark, and slapped a thin, transparent patch over the adhesive label that a service company had placed on the outside of the laptop years before. My addition would be invisible to the naked eye, and it would take a scalpel to prise it off. The relay that would communicate with the patch was larger, about the size of a coat button; I stuck it behind a bookshelf. Unless Campbell was planning to paint the room or put in new carpet, it would probably remain undetected for a couple of years, and I'd already prepaid a two year account with a local wireless internet provider.

I woke not long after dawn, but this un-Bacchanalian early rising was no risk to my cover; Campbell had left the curtains open so the full force of the morning sun struck me in the face, a result that was almost certainly deliberate. I tiptoed around the house for ten minutes or so, not wanting to seem too organized if anyone was listening, then left a scrawled note of thanks and apology on the coffee table by the couch, before letting myself out and heading for the cable car stop.

Down in the city, I sat in a café opposite the backpacker's hostel, and connected to the relay, which in turn had established a successful link with the polymer circuitry of the laptop patch. When noon came and went without Campbell logging on, I sent a message to Kate telling her that I was stuck in the bank for at least another day.

I passed the time browsing the news feeds and buying overpriced snacks; half of the café's other patrons were doing the same. Finally, just after three o'clock, Campbell started up the laptop.

The patch couldn't read his disk drive, but it could pick up currents flowing to and from the keyboard and the display, allowing it to deduce everything he typed and everything he saw. Capturing his password was easy. Better yet, once he was logged in he set about editing one of his files, extending his search program to a new class of models. As he scrolled back and forth, it wasn't long before the patch's screen shots encompassed the entire contents of the file he was working on.

He labored for more than two hours, debugging what he'd written, then set the program running. This creaky old twentieth-century machine, which predated the whole internet-wide search for the defect, had already scored one direct hit on the far side; I just hoped this new class of models were all incompatible with the successful ones from a few days before.

Shortly afterward, the IR sensor in the patch told me that Campbell had left the room. The patch could induce currents in the keyboard connection; I could type into the machine as if I was right there. I started a new process window. The laptop wasn't connected to the internet at all, except through my spyware, but it took me only fifteen minutes to display and record everything there was to see: a few library and header files that the main program depended on, and the data logs listing all of the searches so far. It would not have been hard to hack into the operating system and make provisions to corrupt any future searches, but I decided to wait until I had a better grasp of the whole situation. Even once I was back in Sydney, I'd be able to eavesdrop whenever the laptop was in use, and intervene whenever it was left unattended. I'd only stayed in Wellington in case there'd been a need to return to Campbell's house in person.

When evening fell and I found myself with nothing urgent left to do, I didn't call Kate; it seemed wiser to let her assume that I was slaving away in a windowless computer room. I left the café and lay on my bed in the hostel. The dormitory was deserted; everyone else was out on the town.

I called Alison in Zürich and brought her up to date. In the background, I could hear her husband, Philippe, trying to comfort Laura in another room, calmly talking baby-talk in French while his daughter wailed her head off.

Alison was intrigued. "Campbell's theory can't be perfect, but it must be close. Maybe we'll be able to find a way to make it fit in with the dynamics we've seen." In the ten years since we'd stumbled on the defect, all our work on it had remained frustratingly empirical: running calculations, and observing their effects. We'd never come close to finding any deep underlying principles.

"Do you think Sam knows all this?" she asked.

"I have no idea. If he did, I doubt he'd admit it." Though it was Sam who had given us a taste of far-side mathematics in Shanghai, that had really just been a clip over the ear to let us know that what we were trying to wipe out with Luminous was a civilization, not a wasteland. After that near-disastrous first encounter, he had worked to establish communications with us, learning our languages and happily listening to the accounts we'd volunteered of our world, but he had not been equally forthcoming in return. We knew next to nothing about far-side physics, astronomy, biology, history or culture. That there were living beings occupying the same space as the Earth suggested that the two universes were intimately coupled somehow, in spite of their mutual invisibility. But Sam had hinted that life was much more common on his side of the border than ours; when I'd told him that we seemed to be alone, at least in the solar system, and were surrounded by light-years of sterile vacuum, he'd taken to referring to our side as "Sparseland".

Alison said, "Either way, I think we should keep it to ourselves. The treaty says we should do everything in our power to deal with any breach of territory of which the other side informs us. We're doing that. But we're not obliged to disclose the details of Campbell's activities."

"That's true." I wasn't entirely happy with her suggestion, though. In spite of the attitude Sam and his colleagues had taken—in which they assumed that anything they told us might be exploited, might make them more vulnerable—a part of me had always wondered if there was some gesture of good faith we could make, some way to build trust. Since talking to Campbell, in the back of my mind I'd been building up a faint hope that his discovery might lead to an opportunity to prove, once and for all, that our intentions were honorable.

Alison read my mood. She said, "Bruno, they've given us *nothing*. Shanghai excuses a certain amount of caution, but we also know from

Shanghai that they could brush Luminous aside like a gnat. They have enough computing power to crush us in an instant, and they still cling to every strategic advantage they can get. Not to do the same ourselves would just be stupid and irresponsible."

"So you want us to hold on to this secret weapon?" I was beginning to develop a piercing headache. My usual way of dealing with the surreal responsibility that had fallen on the three of us was to pretend that it didn't exist; having to think about it constantly for three days straight meant more tension than I'd faced for a decade. "Is that what it's come down to? Our own version of the Cold War? Why don't you just march into NATO headquarters on Monday and hand over everything we know?"

Alison said dryly, "Switzerland isn't a member of NATO. The government here would probably charge me with treason."

I didn't want to fight with her. "We should talk about this later. We don't even know exactly what we've got. I need to go through Campbell's files and confirm whether he really did what we think he did."

"OK."

"I'll call you from Sydney."

It took me a while to make sense of everything I'd stolen from Campbell, but eventually I was able to determine which calculations he'd performed on each occasion recorded in his log files. Then I compared the propositions that he'd tested with a rough, static map of the defect; since the event Sam had reported had been deep within the far side, there was no need to take account of the small fluctuations that the border underwent over time.

If my analysis was correct, late on Wednesday night Campbell's calculations had landed in the middle of far-side mathematics. He'd been telling me the truth, though; he'd found nothing out of the ordinary there. Instead, the thing he had been seeking had melted away before his gaze.

In all the calculations Alison and I had done, only at the border had we been able to force propositions to change their allegiance and obey our axioms. It was as if Campbell had dived in from some higher dimension, carrying a hosepipe that sprayed everything with the arithmetic we knew and loved.

For Sam and his colleagues, this was the equivalent of a suitcase nuke appearing out of nowhere, as opposed to the ICBMs they knew how to track and annihilate. Now Alison wanted us to tell them, "Trust us, we've dealt with it," without showing them the weapon itself, without letting them see how it worked, without giving them a chance to devise new defenses against it.

She wanted us to have something up our sleeves, in case the hawks took over the far side, and decided that Sparseland was a ghost world whose lingering, baleful presence they could do without.

Drunken Saturday-night revelers began returning to the hostel, singing off-key and puking enthusiastically. Maybe this was poetic justice for my own faux-inebriation; if so I was being repaid a thousand-fold. I started wishing I'd shelled out for classier accommodation, but since there was no employer picking up my expenses, it was going to be hard enough dealing with my lie to Kate without spending even more on the trip.

Forget the arithmetic of scones; I knew how to make digital currency reproduce like the marching brooms of the sorcerer's apprentice. It might even have been possible to milk the benefits without Sam noticing; I could try to hide my far-sider trading behind the manipulations of the border we used routinely to exchange messages.

I had no idea how to contain the side-effects, though. I had no idea what else such meddling would disrupt, how many people I might kill or maim in the process.

I buried my head beneath the pillows and tried to find a way to get to sleep through the noise. I ended up calculating powers of seven, a trick I hadn't used since childhood. I'd never been a prodigy at mental arithmetic, and the concentration required to push on past the easy cases drained me far faster than any physical labor. *Two hundred and eighty-two million, four hundred and seventy-five thousand, two hundred and forty-nine.* The numbers rose into the stratosphere like bean stalks, until they grew too high and tore themselves apart, leaving behind a cloud of digits drifting through my skull like black confetti.

~~~

"THE PROBLEM is under control," I told Sam. "I've located the source, and I've taken steps to prevent a recurrence."

"Are you sure of that?" As he spoke, the three-holed torus on the screen twisted restlessly. In fact I'd chosen the icon myself, and its appearance wasn't influenced by Sam at all, but it was impossible not to project emotions onto its writhing.

I said, "I'm certain that I know who was responsible for the incursion on Wednesday. It was done without malice; in fact the person who did it doesn't even realize that he crossed the border. I've modified the operating system on his computer so that it won't allow him to do the same thing again; if he tries, it will simply give him the same answers as before, but this time the calculations won't actually be performed."

"That's good to hear," Sam said. "Can you describe these calculations?"

I was as invisible to Sam as he was to me, but out of habit I tried to keep my face composed. "I don't see that as part of our agreement," I replied.

Sam was silent for a few seconds. "That's true, Bruno. But it might provide us with a greater sense of reassurance, if we knew what caused the breach in the first place."

I said, "I understand. But we've made a decision." *We* was Alison and I; Yuen was still in hospital, in no state to do anything. Alison and I, speaking for the world.

"I'll put your position to my colleagues," he said. "We're not your enemy, Bruno." His tone sounded regretful, and these nuances *were* under his control.

"I know that," I replied. "Nor are we yours. Yet you've chosen to keep most of the details of your world from us. We don't view that as evidence of hostility, so you have no grounds to complain if we keep a few secrets of our own."

"I'll contact you again soon," Sam said.

The messenger window closed. I emailed an encrypted transcript to Alison, then slumped across my desk. My head was throbbing, but the encounter really hadn't gone too badly. Of course Sam and his colleagues would have preferred to know everything; of course they were going to be disappointed and reproachful. That didn't mean they were going to abandon the benign policies of the last decade. The important thing was that my assurance would prove to be reliable: the incursion would not be repeated.

I had work to do, the kind that paid bills. Somehow I summoned up the discipline to push the whole subject aside and get on with a report on stochastic methods for resolving distributed programming bottlenecks that I was supposed to be writing for a company in Singapore.

Four hours later, when the doorbell rang, I'd left my desk to raid the kitchen. I didn't bother checking the doorstep camera; I just walked down the hall and opened the door.

Campbell said, "How are you, Bruno?"

"I'm fine. Why didn't you tell me you were coming to Sydney?"

"Aren't you going to ask me how I found your house?"

"How?"

He held up his phone. There was a text message from me, or at least from my phone; it had SMS'd its GPS coordinates to him.

"Not bad," I conceded.

"I believe they recently added 'corrupting communications devices' to the list of terrorism-related offenses in Australia. You could probably get me thrown into solitary confinement in a maximum security prison."

"Only if you know at least ten words of Arabic."

"Actually I spent a month in Egypt once, so anything's possible. But I don't think you really want to go to the police."

I said, "Why don't you come in?"

As I showed him to the living room my mind was racing. Maybe he'd found the relay behind the bookshelf, but surely not before I'd left his house. Had he managed to get a virus into my phone remotely? I'd thought my security was better than that.

Campbell said, "I'd like you to explain why you bugged my computer."

"I'm growing increasingly unsure of that myself. The correct answer might be that you wanted me to."

He snorted. "That's rich! I admit that I deliberately allowed a rumor to start about my work, because I was curious as to why you and Alison Tierney called off your search. I wanted to see if you'd come sniffing around. As you did. But that was hardly an invitation to steal all my work."

"What was the point of the whole exercise for you, then, if not a way of stealing something from Alison and me?"

"You can hardly compare the two. I just wanted to confirm my suspicion that you actually found something."

"And you believe that you've confirmed that?"

He shook his head, but it was with amusement not denial. I said, "Why are you here? Do you think I'm going to publish your crackpot theory as my own? I'm too old to get the Fields Medal, but maybe you think it's Nobel material."

"Oh, I don't think you're interested in fame. As I said, I think you beat me to the prize a long time ago."

I rose to my feet abruptly; I could feel myself scowling, my fists tightening. "So what's the bottom line? You want to press charges against me for the laptop? Go ahead. We can each get a fine *in absentia*."

Campbell said, "I want to know exactly what was so important to you that you crossed the Tasman, lied your way into my house, abused my hospitality, and stole my files. I don't think it was simply curiosity, or jealousy. I think you found something ten years ago, and now you're afraid my work is going to put it at risk."

I sat down again. The rush of adrenalin I'd experienced at being cornered had dissipated. I could almost hear Alison whispering in my ear, "Either you kill him, Bruno, or you recruit him." I had no intention of killing anyone, but I wasn't yet certain that these were the only two choices.

I said, "And if I tell you to mind your own business?"

He shrugged. "Then I'll work harder. I know you've screwed that laptop, and maybe the other computers in my house, but I'm not so broke that I can't get a new machine."

Which would be a hundred times faster. He'd re-run every search, probably with wider parameter ranges. The suitcase nuke from Sparseland that had started this whole mess would detonate again, and for all I knew it could be ten times, a hundred times, more powerful.

I said, "Have you ever wanted to join a secret society?"

Campbell gave an incredulous laugh. "No!"

"Neither did I. Too bad."

I told him everything. The discovery of the defect. Industrial Algebra's pursuit of the result. The epiphany in Shanghai. Sam establishing contact. The treaty, the ten quiet years. Then the sudden jolt of his own work, and the still-unfolding consequences.

Campbell was clearly shaken, but despite the fact that I'd confirmed his original suspicion he wasn't ready to take my word for the whole story.

I knew better than to invite him into my office for a demonstration; faking it there would have been trivial. We walked to the local shopping center, and I handed him two hundred dollars to buy a new notebook. I told him the kind of software he'd need to download, without limiting his choice to any particular package. Then I gave him some further instructions. Within half an hour, he had seen the defect for himself, and nudged the border a short distance in each direction.

We were sitting in the food hall, surrounded by boisterous teenagers who'd just got out from school. Campbell was looking at me as if I'd seized a toy machine gun from his hands, transformed it into solid metal, then bashed him over the head with it.

I said, "Cheer up. There was no war of the worlds after Shanghai; I think we're going to survive this, too." After all these years, the chance to share the burden with someone new was actually making me feel much more optimistic.

"The defect is *dynamic*," he muttered. "That changes everything."

"You don't say."

Campbell scowled. "I don't just mean the politics, the dangers. I'm talking about the underlying physical model."

"Yeah?" I hadn't come close to examining that issue seriously; it had been enough of a struggle coming to terms with his original calculations.

"All along, I've assumed that there were exact symmetries in the Planck scale physics that accounted for a stable boundary between macroscopic arithmetics. It was an artificial restriction, but I took it for granted, because anything else seemed..."

"Unbelievable?"

"Yes." He blinked and looked away, surveying the crowd of diners as if he had no idea how he'd ended up among them. "I'm flying back in a few hours."

"Does Bridget know why you came?"

"Not exactly."

I said, "No one else can know what I've told you. Not yet. The risks are too great, everything's too fluid."

"Yeah." He met my gaze. He wasn't just humoring me; he understood what people like IA might do.

"In the long term," I said, "we're going to have to find a way to make this safe. To make everyone safe." I'd never quite articulated that goal before, but I was only just beginning to absorb the ramifications of Campbell's insights.

"How?" he wondered. "Do we want to build a wall, or do we want to tear one down?"

"I don't know. The first thing we need is a better map, a better feel for the whole territory."

He'd hired a car at the airport in order to drive here and confront me; it was parked in a side street close to my house. I walked him to it.

We shook hands before parting. I said, "Welcome to the reluctant cabal."

Campbell winced. "Let's find a way to change it from reluctant to redundant."

IN THE weeks that followed, Campbell worked on refinements to his theory, emailing Alison and me every few days. Alison had taken my unilateral decision to recruit Campbell with much more equanimity than I'd expected. "Better to have him inside the tent," was all she'd said.

This proved to be an understatement. While the two of us soon caught up with him on all the technicalities, it was clear that his intuition on the subject, hard-won over many years of trial-and-error, was the key to his spectacular progress now. Merely stealing his notes and his algorithms would never have brought us so far.

Gradually, the dynamic version of the theory took shape. As far as macroscopic objects were concerned—and in this context, "macroscopic" stretched all the way down to the quantum states of subatomic particles—all traces of Platonic mathematics were banished. A "proof" concerning the integers was just a class of physical processes, and the result of that proof was neither read from, nor written to, any universal book of truths. Rather, the agreement between proofs was simply a strong, but imperfect, correlation between the different processes that counted as proofs of the same thing. Those correlations arose from the way that the primordial states of Planck-scale physics were carved up—imperfectly—into subsystems that appeared to be distinct objects.

The truths of mathematics *appeared* to be enduring and universal because they persisted with great efficiency within the states of matter and space-time. But there was a built-in flaw in the whole idealization of distinct objects, and the point where the concept finally cracked open was the defect Alison and I had found in our volunteers' data, which appeared to any macroscopic test as the border between contradictory mathematical systems.

We'd derived a crude empirical rule which said that the border shifted when a proposition's neighbors outvoted it. If you managed to prove that $x+1=y+1$ and $x-1=y-1$, then $x=y$ became a sitting duck, even if it hadn't been true before. The consequences of Campbell's search had shown that the reality was more complex, and in his new model, the old border rule became an approximation for a more subtle process, anchored in the dynamics of primordial states that knew nothing of the arithmetic of electrons and apples. The near-side arithmetic Campbell had blasted into the far side hadn't got there by besieging the target with syllogisms; it had got there because he'd gone straight for a far deeper failure in the whole idea of "integers" than Alison and I had ever dreamed of.

Had Sam dreamed of it? I waited for his next contact, but as the weeks passed he remained silent, and the last thing I felt like doing was calling him myself. I had enough people to lie to without adding him to the list.

Kate asked me how work was going, and I waffled about the details of the three uninspiring contracts I'd started recently. When I stopped talking, she looked at me as if I'd just stammered my way through an unconvincing denial of some unspoken crime. I wondered how my mixture of concealed elation and fear was coming across to her. Was that how the most passionate, conflicted adulterer would appear? I didn't actually reach the brink of confession, but I pictured myself approaching it. I had less reason now to think that the secret would bring her harm than when I'd first made my decision to keep her in the dark. But then, what if I told her everything, and the next day Campbell was kidnapped and tortured? If we were all being watched, and the people doing it were good at their jobs, we'd only know about it when it was too late.

Campbell's emails dropped off for a while, and I assumed he'd hit a roadblock. Sam had offered no further complaints. Perhaps, I thought, this was the new *status quo*, the start of another quiet decade. I could live with that.

Then Campbell flung his second grenade. He reached me by IM and said, "I've started making maps."

"Of the defect?" I replied.

"Of the planets."

I stared at his image, uncomprehending.

"The far-side planets," he said. "*The physical worlds.*"

He'd bought himself some time on a geographically scattered set of processor clusters. He was no longer repeating his dangerous incursions, of course, but by playing around in the natural ebb and flow at the border, he'd made some extraordinary discoveries.

Alison and I had realized long ago that random "proofs" in the natural world would influence what happened at the border, but Campbell's theory made that notion more precise. By looking at the exact timing of changes to propositions at the border, measured in a dozen different computers world-wide, he had set up a kind of…radar? CT machine? Whatever you called it, it allowed him to deduce the locations where the relevant natural processes were occurring, and his model allowed him to distinguish between both near-side and far-side processes, and processes in matter and those in vacuum. He could measure the density of far-side matter, out to a distance of several light-hours, and crudely image nearby planets.

"Not just on the far side," he said. "I validated the technique by imaging our own planets." He sent me a data log, with comparisons to an online almanac. For Jupiter, the farthest of the planets he'd located, the positions were out by as much as a hundred thousand kilometers; not exactly GPS quality, but that was a bit like complaining that your abacus couldn't tell north from north-west.

"Maybe that's how Sam found us in Shanghai?" I wondered. "The same kind of thing, only more refined?"

Campbell said, "Possibly."

"So what about the far-side planets?"

"Well, here's the first interesting thing. None of the planets coincide with ours. Nor does their sun with our sun." He sent me an image of the far-side system, one star and its six planets, overlaid on our own.

"But Sam's time lags," I protested, "when we communicate—"

"Make no sense if he's too far away. Exactly. So he is *not* living on any of these planets, and he's not even in a natural orbit around their star. He's in powered flight, moving with the Earth. Which suggests to me that they've known about us for much longer than Shanghai."

"Known about us," I said, "but maybe they still didn't anticipate anything like Shanghai." When we'd set Luminous on to the task of eliminating the defect—not knowing that we were threatening anyone—it had taken several minutes before the far side had responded. Computers on board a spacecraft moving with the Earth would have detected the assault quickly, but it might have taken the recruitment of larger, planetbound machines, minutes away at lightspeed, to repel it.

Until I'd encountered Campbell's theories, my working assumption had been that Sam's world was like a hidden message encoded in the Earth, with the different arithmetic giving different meanings to all the air, water and rock around us. But their matter was not bound to our matter; they didn't need our specks of dust or molecules of air to represent the dark integers. The two worlds split apart at a much lower level; vacuum could be rock, and rock, vacuum.

I said, "So do you want the Nobel for physics, or peace?"

Campbell smiled modestly. "Can I hold out for both?"

"That's the answer I was looking for." I couldn't get the stupid Cold War metaphors out of my brain: what would Sam's hot-headed colleagues think, if they knew that we were now flying spy planes over their territory? Saying "screw them, they were doing it first!" might have been a fair response, but it was not a particularly helpful one.

I said, "We're never going to match their Sputnik, unless you happen to know a trustworthy billionaire who wants to help us launch a space probe on a very strange trajectory. Everything we want to do has to work from Earth."

"I'll tear up my letter to Richard Branson then, shall I?"

I stared at the map of the far-side solar system. "There must be some relative motion between their star and ours. It can't have been this close for all that long."

"I don't have enough accuracy in my measurements to make a meaningful estimate of the velocity," Campbell said. "But I've done some crude estimates of the distances between their stars, and it's much smaller than ours. So it's not all that unlikely to find *some* star this close to us, even if it's unlikely to be the same one that was close a thousand years ago. Then again, there might be a selection effect at work here: the whole reason Sam's civilization managed to notice us at all was *because* we weren't shooting past them at a substantial fraction of lightspeed."

"OK. So *maybe* this is their home system, but it could just as easily be an expeditionary base for a team that's been following our sun for thousands of years."

"Yes."

I said, "Where do we go with this?"

"I can't increase the resolution much," Campbell replied, "without buying time on a lot more clusters." It wasn't that he needed much processing power for the calculations, but there were minimum prices to be paid to do anything at all, and what would give us clearer pictures would be more computers, not more time on each one.

I said, "We can't risk asking for volunteers, like the old days. We'd have to lie about what the download was for, and you can be certain that somebody would reverse-engineer it and catch us out."

"Absolutely."

I slept on the problem, then woke with an idea at four a.m. and went to my office, trying to flesh out the details before Campbell responded to my email. He was bleary-eyed when the messenger window opened; it was later in Wellington than in Sydney, but it looked as if he'd had as little sleep as I had.

I said, "We use the internet."

"I thought we decided that was too risky."

"Not screensavers for volunteers; I'm talking about *the internet itself.* We work out a way to do the calculations using nothing but data packets and network routers. We bounce traffic all around the world, and we get the geographical resolution for free."

"You've got to be joking, Bruno—"

"Why? *Any* computing circuit can be built by stringing together enough NAND gates; you think we can't leverage packet switching into a NAND gate? But that's just the proof that it's possible; I expect we can actually make it a thousand times tighter."

Campbell said, "I'm going to get some aspirin and come back."

We roped in Alison to help, but it still took us six weeks to get a workable design, and another month to get it functioning. We ended up exploiting authentication and error-correction protocols built into the internet at several different layers; the heterogeneous approach not only helped us do all the calculations we needed, but made our gentle siphoning of computing power less likely to be detected and mistaken for anything malicious. In fact we were "stealing" far less from the routers and servers of the net than if we'd sat down for a hardcore 3D multiplayer gaming session, but security systems had their own ideas about what constituted fair use and what was suspicious. The most important thing was not the size of the burden we imposed, but the signature of our behavior.

Our new globe-spanning arithmetical telescope generated pictures far sharper than before, with kilometer-scale resolution out to a billion kilometers. This gave us crude relief-maps of the far-side planets, revealing mountains on four of them, and what might have been oceans on two of those four. If there were any artificial structures, they were either too small to see, or too subtle in their artificiality.

The relative motion of our sun and the star these planets orbited turned out to be about six kilometers per second. In the decade since Shanghai, the two solar systems had changed their relative location by about two billion kilometers. Wherever the computers were now that had fought with Luminous to control the border, they certainly hadn't been on any of these planets at the time. Perhaps there were two ships, with one following the Earth, and the other, heavier one saving fuel by merely following the sun.

Yuen had finally recovered his health, and the full cabal held an IM conference to discuss these results.

"We should be showing these to geologists, xenobiologists…everyone," Yuen lamented. He wasn't making a serious proposal, but I shared his sense of frustration.

Alison said, "What I regret most is that we can't rub Sam's face in these pictures, just to show him that we're not as stupid as he thinks."

"I imagine his own pictures are sharper," Campbell replied.

"Which is as you'd expect," Alison retorted, "given a head start of a few centuries. If they're so brilliant on the far side, why do they need *us* to tell them what you did to jump the border?"

"They might have guessed precisely what I did," he countered, "but they could still be seeking confirmation. Perhaps what they really want is to rule out the possibility that we've discovered something different, something they've never even thought of."

I gazed at the false colors of one contoured sphere, imagining gray-blue oceans, snow-topped mountains with alien forests, strange cities, wondrous machines. Even if that was pure fantasy and this temporary neighbor was barren, there had to be a living home world from which the ships that pursued us had been launched.

After Shanghai, Sam and his colleagues had chosen to keep us in the dark for ten years, but it had been our own decision to cement the mistrust by holding on to the secret of our accidental weapon. If they'd already guessed its nature, then they might already have found a defense against it, in which case our silence bought us no advantage at all to compensate for the suspicion it engendered.

If that assumption was wrong, though? Then handing over the details of Campbell's work could be just what the far-side hawks were waiting for, before raising their shields and crushing us.

I said, "We need to make some plans. I want to stay hopeful, I want to keep looking for the best way forward, but we need to be prepared for the worst."

TRANSFORMING THAT suggestion into something concrete required far more work than I'd imagined; it was three months before the pieces started coming together. When I finally shifted my gaze back to the everyday world, I decided that I'd earned a break. Kate had a free weekend approaching; I suggested a day in the Blue Mountains.

Her initial response was sarcastic, but when I persisted she softened a little, and finally agreed.

On the drive out of the city, the chill that had developed between us slowly began to thaw. We played JJJ on the car radio—laughing with disbelief as we realized that today's cutting-edge music consisted mostly of cover versions and re-samplings of songs that had been hits when we were in our twenties—and resurrected old running jokes from the time when we'd first met.

As we wound our way into the mountains, though, it proved impossible simply to turn back the clock. Kate said, "Whoever you've been working for these last few months, can you put them on your blacklist?"

I laughed. "That will scare them." I switched to my best Brando voice. "You're on Bruno Costanzo's blacklist. You'll never run distributed software efficiently in this town again."

She said, "I'm serious. I don't know what's so stressful about the work, or the people, but it's really screwing you up."

I could have made her a promise, but it would have been hard enough to sound sincere as I spoke the words, let alone live up to them. I said, "Beggars can't be choosers."

She shook her head, her mouth tensed in frustration. "If you really want a heart attack, fine. But don't pretend that it's all about money. We're never that broke, and we're never that rich. Unless it's all going into your account in Zürich."

It took me a few seconds to convince myself that this was nothing more than a throw-away reference to Swiss banks. Kate knew about Alison, knew that we'd once been close, knew that we still kept in touch. She had plenty of male friends from her own past, and they all lived in Sydney; for more than five years, Alison and I hadn't even set foot on the same continent.

We parked the car, then walked along a scenic trail for an hour, mostly in silence. We found a spot by a stream, with tiered rocks smoothed by some ancient river, and ate the lunch I'd packed.

Looking out into the blue haze of the densely wooded valley below, I couldn't keep the image of the crowded skies of the far side from my mind. A dazzling richness surrounded us: alien worlds, alien life, alien culture. There had to be a way to end our mutual suspicion, and work toward a genuine exchange of knowledge.

As we started back toward the car, I turned to Kate. "I know I've neglected you," I said. "I've been going through a rough patch, but everything's going to change. I'm going to make things right."

I was prepared for a withering rebuff, but for a long time she·was silent. Then she nodded slightly and said, "OK."

As she reached across and took my hand, my wrist began vibrating. I'd buckled to the pressure and bought a watch that shackled me to the net twenty four hours a day.

I freed my hand from Kate's and lifted the watch to my face. The bandwidth reaching me out in the sticks wasn't enough for video, but a stored snapshot of Alison appeared on the screen.

"This is for *emergencies only*," I snarled.

"Check out a news feed," she replied. The acoustics were focused on my ears; Kate would get nothing but the bad-hearing-aid-at-a-party impression that made so many people want to punch their fellow commuters on trains.

"Why don't you just summarise whatever it is I'm meant to have noticed?"

Financial computing systems were going haywire, to an extent that was already being described as terrorism. Most trading was closed for the weekend, but some experts were predicting the crash of the century, come Monday.

I wondered if the cabal itself was to blame; if we'd inadvertently corrupted the whole internet by coupling its behavior to the defect. That was nonsense, though. Half the transactions being garbled were taking place on secure, interbank networks that shared no hardware with our global computer. This was coming from the far side.

"Have you contacted Sam?" I asked her.

"I can't raise him."

"Where are you going?" Kate shouted angrily. I'd unconsciously broken into a jog; I wanted to get back to the car, back to the city, back to my office.

I stopped and turned to her. "Run with me? Please? This is important."

"You're joking! I've spent half a day hiking, I'm not running anywhere!"

I hesitated, fantasizing for a moment that I could sit beneath a gum tree and orchestrate everything with my Dick Tracy watch before its battery went flat.

I said, "You'd better call a taxi when you get to the road."

"You're taking the car?" Kate stared at me, incredulous. "You piece of shit!"

"I'm sorry." I tossed my backpack on the ground and started sprinting. "We need to deploy," I told Alison.

"I know," she said. "We've already started."

It was the right decision, but hearing it still loosened my bowels far more than the realization that the far side were attacking us. Whatever their motives, at least they were unlikely to do more harm than they intended. I was much less confident about our own abilities.

"Keep trying to reach Sam," I insisted. "This is a thousand times more useful if they know about it."

Alison said, "I guess this isn't the time for *Dr. Strangelove* jokes."

Over the last three months, we'd worked out a way to augment our internet "telescope" software to launch a barrage of Campbell-style attacks on far-side propositions if it saw our own mathematics being encroached upon. The software couldn't protect the whole border, but there were millions of individual trigger points, forming a randomly shifting minefield. The plan had been to buy ourselves some security, without ever reaching the point of actual retaliation. We'd been waiting to complete a final round of tests before unleashing this version live on the net, but it would only take a matter of minutes to get it up and running.

"Anything being hit besides financials?" I asked.

"Not that I'm picking up."

If the far side was deliberately targeting the markets, that was infinitely preferable to the alternative: that financial systems had simply been the most fragile objects in the path of a much broader assault. Most modern engineering and aeronautical systems were more interested in resorting to fall-backs than agonizing over their failures. A bank's computer might declare itself irretrievably compromised and shut down completely, the instant certain totals failed to reconcile; those in a chemical plant or an airliner would be designed to fail more gracefully, trying simpler alternatives and bringing all available humans into the loop.

I said, "Yuen and Tim—?"

"Both on board," Alison confirmed. "Monitoring the deployment, ready to tweak the software if necessary."

"Good. You really won't need me at all, then, will you?"

Alison's reply dissolved into digital noise, and the connection cut out. I refused to read anything sinister into that; given my location, I was lucky to have any coverage at all. I ran faster, trying not to think about the time in Shanghai when Sam had taken a mathematical scalpel to all of our brains. Luminous had been screaming out our position like a beacon; we would not be so easy to locate this time. Still, with a cruder approach, the hawks could take a hatchet to everyone's head. *Would they go that far?* Only if this was meant as much more than a threat, much more than intimidation to make us hand over Campbell's algorithm. Only if this was the end game: no warning, no negotiations, just Sparseland wiped off the map forever.

Fifteen minutes after Alison's call, I reached the car. Apart from the entertainment console it didn't contain a single microchip; I remembered the salesman laughing when I'd queried that twice. "What are you afraid of? Y3K?" The engine started immediately.

I had an ancient second-hand laptop in the trunk; I put it beside me on the passenger seat and started it booting up while I drove out on to the access road, heading for the highway. Alison and I had worked for a fortnight on a stripped-down operating system, as simple and robust as possible, to run on these old computers; if the far side kept reaching down from the arithmetic stratosphere, these would be like concrete bunkers compared to the glass skyscrapers of more modern machines. The four of us would also be running different versions of the OS, on CPUs with different instruction sets; our bunkers were scattered mathematically as well as geographically.

As I drove on to the highway, my watch stuttered back to life. Alison said, "Bruno? Can you hear me?"

"Go ahead."

"Three passenger jets have crashed," she said. "Poland, Indonesia, South Africa."

I was dazed. Ten years before, when I'd tried to bulldoze his whole mathematical world into the sea, Sam had spared my life. Now the far side was slaughtering innocents.

"Is our minefield up?"

"It's been up for ten minutes, but nothing's tripped it yet."

"You think they're steering through it?"

Alison hesitated. "I don't see how. There's no way to predict a safe path." We were using a quantum noise server to randomize the propositions we tested.

I said, "We should trigger it manually. One counter-strike to start with, to give them something to think about." I was still hoping that the downed jets were unintended, but we had no choice but to retaliate.

"Yeah." Alison's image was live now; I saw her reach down for her mouse. She said, "It's not responding. The net's too degraded." All the fancy algorithms that the routers used, and that we'd leveraged so successfully for our imaging software, were turning them into paperweights. The internet was robust against high levels of transmission noise and the loss of thousands of connections, but not against the decay of arithmetic itself.

My watch went dead. I looked to the laptop; it was still working. I reached over and hit a single hotkey, launching a program that would try to reach Alison and the others the same way we'd talked to Sam: by modulating part of the border. In theory, the hawks might have moved the whole border—in which case we were screwed—but the border was vast, and it made more sense for them to target their computing resources on the specific needs of the assault itself.

A small icon appeared on the laptop's screen, a single letter A in reversed monochrome. I said, "Is this working?"

"Yes," Alison replied. The icon blinked out, then came back again. We were doing a Hedy Lamarr, hopping rapidly over a predetermined sequence of border points to minimize the chance of detection. Some of those points would be missing, but it looked as if enough of them remained intact.

The A was joined by a Y and a T. The whole cabal was online now, whatever that was worth. What we needed was S, but S was not answering.

Campbell said grimly, "I heard about the planes. I've started an attack." The tactic we had agreed upon was to take turns running different variants of Campbell's border-jumping algorithm from our scattered machines.

I said, "The miracle is that they're not hitting us the same way we're hitting them. They're just pushing down part of the border with the old voting method, step by step. If we'd given them what they'd asked for, we'd all be dead by now."

"Maybe not," Yuen replied. "I'm only halfway through a proof, but I'm ninety percent sure that Tim's method is asymmetrical. It only works in one direction. Even if we'd told them about it, they couldn't have turned it against us."

I opened my mouth to argue, but if Yuen was right that made perfect sense. The far side had probably been working on the same branch of mathematics for centuries; if there had been an equivalent weapon that could be used from their vantage point, they would have discovered it long ago.

My machine had synchronized with Campbell's, and it took over the assault automatically. We had no real idea what we were hitting, except that the propositions were further from the border, describing far simpler arithmetic on the dark integers than anything of ours that the far side had yet touched. *Were we crippling machines? Taking lives?* I was torn between a triumphant vision of retribution, and a sense of shame that we'd allowed it to come to this.

Every hundred meters or so, I passed another car sitting motionless by the side of the highway. I was far from the only person still driving, but I had a feeling Kate wouldn't have much luck getting a taxi. She had water in her backpack, and there was a small shelter at the spot where we'd parked. There was little to be gained by reaching my office now; the laptop could do everything that mattered, and I could run it from the car battery if necessary. If I turned around and went back for Kate, though, I'd have so much explaining to do that there'd be no time for anything else.

I switched on the car radio, but either its digital signal processor was too sophisticated for its own good, or all the local stations were out.

"Anyone still getting news?" I asked.

"I still have radio," Campbell replied. "No TV, no internet. Landlines and mobiles here are dead." It was the same for Alison and Yuen. There'd been no more reports of disasters on the radio, but the stations were probably as isolated now as their listeners. Ham operators would still be calling each other, but journalists and newsrooms would not be in the loop. I didn't want to think about the contingency plans that might have been in place, given ten years' preparation and an informed population.

By the time I reached Penrith there were so many abandoned cars that the remaining traffic was almost gridlocked. I decided not to even try to reach home. I didn't know if Sam had literally scanned my brain in Shanghai and used that to target what he'd done to me then, and whether or not he could use the same neuroanatomical information against me now, wherever I was, but staying away from my usual haunts seemed like one more small advantage to cling to.

I found a petrol station, and it was giving priority to customers with functioning cars over hoarders who'd appeared on foot with empty cans. Their EFTPOS wasn't working, but I had enough cash for the petrol and some chocolate bars.

As dusk fell the streetlights came on; the traffic lights had never stopped working. All four laptops were holding up, hurling their grenades into the far side. The closer the attack front came to simple arithmetic, the more resistance it would face from natural processes voting at the border for near-side results. Our enemy had their supercomputers; we had every every atom of the Earth, following its billion-year-old version of the truth.

We had modeled this scenario. The sheer arithmetical inertia of all that matter would buy us time, but in the long run a coherent, sustained, computational attack could still force its way through.

How would we die? Losing consciousness first, feeling no pain? Or was the brain more robust than that? Would all the cells of our bodies start committing apoptosis, once their biochemical errors mounted up beyond repair? Maybe it would be just like radiation sickness. We'd be burned by decaying arithmetic, just as if it was nuclear fire.

My laptop beeped. I swerved off the road and parked on a stretch of concrete beside a dark shopfront. A new icon had appeared on the screen: the letter S.

Sam said, "Bruno, this was not my decision."

"I believe you," I said. "But if you're just a messenger now, what's your message?"

"If you give us what we asked for, we'll stop the attack."

"We're hurting you, aren't we?"

"We know we're hurting *you*," Sam replied. Point taken: we were guessing, firing blind. He didn't have to ask about the damage we'd suffered.

I steeled myself, and followed the script the cabal had agreed upon. "We'll give you the algorithm, but only if you retreat back to the old border, and then seal it."

Sam was silent for four long heartbearts.

"Seal it?"

"I think you know what I mean." In Shanghai, when we'd used Luminous to try to ensure that Industrial Algebra could not exploit the defect, we'd contemplated trying to seal the border rather than eliminating the defect altogether. The voting effect could only shift the border if it was crinkled in such a way that propositions on one side could be outnumbered by those on the other side. It was possible—given enough time and computing power—to smooth the border, to iron it flat. Once that was done, everywhere, the whole thing would become immovable. No force in the universe could shift it again.

Sam said, "You want to leave us with no weapon against you, while you still have the power to harm us."

"We won't have that power for long. Once you know exactly what we're using, you'll find a way to block it."

There was a long pause. Then, "Stop your attacks on us, and we'll consider your proposal."

"We'll stop our attacks when you pull the border back to the point where our lives are no longer at risk."

"How would you even know that we've done that?" Sam replied. I wasn't sure if the condescension was in his tone or just his words, but either way I welcomed it. The lower the far side's opinion of our abilities, the more attractive the deal became for them.

I said, "Then you'd better back up far enough for all our communications systems to recover. When I can get news reports and see that there are no more planes going down, no power plants exploding, then we'll start the ceasefire."

Silence again, stretching out beyond mere hesitancy. His icon was still there, though, the S unblinking. I clutched at my shoulder, hoping that the burning pain was just tension in the muscle.

Finally: "All right. We agree. We'll start shifting the border."

I DROVE around looking for an all-night convenience store that might have had an old analog TV sitting in a corner to keep the cashier awake—that seemed like a good bet to start working long before the wireless connection to my laptop—but Campbell beat me to it. New Zealand radio and TV were reporting that the "digital blackout" appeared to be lifting, and ten minutes later Alison announced that she had internet access. A lot of the major servers were still down, or their sites weirdly garbled, but Reuters was starting to post updates on the crisis.

Sam had kept his word, so we halted the counter-strikes. Alison read from the Reuters site as the news came in. Seventeen planes had crashed, and four trains. There'd been fatalities at an oil refinery, and half a dozen manufacturing plants. One analyst put the global death toll at five thousand, and rising.

I muted the microphone on my laptop, and spent thirty seconds shouting obscenities and punching the dashboard. Then I rejoined the cabal.

Yuen said, "I've been reviewing my notes. If my instinct is worth anything, the theorem I mentioned before is correct: if the border is sealed, they'll have no way to touch us."

"What about the upside for them?" Alison asked. "Do you think they can protect themselves against Tim's algorithm, once they understand it?"

Yuen hesitated. "Yes and no. Any cluster of near-side truth values it injects into the far side will have a non-smooth border, so they'll be able to remove it with sheer computing power. In that sense, they'll never be defenseless. But I don't see how there's anything they can do to prevent the attacks in the first place."

"Short of wiping us out," Campbell said.

I heard an infant sobbing. Alison said, "That's Laura. I'm alone here. Give me five minutes."

I buried my head in my arms. I still had no idea what the right course would have been. If we'd handed over Campbell's algorithm immediately, might the good will that bought us have averted the war? Or would the same attack merely have come sooner? What criminal vanity had ever made the three of us think we could shoulder this responsibility on our own? Five thousand people were dead. The hawks who had taken over on the far side would weigh up our offer, and decide that they had no choice but to fight on.

And if the reluctant cabal had passed its burden to Canberra, to Zürich, to Beijing? Would there really have been peace? Or was I just wishing that there had been more hands steeped in the same blood, to share the guilt around?

The idea came from nowhere, sweeping away every other thought. I said, "Is there any reason why the far side has to stay *connected*?"

"Connected to what?" Campbell asked.

"Connected to itself. Connected topologically. They should be able to send down a spike, then withdraw it, but leave behind a bubble of altered truth values: a kind of outpost, sitting within the near side, with a perfect, smooth border making it impregnable. Right?"

Yuen said, "Perhaps. With both sides collaborating on the construction, that might be possible."

"Then the question is, can we find a place where we can do that so that it kills off the chance to use Tim's method completely—without crippling any process that we need just to survive?"

"*Fuck you*, Bruno!" Campbell exclaimed happily. "We give them one small Achilles' tendon to slice…and then they've got nothing to fear from us!"

Yuen said, "A watertight proof of something like that is going to take weeks, months."

"Then we'd better start work. And we'd better feed Sam the first plausible conjecture we get, so they can use their own resources to help us with the proof."

Alison came back online, and greeted the suggestion with cautious approval. I drove around until I found a quiet coffee shop. Electronic banking still wasn't working, and I had no cash left, but the waiter agreed to take my credit card number and a signed authority for a deduction of one hundred dollars; whatever I didn't eat and drink would be his tip.

I sat in the café, blanking out the world, steeping myself in the mathematics. Sometimes the four of us worked on separate tasks; sometimes we paired up, dragging each other out of dead ends and ruts. There were an infinite number of variations that could be made to Campbell's algorithm, but hour by hour we whittled away at the concept, finding the common ground that no version of the weapon could do without.

By four in the morning, we had a strong conjecture. I called Sam, and explained what we were hoping to achieve.

He said, "This is a good idea. We'll consider it."

The café closed. I sat in the car for a while, drained and numb, then I called Kate to find out where she was. A couple had given her a lift almost as far as Penrith, and when their car failed she'd walked the rest of the way home.

ᴡᴠᴠ

FOR CLOSE to four days, I spent most of my waking hours just sitting at my desk, watching as a wave of red inched its way across a map of the defect. The change of hue was not being rendered lightly; before each pixel turned red, twelve separate computers needed to confirm that the region of the border it represented was flat.

On the fifth day, Sam shut off his computers and allowed us to mount an attack from our side on the narrow corridor linking the bulk of the far side with the small enclave that now surrounded our Achilles' Heel. We wouldn't have suffered any real loss of essential arithmetic if this slender thread had remained, but keeping the corridor both small and impregnable had turned out to be impossible. The original plan was the only route to finality: to seal the border perfectly, the far side proper could not remain linked to its offshoot.

In the next stage, the two sides worked together to seal the enclave completely, polishing the scar where its umbilical had been sheared away. When that task was complete, the map showed it as a single burnished ruby. No known process could reshape it now. Campbell's method could have breached its border without touching it, reaching inside to reclaim it from within—but Campbell's method was exactly what this jewel ruled out.

At the other end of the vanished umbilical, Sam's machines set to work smoothing away the blemish. By early evening that, too, was done.

Only one tiny flaw in the border remained, now: the handful of propositions that enabled communication between the two sides. The cabal had debated the fate of this for hours. So long as this small wrinkle persisted, in principle it could be used to unravel everything, to mobilize the entire border again. It was true that, compared to the border as a whole, it would be relatively easy to monitor and defend such a small site, but a sustained burst of brute-force computing from either side could still overpower any resistance and exploit it.

In the end, Sam's political masters had made the decision for us. What they had always aspired to was certainty, and even if their strength favored them, this wasn't a gamble they were prepared to take.

I said, "Good luck with the future."

"Good luck to Sparseland," Sam replied. I believed he'd tried to hold out against the hawks, but I'd never been certain of his friendship. When his icon faded from my screen, I felt more relief than regret.

I'd learned the hard way not to assume that anything was permanent. Perhaps in a thousand years, someone would discover that Campbell's model was just an approximation to something deeper, and find a way to fracture these allegedly perfect walls. With any luck, by then both sides might also be better prepared to find a way to co-exist.

I found Kate sitting in the kitchen. I said, "I can answer your questions now, if that's what you want." On the morning after the disaster, I'd promised her this time would come—within weeks, not months—and she'd agreed to stay with me until it did.

She thought for a while.

"Did you have something to do with what happened last week?"

"Yes."

"Are you saying you unleashed the virus? You're the terrorist they're looking for?" To my great relief, she asked this in roughly the tone she might have used if I'd claimed to be Genghis Khan.

"No, I'm not the cause of what happened. It was my job to try and stop it, and I failed. But it wasn't any kind of computer virus."

She searched my face. "What was it, then? Can you explain that to me?"

"It's a long story."

"I don't care. We've got all night."

I said, "It started in university. With an idea of Alison's. One brilliant, beautiful, crazy idea."

Kate looked away, her face flushing, as if I'd said something deliberately humiliating. She knew I was not a mass-murderer. But there were other things about me of which she was less sure.

"The story starts with Alison," I said. "But it ends here, with you."

GLORY

1

An ingot of metallic hydrogen gleamed in the starlight, a narrow cylinder half a meter long with a mass of about a kilogram. To the naked eye it was a dense, solid object, but its lattice of tiny nuclei immersed in an insubstantial fog of electrons was one part matter to two hundred trillion parts empty space. A short distance away was a second ingot, apparently identical to the first, but composed of antihydrogen.

A sequence of finely tuned gamma rays flooded into both cylinders. The protons that absorbed them in the first ingot spat out positrons and were transformed into neutrons, breaking their bonds to the electron cloud that glued them in place. In the second ingot, antiprotons became antineutrons.

A further sequence of pulses herded the neutrons together and forged them into clusters; the antineutrons were similarly rearranged. Both kinds of cluster were unstable, but in order to fall apart they first had to pass through a quantum state that would have strongly absorbed a component of the gamma rays constantly raining down on them. Left to themselves, the probability of them being in this state would have increased rapidly, but each time they measurably failed to absorb the

149

gamma rays, the probability fell back to zero. The quantum Zeno effect endlessly reset the clock, holding the decay in check.

The next series of pulses began shifting the clusters into the space that had separated the original ingots. First neutrons, then antineutrons, were sculpted together in alternating layers. Though the clusters were ultimately unstable, while they persisted they were inert, sequestering their constituents and preventing them from annihilating their counterparts. The end point of this process of nuclear sculpting was a sliver of compressed matter and antimatter, sandwiched together into a needle one micron wide.

The gamma ray lasers shut down, the Zeno effect withdrew its prohibitions. For the time it took a beam of light to cross a neutron, the needle sat motionless in space. Then it began to burn, and it began to move.

The needle was structured like a meticulously crafted firework, and its outer layers ignited first. No external casing could have channeled this blast, but the pattern of tensions woven into the needle's construction favored one direction for the debris to be expelled. Particles streamed backward; the needle moved forward. The shock of acceleration could not have been borne by anything built from atomic-scale matter, but the pressure bearing down on the core of the needle prolonged its life, delaying the inevitable.

Layer after layer burned itself away, blasting the dwindling remnant forward ever faster. By the time the needle had shrunk to a tenth of its original size it was moving at ninety-eight per cent of light speed; to a bystander this could scarcely have been improved upon, but from the needle's perspective there was still room to slash its journey's duration by orders of magnitude.

When just one thousandth of the needle remained, its time, compared to the neighboring stars, was passing five hundred times more slowly. Still the layers kept burning, the protective clusters unraveling as the pressure on them was released. The needle could only reach close enough to light speed to slow down time as much as it required if it could sacrifice a large enough proportion of its remaining mass. The core of the needle could only survive for a few trillionths of a second, while its journey would take two hundred million seconds as judged by the stars. The proportions had been carefully matched, though: out of the two kilograms of matter and antimatter that had been woven together at the launch, only a few million neutrons were needed as the final payload.

By one measure, seven years passed. For the needle, its last trillionths of a second unwound, its final layers of fuel blew away, and at the moment its core was ready to explode it reached its destination, plunging from the near-vacuum of space straight into the heart of a star.

Even here, the density of matter was insufficient to stabilize the core, yet far too high to allow it to pass unhindered. The core was torn apart. But it did not go quietly, and the shock waves it carved through the fusing plasma endured for a million kilometers: all the way through to the cooler outer layers on the opposite side of the star. These shock waves were shaped by the payload that had formed them, and though the initial pattern imprinted on them by the disintegrating cluster of neutrons was enlarged and blurred by its journey, on an atomic scale it remained sharply defined. Like a mold stamped into the seething plasma it encouraged ionized molecular fragments to slip into the troughs and furrows that matched their shape, and then brought them together to react in ways that the plasma's random collisions would never have allowed. In effect, the shock waves formed a web of catalysts, carefully laid out in both time and space, briefly transforming a small corner of the star into a chemical factory operating on a nanometer scale.

The products of this factory sprayed out of the star, riding the last traces of the shock wave's momentum: a few nanograms of elaborate, carbon-rich molecules, sheathed in a protective fullerene weave. Traveling at seven hundred kilometers per second, a fraction below the velocity needed to escape from the star completely, they climbed out of its gravity well, slowing as they ascended.

Four years passed, but the molecules were stable against the ravages of space. By the time they'd traveled a billion kilometers they had almost come to a halt, and they would have fallen back to die in the fires of the star that had forged them if their journey had not been timed so that the star's third planet, a gas giant, was waiting to urge them forward. As they fell toward it, the giant's third moon moved across their path. Eleven years after the needle's launch, its molecular offspring rained down on to the methane snow.

The tiny heat of their impact was not enough to damage them, but it melted a microscopic puddle in the snow. Surrounded by food, the molecular seeds began to grow. Within hours, the area was teeming with nanomachines, some mining the snow and the minerals beneath it, others assembling the bounty into an intricate structure, a rectangular panel a couple of meters wide.

From across the light years, an elaborate sequence of gamma ray pulses fell upon the panel. These pulses were the needle's true payload, the passengers for whom it had merely prepared the way, transmitted in its wake four years after its launch. The panel decoded and stored the data, and the army of nanomachines set to work again, this time following a far more elaborate blueprint. The miners were forced to look further afield to find all the elements that were needed, while the assemblers labored to reach their goal through a sequence of intermediate stages, carefully designed to protect the final product from the vagaries of the local chemistry and climate.

After three months' work, two small fusion-powered spacecraft sat in the snow. Each one held a single occupant, waking for the first time in their freshly minted bodies, yet endowed with memories of an earlier life.

Joan switched on her communications console. Anne appeared on the screen, three short pairs of arms folded across her thorax in a posture of calm repose. They had both worn virtual bodies with the same anatomy before, but this was the first time they had become Noudah in the flesh.

"We're here. Everything worked," Joan marveled. The language she spoke was not her own, but the structure of her new brain and body made it second nature.

Anne said, "Now comes the hard part."

"Yes." Joan looked out from the spacecraft's cockpit. In the distance, a fissured blue-gray plateau of water ice rose above the snow. Nearby, the nanomachines were busy disassembling the gamma ray receiver. When they had erased all traces of their handiwork they would wander off into the snow and catalyze their own destruction.

Joan had visited dozens of planet-bound cultures in the past, taking on different bodies and languages as necessary, but those cultures had all been plugged in to the Amalgam, the meta-civilization that spanned the galactic disk. However far from home she'd been, the means to return to familiar places had always been close at hand. The Noudah had only just mastered interplanetary flight, and they had no idea that the Amalgam existed. The closest node in the Amalgam's network was seven light years away, and even that was out of bounds to her and Anne now: they had agreed not to risk disclosing its location to the Noudah, so any transmission they sent could only be directed to a decoy node that they'd set up more than twenty light years away.

"It will be worth it," Joan said.

Anne's Noudah face was immobile, but chromatophores sent a wave of violet and gold sweeping across her skin in an expression of cautious optimism. "We'll see." She tipped her head to the left, a gesture preceding a friendly departure.

Joan tipped her own head in response, as if she'd been doing so all her life. "Be careful, my friend," she said.

"You too."

Anne's ship ascended so high on its chemical thrusters that it shrank to a speck before igniting its fusion engine and streaking away in a blaze of light. Joan felt a pang of loneliness; there was no predicting when they would be reunited.

Her ship's software was primitive; the whole machine had been scrupulously matched to the Noudah's level of technology. Joan knew how to fly it herself if necessary, and on a whim she switched off the autopilot and manually activated the ascent thrusters. The control panel was crowded, but having six hands helped.

2

THE WORLD the Noudah called home was the closest of the system's five planets to their sun. The average temperature was one hundred and twenty degrees Celsius, but the high atmospheric pressure allowed liquid water to exist across the entire surface. The chemistry and dynamics of the planet's crust had led to a relatively flat terrain, with a patchwork of dozens of disconnected seas but no globe-spanning ocean. From space, these seas appeared as silvery mirrors, bordered by a violet and brown tarnish of vegetation.

The Noudah were already leaving their most electromagnetically promiscuous phase of communications behind, but the short-lived oasis of Amalgam-level technology on Baneth, the gas giant's moon, had had no trouble eavesdropping on their chatter and preparing an updated cultural briefing which had been spliced into Joan's brain.

The planet was still divided into the same eleven political units as it had been fourteen years before, the time of the last broadcasts that had reached the node before Joan's departure. Tira and Ghahar, the two dominant nations in terms of territory, economic activity and military power, also occupied the vast majority of significant Niah archaeological sites.

Joan had expected that they'd be noticed as soon as they left Baneth—the exhaust from their fusion engines glowed like the sun— but their departure had triggered no obvious response, and now that they were coasting they'd be far harder to spot. As Anne drew closer to the home world, she sent a message to Tira's traffic control center. Joan tuned in to the exchange.

"I come in peace from another star," Anne said. "I seek permission to land."

There was a delay of several seconds more than the light-speed lag, then a terse response. "Please identify yourself and state your location."

Anne transmitted her coordinates and flight plan.

"We confirm your location, please identify yourself."

"My name is Anne. I come from another star."

There was a long pause, then a different voice answered. "If you are from Ghahar, please explain your intentions."

"I am not from Ghahar."

"Why should I believe that? Show yourself."

"I've taken the same shape as your people, in the hope of living among you for a while." Anne opened a video channel and showed them her unremarkable Noudah face. "But there's a signal being transmitted from these coordinates that might persuade you that I'm telling the truth." She gave the location of the decoy node, twenty light years away, and specified a frequency. The signal coming from the node contained an image of the very same face.

This time, the silence stretched out for several minutes. It would take a while for the Tirans to confirm the true distance of the radio source.

"You do not have permission to land. Please enter this orbit, and we will rendezvous and board your ship."

Parameters for the orbit came through on the data channel. Anne said, "As you wish."

Minutes later, Joan's instruments picked up three fusion ships being launched from Tiran bases. When Anne reached the prescribed orbit, Joan listened anxiously to the instructions the Tirans issued. Their tone sounded wary, but they were entitled to treat this stranger with caution, all the more so if they believed Anne's claim.

Joan was accustomed to a very different kind of reception, but then the members of the Amalgam had spent hundreds of millennia establishing a framework of trust. They also benefited from a milieu in which most kinds of force had been rendered ineffectual; when everyone had backups of themselves scattered around the galaxy, it required a vastly disproportionate effort to inconvenience someone, let alone kill them. By any reasonable measure, honesty and cooperation yielded far richer rewards than subterfuge and slaughter.

Nonetheless, each individual culture had its roots in a biological heritage that gave rise to behavior governed more by ancient urges than contemporary realities, and even when they mastered the technology to choose their own nature, the precise set of traits they preserved was up to them. In the worst case, a species still saddled with inappropriate drives but empowered by advanced technology could wreak havoc. The Noudah deserved to be treated with courtesy and respect, but they did not yet belong in the Amalgam.

The Tirans' own exchanges were not on open channels, so once they had entered Anne's ship Joan could only guess what was happening. She waited until two of the ships had returned to the surface, then sent her own message to Ghahar's traffic control.

"I come in peace from another star. I seek permission to land."

3

THE GHAHARI allowed Joan to fly her ship straight down to the surface. She wasn't sure if this was because they were more trusting, or if they were afraid that the Tirans might try to interfere if she lingered in orbit.

The landing site was a bare plain of chocolate colored sand. The air shimmered in the heat, the distortions intensified by the thickness of the atmosphere, making the horizon waver as if seen through molten glass. Joan waited in the cockpit as three trucks approached; they all came to a halt some twenty meters away. A voice over the radio instructed her to leave the ship; she complied, and after she'd stood in the open for a minute, a lone Noudah left one of the trucks and walked toward her.

"I'm Pirit," she said. "Welcome to Ghahar." Her gestures were courteous but restrained.

"I'm Joan. Thank you for your hospitality."

"Your impersonation of our biology is impeccable." There was a trace of skepticism in Pirit's tone; Joan had pointed the Ghahari to her own portrait being broadcast from the decoy node, but she had to admit that in the context her lack of exotic technology and traits would make it harder to accept the implications of that transmission.

"In my culture, it's a matter of courtesy to imitate one's hosts as closely as possible."

Pirit hesitated, as if pondering whether to debate the merits of such a custom, but then rather than quibbling over the niceties of interspecies etiquette she chose to confront the real issue head on. "If you're a Tiran spy, or a defector, the sooner you admit that the better."

"That's very sensible advice, but I'm neither."

The Noudah wore no clothing as such, but Pirit had a belt with a number of pouches. She took a hand-held scanner from one and ran it over Joan's body. Joan's briefing suggested that it was probably only checking for metal, volatile explosives and radiation; the technology to image her body or search for pathogens would not be so portable. In any case, she was a healthy, unarmed Noudah down to the molecular level.

Pirit escorted her to one of the trucks, and invited her to recline in a section at the back. Another Noudah drove while Pirit watched over Joan. They soon arrived at a small complex of buildings a couple of kilometers from where the ship had touched down. The walls, roofs and floors of the buildings were all made from the local sand, cemented with an adhesive that the Noudah secreted from their own bodies.

Inside, Joan was given a thorough medical examination, including three kinds of full-body scan. The Noudah who examined her treated her with a kind of detached efficiency devoid of any pleasantries; she wasn't sure if that was their standard bedside manner, or a kind of glazed shock at having been told of her claimed origins.

Pirit took her to an adjoining room and offered her a couch. The Noudah anatomy did not allow for sitting, but they liked to recline.

Pirit remained standing. "How did you come here?" she asked.

"You've seen my ship. I flew it from Baneth."

"And how did you reach Baneth?"

"I'm not free to discuss that," Joan replied cheerfully.

"Not free?" Pirit's face clouded with silver, as if she was genuinely perplexed.

Joan said, "You understand me perfectly. Please don't tell me there's nothing *you're* not free to discuss with me."

"You certainly didn't fly that ship twenty light years."

"No, I certainly didn't."

Pirit hesitated. "Did you come through the Cataract?" The Cataract was a black hole, a remote partner to the Noudah's sun; they orbited each other at a distance of about eighty billion kilometers. The name came from its telescopic appearance: a dark circle ringed by a distortion in the background of stars, like some kind of visual aberration. The Tirans and Ghahari were in a race to be the first to visit this extraordinary neighbor, but as yet neither of them were quite up to the task.

"*Through* the Cataract? I think your scientists have already proven that black holes aren't shortcuts to anywhere."

"Our scientists aren't always right."

"Neither are ours," Joan admitted, "but all the evidence points in one direction: black holes aren't doorways, they're shredding machines."

"So you traveled the whole twenty light years?"

"More than that," Joan said truthfully, "from my original home. I've spent half my life traveling."

"Faster than light?" Pirit suggested hopefully.

"No. That's impossible."

They circled around the question a dozen more times, before Pirit finally changed her tune from *how* to *why?*

"I'm a xenomathematician," Joan said. "I've come here in the hope of collaborating with your archaeologists in their study of Niah artifacts."

Pirit was stunned. "What do you know about the Niah?"

"Not as much as I'd like to." Joan gestured at her Noudah body. "As I'm sure you've already surmised, we've listened to your broadcasts for some time, so we know pretty much what an ordinary Noudah knows. That includes the basic facts about the Niah. Historically they've been referred to as your ancestors, though the latest studies suggest that you and they really just have an earlier common ancestor. They died out about a million years ago, but there's evidence that they might have had a sophisticated culture for as long as three million years. There's no indication that they ever developed space flight. Basically, once they achieved material comfort, they seem to have devoted themselves to various artforms, including mathematics."

"So you've traveled twenty light years just to look at Niah tablets?" Pirit was incredulous.

"Any culture that spent three million years doing mathematics must have something to teach us."

"Really?" Pirit's face became blue with disgust. "In the ten thousand years since we discovered the wheel, we've already reached halfway to the Cataract. They wasted their time on useless abstractions."

Joan said, "I come from a culture of spacefarers myself, so I respect your achievements. But I don't think anyone really knows what the Niah achieved. I'd like to find out, with the help of your people."

Pirit was silent for a while. "What if we say no?"

"Then I'll leave empty-handed."

"What if we insist that you remain with us?"

"Then I'll die here, empty-handed." On her command, this body would expire in an instant; she could not be held and tortured.

Pirit said angrily, "You must be willing to trade *something* for the privilege you're demanding!"

"Requesting, not demanding," Joan insisted gently. "And what I'm willing to offer is my own culture's perspective on Niah mathematics. If you ask your archaeologists and mathematicians, I'm sure they'll tell you that there are many things written in the Niah tablets that they don't yet understand. My colleague and I—" neither of them had mentioned Anne before, but Joan was sure that Pirit knew all about her "—simply want to shed as much light as we can on this subject."

Pirit said bitterly, "You won't even tell us how you came to our world. Why should we trust you to share whatever you discover about the Niah?"

"Interstellar travel is no great mystery," Joan countered. "You know all the basic science already; making it work is just a matter of persistence. If you're left to develop your own technology, you might even come up with better methods than we have."

"So we're expected to be patient, to discover these things for ourselves…but you can't wait a few centuries for us to decipher the Niah artifacts?"

Joan said bluntly, "The present Noudah culture, both here and in Tira, seems to hold the Niah in contempt. Dozens of partially excavated sites containing Niah artifacts are under threat from irrigation projects and other developments. That's the reason we couldn't wait. We needed to come here and offer our assistance, before the last traces of the Niah disappeared forever."

Pirit did not reply, but Joan hoped she knew what her interrogator was thinking: *Nobody would cross twenty light years for a few worthless scribblings. Perhaps we've underestimated the Niah. Perhaps our ancestors have left us a great secret, a great legacy. And perhaps the fastest—perhaps the only—way to uncover it is to give this impertinent, irritating alien exactly what she wants.*

4

THE SUN was rising ahead of them as they reached the top of the hill. Sando turned to Joan, and his face became green with pleasure. "Look behind you," he said.

Joan did as he asked. The valley below was hidden in fog, and it had settled so evenly that she could see their shadows in the dawn light, stretched out across the top of the fog layer. Around the shadow of her head was a circular halo like a small rainbow.

"We call it the Niah's light," Sando said. "In the old days, people used to say that the halo proved that the Niah blood was strong in you."

Joan said, "The only trouble with that hypothesis being that *you* see it around *your* head…and I see it around mine." On Earth, the phenomenon was known as a "glory". The particles of fog were scattering the sunlight back toward them, turning it one hundred and eighty degrees. To look at the shadow of your own head was to face directly away from the sun, so the halo always appeared around the observer's shadow.

"I suppose you're the final proof that Niah blood has nothing to do with it," Sando mused.

"That's assuming I'm telling you the truth, and I really can see it around my own head."

"And assuming," Sando added, "that the Niah really did stay at home, and didn't wander around the galaxy spreading their progeny."

They came over the top of the hill and looked down into the adjoining riverine valley. The sparse brown grass of the hillside gave way to a lush violet growth closer to the water. Joan's arrival had delayed the flooding of the valley, but even alien interest in the Niah had only bought the archaeologists an extra year. The dam was part of a long-planned agricultural development, and however tantalizing the possibility that Joan might reveal some priceless insight hidden among the Niah's "useless abstractions", that vague promise could only compete with more tangible considerations for a limited time.

Part of the hill had fallen away in a landslide a few centuries before, revealing more than a dozen beautifully preserved strata. When Joan and Sando reached the excavation site, Rali and Surat were already at work, clearing away soft sedimentary rock from a layer that Sando had dated as belonging to the Niah's "twilight" period.

Pirit had insisted that only Sando, the senior archaeologist, be told about Joan's true nature; Joan refused to lie to anyone, but had agreed to tell her colleagues only that she was a mathematician and that she was not permitted to discuss her past. At first this had made them guarded and resentful, no doubt because they assumed that she was some kind of spy sent by the authorities to watch over them. Later it had dawned on them that she was genuinely interested in their work, and that the absurd restrictions on her topics of conversation were not of her own choosing. Nothing about the Noudah's language or appearance correlated strongly with their recent division into nations—with no oceans to cross, and a long history of migration they were more or less geographically homogeneous—but Joan's odd name and occasional *faux pas* could still be ascribed to some mysterious exoticism. Rali and Surat seemed content to assume that she was a defector from one of the smaller nations, and that her history could not be made explicit for obscure political reasons.

"There are more tablets here, very close to the surface," Rali announced excitedly. "The acoustics are unmistakable." Ideally they would have excavated the entire hillside, but they did not have the time or the labor, so they were using acoustic tomography to identify likely deposits of accessible Niah writing, and then concentrating their efforts on those spots.

The Niah had probably had several ephemeral forms of written communication, but when they found something worth publishing, it stayed published: they carved their symbols into a ceramic that made diamond seem like tissue paper. It was almost unheard of for the tablets to be broken, but they were small, and multi-tablet works were sometimes widely dispersed. Niah technology could probably have carved three million years' worth of knowledge on to the head of a pin—they seemed not to have invented nanomachines, but they were into high quality bulk materials and precision engineering—but for whatever reason they had chosen legibility to the naked eye above other considerations.

Joan made herself useful, taking acoustic readings further along the slope, while Sando watched over his students as they came closer to the buried Niah artifacts. She had learned not to hover around expectantly when a discovery was imminent; she was treated far more warmly if she waited to be summoned. The tomography unit was almost foolproof, using satellite navigation to track its position and software to analyze the signals it gathered; all it really needed was someone to drag it along the rock face at a suitable pace.

Through the corner of her eye, Joan noticed her shadow on the rocks flicker and grow complicated. She looked up to see three dazzling beads of light flying west out of the sun. She might have assumed that the fusion ships were doing something useful, but the media was full of talk of "military exercises", which meant the Tirans and the Ghahari engaging in expensive, belligerent gestures in orbit, trying to convince each other of their superior skills, technology, or sheer strength of numbers. For people with no real differences apart from a few centuries of recent history, they could puff up their minor political disputes into matters of the utmost solemnity. It might almost have been funny, if the idiots hadn't incinerated hundreds of thousands of each other's citizens every few decades, not to mention playing callous and often deadly games with the lives of the inhabitants of smaller nations.

"Jown! Jown! Come and look at this!" Surat called to her. Joan switched off the tomography unit and jogged toward the archaeologists, suddenly conscious of her body's strangeness. Her legs were stumpy but strong, and her balance as she ran came not from arms and shoulders but from the swish of her muscular tail.

"It's a significant mathematical result," Rali informed her proudly when she reached them. He'd pressure-washed the sandstone away from the near-indestructible ceramic of the tablet, and it was only a matter of holding the surface at the right angle to the light to see the etched writing stand out as crisply and starkly as it would have a million years before.

Rali was not a mathematician, and he was not offering his own opinion on the theorem the tablet stated; the Niah themselves had a clear set of typographical conventions which they used to distinguish between everything from minor lemmas to the most celebrated theorems. The size and decorations of the symbols labelling the theorem attested to its value in the Niah's eyes.

Joan read the theorem carefully. The proof was not included on the same tablet, but the Niah had a way of expressing their results that made you believe them as soon as you read them; in this case the definitions of the terms needed to state the theorem were so beautifully chosen that the result seemed almost inevitable.

The theorem itself was expressed as a commuting hypercube, one of the Niah's favorite forms. You could think of a square with four different sets of mathematical objects associated with each of its corners, and a way of mapping one set into another associated with each edge of the square. If the maps commuted, then going across the top of the square, then down, had exactly the same effect as going down the left edge of the square, then across: either way, you mapped each element from the top-left set into the same element of the bottom-right set. A similar kind of result might hold for sets and maps that could naturally be placed at the corners and edges of a cube, or a hypercube of any dimension. It was also possible for the square faces in these structures to stand for relationships that held between the maps between sets, and for cubes to describe relationships between those relationships, and so on.

That a theorem took this form didn't guarantee its importance; it was easy to cook up trivial examples of sets and maps that commuted. The Niah didn't carve trivia into their timeless ceramic, though, and this theorem was no exception. The seven-dimensional commuting hypercube established a dazzlingly elegant correspondence between seven distinct, major branches of Niah mathematics, intertwining their most important concepts into a unified whole. It was a result Joan had never seen before: no mathematician anywhere in the Amalgam, or in any ancestral culture she had studied, had reached the same insight.

She explained as much of this as she could to the three archaeologists; they couldn't take in all the details, but their faces became orange with fascination when she sketched what she thought the result would have meant to the Niah themselves.

"This isn't quite the Big Crunch," she joked, "but it must have made them think they were getting closer." *The Big Crunch* was her nickname for the mythical result that the Niah had aspired to reach: a unification of every field of mathematics that they considered significant. To find such a thing would not have meant the end of mathematics—it would not have subsumed every last conceivable, interesting mathematical truth—but it would certainly have marked a point of closure for the Niah's own style of investigation.

"I'm sure they found it," Surat insisted. "They reached the Big Crunch, then they had nothing more to live for."

Rali was scathing. "So the whole culture committed collective suicide?"

"Not actively, no," Surat replied. "But it was the search that had kept them going."

"Entire cultures don't lose the will to live," Rali said. "They get wiped out by external forces: disease, invasion, changes in climate."

"The Niah survived for three million years," Surat countered. "They had the means to weather all of those forces. Unless they were wiped out by alien invaders with vastly superior technology." She turned to Joan. "What do you think?"

"About aliens destroying the Niah?"

"I was joking about the aliens. But what about the mathematics? What if they found the Big Crunch?"

"There's more to life than mathematics," Joan said. "But not much more."

Sando said, "And there's more to this find than one tablet. If we get back to work, we might have the proof in our hands before sunset."

5

JOAN BRIEFED Halzoun by video link while Sando prepared the evening meal. Halzoun was the mathematician Pirit had appointed to supervise her, but apparently his day job was far too important to allow him to travel. Joan was grateful; Halzoun was the most tedious Noudah she had encountered. He could understand the Niah's work when she explained it to him, but he seemed to have no interest in it for its own sake. He spent most of their conversations trying to catch her out in some deception or contradiction, and the rest pressing her to imagine military or commercial applications of the Niah's gloriously useless insights. Sometimes she played along with this infantile fantasy, hinting at potential superweapons based on exotic physics that might come tumbling out of the vacuum, if only one possessed the right Niah theorems to coax them into existence.

Sando was her minder too, but at least he was more subtle about it. Pirit had insisted that she stay in his shelter, rather than sharing Rali and Surat's; Joan didn't mind, because with Sando she didn't have the stress of having to keep quiet about everything. Privacy and modesty were non-issues for the Noudah, and Joan had become Noudah enough not to care herself. Nor was there any danger of their proximity leading to a sexual bond; the Noudah had a complex system of biochemical cues that meant desire only arose in couples with a suitable mixture of genetic differences and similarities. She would have had to search a crowded Noudah city for a week to find someone to lust after, though at least it would have been guaranteed to be mutual.

After they'd eaten, Sando said, "You should be happy. That was our best find yet."

"I am happy." Joan made a conscious effort to exhibit a viridian tinge. "It was the first new result I've seen on this planet. It was the reason I came here, the reason I traveled so far."

"Something's wrong, though, I think."

"I wish I could have shared the news with my friend," Joan admitted. Pirit claimed to be negotiating with the Tirans to allow Anne to communicate with her, but Joan was not convinced that she was genuinely trying. She was sure that she would have relished the thought of listening in on a conversation between the two of them—while forcing them to speak Noudah, of course—in the hope that they'd slip up and reveal something useful, but at the same time she would have had to face the fact that the Tirans would be listening too. What an excruciating dilemma.

"You should have brought a communications link with you," Sando suggested. "A home-style one, I mean. Nothing we could eavesdrop on."

"We couldn't do that," Joan said.

He pondered this. "You really are afraid of us, aren't you? You think the smallest technological trinket will be enough to send us straight to the stars, and then you'll have a horde of rampaging barbarians to deal with."

"We know how to deal with barbarians," Joan said coolly.

Sando's face grew dark with mirth. "Now *I'm* afraid."

"I just wish I knew what was happening to her," Joan said. "What she was doing, how they were treating her."

"Probably much the same as we're treating you," Sando suggested. "We're really not that different." He thought for a moment. "There was something I wanted to show you." He brought over his portable console, and summoned up an article from a Tiran journal. "See what a border-less world we live in," he joked.

The article was entitled "Seekers and Spreaders: What We Must Learn from the Niah". Sando said, "This might give you some idea of how they're thinking over there. Jaqad is an academic archaeologist, but she's also very close to the people in power."

Joan read from the console while Sando made repairs to their shelter, secreting a molasses-like substance from a gland at the tip of his tail and spreading it over the cracks in the walls.

There were two main routes a culture could take, Jaqad argued, once it satisfied its basic material needs. One was to think and study: to stand back and observe, to seek knowledge and insight from the world around it. The other was to invest its energy in entrenching its good fortune.

The Niah had learned a great deal in three million years, but in the end it had not been enough to save them. Exactly what had killed them was still a matter of speculation, but it was hard to believe that if they had colonized other worlds they would have vanished on all of them. "Had the Niah been Spreaders," Jaqad wrote, "we might expect a visit from them, or them from us, sometime in the coming centuries."

The Noudah, in contrast, were determined Spreaders. Once they had the means, they would plant colonies across the galaxy. They would, Jaqad was sure, create new biospheres, re-engineer stars, and even alter space and time to guarantee their survival. The growth of their empire would come first; any knowledge that failed to serve that purpose would be a mere distraction. "In any competition between Seekers and Spreaders, it is a Law of History that the Spreaders must win out in the end. Seekers, such as the Niah, might hog resources and block the way, but in the long run their own nature will be their downfall."

Joan stopped reading. "When you look out into the galaxy with your telescopes," she asked Sando, "how many *re-engineered stars* do you see?"

"Would we recognize them?"

"Yes. Natural stellar processes aren't that complicated; your scientists already know everything there is to know about the subject."

"I'll take your word for that. So…you're saying Jaqad is wrong? The Niah themselves never left this world, but the galaxy already belongs to creatures more like them than like us?"

"It's not Noudah versus Niah," Joan said. "It's a matter of how a culture's perspective changes with time. Once a species conquers disease, modifies their biology, and spreads even a short distance beyond their home world, they usually start to relax a bit. The territorial imperative isn't some timeless Law of History; it belongs to a certain phase."

"What if it persists, though? Into a later phase?"

"That can cause friction," Joan admitted.

"Nevertheless, no Spreaders have conquered the galaxy?"

"Not yet."

Sando went back to his repairs; Joan read the rest of the article. She'd thought she'd already grasped the lesson demanded by the subtitle, but it turned out that Jaqad had something more specific in mind.

"Having argued this way, how can I defend my own field of study from the very same charges as I have brought against the Niah? Having grasped the essential character of this doomed race, why should we waste our time and resources studying them further?

"The answer is simple. We still do not know exactly how and why the Niah died, but when we do, that could turn out to be the most important discovery in history. When we finally leave our world behind, we should not expect to find only other Spreaders to compete with us, as honorable opponents in battle. There will be Seekers as well, blocking the way: tired, old races squatting uselessly on their hoards of knowledge and wealth.

"Time will defeat them in the end, but we already waited three million years to be born; we should have no patience to wait again. If we can learn how the Niah died, that will be our key, that will be our weapon. If we know the Seekers' weakness, we can find a way to hasten their demise."

6

THE PROOF of the Niah's theorem turned out to be buried deep in the hillside, but over the following days they extracted it all.

It was as beautiful and satisfying as Joan could have wished, merging six earlier, simpler theorems while extending the techniques used in their proofs. She could even see hints at how the same methods might be stretched further to yield still stronger results. "The Big Crunch" had always been a slightly mocking, irreverent term, but now she was struck anew by how little justice it did to the real trend that had fascinated the Niah. It was not a matter of everything in mathematics collapsing in on itself, with one branch turning out to have been merely a recapitulation of another under a different guise. Rather, the principle was that every sufficiently beautiful mathematical system was rich enough to mirror *in part*—and sometimes in a complex and distorted fashion—every other sufficiently beautiful system. Nothing became sterile and redundant, nothing proved to have been a waste of time, but everything was shown to be magnificently intertwined.

After briefing Halzoun, Joan used the satellite dish to transmit the theorem and its proof to the decoy node. That had been the deal with Pirit: anything she learned from the Niah belonged to the whole galaxy, as long as she explained it to her hosts first.

The archaeologists moved across the hillside, hunting for more artifacts in the same layer of sediment. Joan was eager to see what else the same group of Niah might have published. One possible eight-dimensional hypercube was hovering in her mind; if she'd sat down and thought about it for a few decades she might have worked out the details herself, but the Niah did what they did so well that it would have seemed crass to try to follow clumsily in their footsteps when their own immaculately polished results might simply be lying in the ground, waiting to be uncovered.

A month after the discovery, Joan was woken by the sound of an intruder moving through the shelter. She knew it wasn't Sando; even as she slept an ancient part of her Noudah brain was listening to his heartbeat. The stranger's heart was too quiet to hear, which required great discipline, but the shelter's flexible adhesive made the floor emit a characteristic squeak beneath even the gentlest footsteps. As she rose from her couch she heard Sando waking, and she turned in his direction.

Bright torchlight on his face dazzled her for a moment. The intruder held two knives to Sando's respiratory membranes; a deep enough cut there would mean choking to death, in excruciating pain. The nanomachines that had built Joan's body had wired extensive skills in unarmed combat into her brain, and one scenario involving a feigned escape attempt followed by a sideways flick of her powerful tail was already playing out in the back of her mind, but as yet she could see no way to guarantee that Sando came through it all unharmed.

She said, "What do you want?"

The intruder remained in darkness. "Tell me about the ship that brought you to Baneth."

"Why?"

"Because it would be a shame to shred your colleague here, just when his work was going so well." Sando refused to show any emotion on his face, but the blank pallor itself was as stark an expression of fear as anything Joan could imagine.

She said, "There's a coherent state that can be prepared for a quark-gluon plasma in which virtual black holes catalyze baryon decay. In effect, you can turn all of your fuel's rest mass into photons, yielding the most efficient exhaust stream possible." She recited a long list of technical details. The claimed baryon decay process didn't actually exist, but the pseudo-physics underpinning it was mathematically consistent, and could not be ruled out by anything the Noudah had yet observed. She and Anne had prepared an entire fictitious science and technology, and even a fictitious history of their culture, precisely for emergencies like this; they could spout red herrings for a decade if necessary, and never get caught out contradicting themselves.

"That wasn't so hard, was it?" the intruder gloated.

"What now?"

"You're going to take a trip with me. If you do this nicely, nobody needs to get hurt."

Something moved in the shadows, and the intruder screamed in pain. Joan leaped forward and knocked one of the knives out of his hand with her tail; the other knife grazed Sando's membrane, but a second tail whipped out of the darkness and intervened. As the intruder fell backward, the beam of his torch revealed Surat and Rali tensed beside him, and a pick buried deep in his side.

Joan's rush of combat hormones suddenly faded, and she let out a long, deep wail of anguish. Sando was unscathed, but a stream of dark liquid was pumping out of the intruder's wound.

Surat was annoyed. "Stop blubbing, and help us tie up this Tiran cousin-fucker."

"Tie him up? You've killed him!"

"Don't be stupid, that's just sheath fluid." Joan recalled her Noudah anatomy; sheath fluid was like oil in a hydraulic machine. You could lose it all and it would cost you most of the strength in your limbs and tail, but you wouldn't die, and your body would make more eventually.

Rali found some cable and they trussed up the intruder. Sando was shaken, but he seemed to be recovering. He took Joan aside. "I'm going to have to call Pirit."

"I understand. But what will she do to these two?" She wasn't sure exactly how much Rali and Surat had heard, but it was certain to have been more than Pirit wanted them to know.

"Don't worry about that, I can protect them."

Just before dawn someone sent by Pirit arrived in a truck to take the intruder away. Sando declared a rest day, and Rali and Surat went back to their shelter to sleep. Joan went for a walk along the hillside; she didn't feel like sleeping.

Sando caught up with her. He said, "I told them you'd been working on a military research project, and you were exiled here for some political misdemeanor."

"And they believed you?"

"All they heard was half of a conversation full of incomprehensible physics. All they know is that someone thought you were worth kidnapping."

Joan said, "I'm sorry about what happened."

Sando hesitated. "What did you expect?"

Joan was stung. "One of us went to Tira, one of us came here. We thought that would keep everyone happy!"

"We're Spreaders," said Sando. "Give us one of anything, and we want two. Especially if our enemy has the other one. Did you really think you could come here, do a bit of fossicking, and then simply fly away without changing a thing?"

"Your culture has always believed there were other civilizations in the galaxy. Our existence hardly came as a shock."

Sando's face became yellow, an expression of almost parental reproach. "Believing in something in the abstract is not the same as having it dangled in front of you. We were never going to have an existential crisis at finding out that we're not unique; the Niah might be related to us, but they were still alien enough to get us used to the idea. But did you really think we were just going to relax and accept your refusal to share your technology? That one of you went to the Tirans only makes it worse for the Ghahari, and vice versa. Both governments are going absolutely crazy, each one terrified that the other has found a way to make its alien talk."

Joan stopped walking. "The war games, the border skirmishes? You're blaming all of that on Anne and me?"

Sando's body sagged wearily. "To be honest, I don't know all the details. And if it's any consolation, I'm sure we would have found another reason if you hadn't come along."

Joan said, "Maybe I should leave." She was tired of these people, tired of her body, tired of being cut off from civilization. She had rescued one beautiful Niah theorem and sent it out into the Amalgam. Wasn't that enough?

"It's up to you," Sando replied. "But you might as well stay until they flood the valley. Another year isn't going to change anything. What you've done to this world has already been done. For us, there's no going back."

7

JOAN STAYED with the archaeologists as they moved across the hillside. They found tablets bearing Niah drawings and poetry, which no doubt had their virtues but to Joan seemed bland and opaque. Sando and his students relished these discoveries as much as the theorems; to them, the Niah culture was a vast jigsaw puzzle, and any clue that filled in the details of their history was as good as any other.

Sando would have told Pirit everything he'd heard from Joan the night the intruder came, so she was surprised that she hadn't been summoned for a fresh interrogation to flesh out the details. Perhaps the Ghahari physicists were still digesting her elaborate gobbledygook, trying to decide if it made sense. In her more cynical moments she wondered if the intruder might have been Ghahari himself, sent by Pirit to exploit her friendship with Sando. Perhaps Sando had even been in on it, and Rali and Surat as well. The possibility made her feel as if she was living in a fabricated world, a scape in which nothing was real and nobody could be trusted. The only thing she was certain that the Ghaharis could not have faked was the Niah artifacts. The mathematics verified itself; everything else was subject to doubt and paranoia.

Summer came, burning away the morning fogs. The Noudah's idea of heat was very different from Joan's previous perceptions, but even the body she now wore found the midday sun oppressive. She willed herself to be patient. There was still a chance that the Niah had taken a few more steps toward their grand vision of a unified mathematics, and carved their final discoveries into the form that would outlive them by a million years.

When the lone fusion ship appeared high in the afternoon sky, Joan resolved to ignore it. She glanced up once, but she kept dragging the tomography unit across the ground. She was sick of thinking about Tiran-Ghahari politics. They had played their childish games for centuries; she would not take the blame for this latest outbreak of provocation.

Usually the ships flew by, disappearing within minutes, showing off their power and speed. This one lingered, weaving back and forth across the sky like some dazzling insect performing an elaborate mating dance. Joan's second shadow darted around her feet, hammering a strangely familiar rhythm into her brain.

She looked up, disbelieving. The motion of the ship was following the syntax of a gestural language she had learned on another planet, in another body, a dozen lifetimes ago. The only other person on this world who could know that language was Anne.

She glanced toward the archaeologists a hundred meters away, but they seemed to be paying no attention to the ship. She switched off the tomography unit and stared into the sky. *I'm listening, my friend. What's happening? Did they give you back your ship? Have you had enough of this world, and decided to go home?*

Anne told the story in shorthand, compressed and elliptic. The Tirans had found a tablet bearing a theorem: the last of the Niah's discoveries, the pinnacle of their achievements. Her minders had not let her study it, but they had contrived a situation making it easy for her to steal it, and to steal this ship. They had wanted her to take it and run, in the hope that she would lead them to something they valued far more than any ancient mathematics: an advanced spacecraft, or some magical stargate at the edge of the system.

But Anne wasn't fleeing anywhere. She was high above Ghahar, reading the tablet, and now she would paint what she read across the sky for Joan to see.

Sando approached. "We're in danger, we have to move."

"Danger? That's my friend up there! She's not going to shoot a missile at us!"

"Your friend?" Sando seemed confused. As he spoke, three more ships came into view, lower and brighter than the first. "I've been told that the Tirans are going to strike the valley, to bury the Niah sites. We need to get over the hill and indoors, to get some protection from the blast."

"Why would the Tirans attack the Niah sites? That makes no sense to me."

Sando said, "Nor me, but I don't have time to argue."

The three ships were menacing Anne's, pursuing her, trying to drive her away. Joan had no idea if they were Ghahari defending their territory, or Tirans harassing her in the hope that she would flee and reveal the non-existent shortcut to the stars, but Anne was staying put, still weaving the same gestural language into her maneuvers even as she dodged her pursuers, spelling out the Niah's glorious finale.

Joan said, "You go. I have to see this." She tensed, ready to fight him if necessary.

Sando took something from his tool belt and peppered her side with holes. Joan gasped with pain and crumpled to the ground as the sheath fluid poured out of her.

Rali and Surat helped carry her to the shelter. Joan caught glimpses of the fiery ballet in the sky, but not enough to make sense of it, let alone reconstruct it.

They put her on her couch inside the shelter. Sando bandaged her side and gave her water to sip. He said, "I'm sorry I had to do that, but if anything had happened to you I would have been held responsible."

Surat kept ducking outside to check on the "battle", then reporting excitedly on the state of play. "The Tiran's still up there, they can't get rid of it. I don't know why they haven't shot it down yet."

Because the Tirans were the ones pursuing Anne, and they didn't want her dead. But for how long would the Ghahari tolerate this violation?

Anne's efforts could not be allowed to come to nothing. Joan struggled to recall the constellations she'd last seen in the night sky. At the node they'd departed from, powerful telescopes were constantly trained on the Noudah's home world. Anne's ship was easily bright enough, its gestures wide enough, to be resolved from seven light years away—if the planet itself wasn't blocking the view, if the node was above the horizon.

The shelter was windowless, but Joan saw the ground outside the doorway brighten for an instant. The flash was silent; no missile had struck the valley, the explosion had taken place high above the atmosphere.

Surat went outside. When she returned she said quietly, "All clear. They got it."

Joan put all her effort into spitting out a handful of words. "I want to see what happened."

Sando hesitated, then motioned to the others to help him pick up the couch and carry it outside.

A shell of glowing plasma was still visible, drifting across the sky as it expanded, a ring of light growing steadily fainter until it vanished into the afternoon glare.

Anne was dead in this embodiment, but her backup would wake and go on to new adventures. Joan could at least tell her the story of her local death: of virtuoso flying and a spectacular end.

She'd recovered her bearings now, and she recalled the position of the stars. The node was still hours away from rising. The Amalgam was full of powerful telescopes, but no others would be aimed at this obscure planet, and no plea to redirect them could outrace the light they would need to capture in order to bring the Niah's final theorem back to life.

8

SANDO WANTED to send her away for medical supervision, but Joan insisted on remaining at the site.

"The fewer officials who get to know about this incident, the fewer problems it makes for you," she reasoned.

"As long as you don't get sick and die," he replied.

"I'm not going to die." Her wounds had not become infected, and her strength was returning rapidly.

They compromised. Sando hired someone to drive up from the nearest town to look after her while he was out at the excavation. Daya had basic medical training and didn't ask awkward questions; he seemed happy to tend to Joan's needs, and then lie outside daydreaming the rest of the time.

There was still a chance, Joan thought, that the Niah had carved the theorem on a multitude of tablets and scattered them all over the planet. There was also a chance that the Tirans had made copies of the tablet before letting Anne abscond with it. The question, though, was whether she had the slightest prospect of getting her hands on these duplicates.

Anne might have made some kind of copy herself, but she hadn't mentioned it in the prologue to her aerobatic rendition of the theorem. If she'd had any time to spare, she wouldn't have limited herself to an audience of one: she would have waited until the node had risen over Ghahar.

On her second night as an invalid, Joan dreamed that she saw Anne standing on the hill looking back into the fog-shrouded valley, her shadow haloed by the Niah light.

When she woke, she knew what she had to do.

When Sando left, she asked Daya to bring her the console that controlled the satellite dish. She had enough strength in her arms now to operate it, and Daya showed no interest in what she did. That was naive, of course: whether or not Daya was spying on her, Pirit would know exactly where the signal was sent. So be it. Seven light years was still far beyond the Noudah's reach; the whole node could be disassembled and erased long before they came close.

No message could outrace light directly, but there were more ways for light to reach the node than the direct path, the fastest one. Every black hole had its glory, twisting light around it in a tight, close orbit and flinging it back out again. Seventy-four hours after the original image was lost to them, the telescopes at the node could still turn to the Cataract and scour the distorted, compressed image of the sky at the rim of the hole's black disk to catch a replay of Anne's ballet.

Joan composed the message and entered the coordinates of the node. *You didn't die for nothing, my friend. When you wake and see this, you'll be proud of us both.*

She hesitated, her hand hovering above the send key. The Tirans had wanted Anne to flee, to show them the way to the stars, but had they really been indifferent to the loot they'd let her carry? The theorem had come at the end of the Niah's three-million-year reign. To witness this beautiful truth would not destroy the Amalgam, but might it not weaken it? If the Seekers' thirst for knowledge was slaked, their sense of purpose corroded, might not the most crucial strand of the culture fall into a twilight of its own? There was no shortcut to the stars, but the Noudah had been goaded by their alien visitors, and the technology would come to them soon enough.

The Amalgam had been goaded, too: the theorem she'd already transmitted would send a wave of excitement around the galaxy, strengthening the Seekers, encouraging them to complete the unification by their own efforts. The Big Crunch might be inevitable, but at least she could delay it, and hope that the robustness and diversity of the Amalgam would carry them through it, and beyond.

She erased the message and wrote a new one, addressed to her backup via the decoy node. It would have been nice to upload all her memories, but the Noudah were ruthless, and she wasn't prepared to stay any longer and risk being used by them. This sketch, this postcard, would have to be enough.

When the transmission was complete she left a note for Sando in the console's memory.

Daya called out to her, "Jown? Do you need anything?"

She said, "No. I'm going to sleep for a while."

OCEANIC

1

he swell was gently lifting and lowering the boat. My breathing grew slower, falling into step with the creaking of the hull, until I could no longer tell the difference between the faint rhythmic motion of the cabin and the sensation of filling and emptying my lungs. It was like floating in darkness: every inhalation buoyed me up, slightly; every exhalation made me sink back down again.

In the bunk above me, my brother Daniel said distinctly, "Do you believe in God?"

My head was cleared of sleep in an instant, but I didn't reply straight away. I'd never closed my eyes, but the darkness of the unlit cabin seemed to shift in front of me, grains of phantom light moving like a cloud of disturbed insects.

"Martin?"

"I'm awake."

"Do you believe in God?"

"Of course." Everyone I knew believed in God. Everyone talked about Her, everyone prayed to Her. Daniel most of all. Since he'd joined the Deep Church the previous summer, he prayed every morning for a

179

kilotau before dawn. I'd often wake to find myself aware of him kneeling by the far wall of the cabin, muttering and pounding his chest, before I drifted gratefully back to sleep.

Our family had always been Transitional, but Daniel was fifteen, old enough to choose for himself. My mother accepted this with diplomatic silence, but my father seemed positively proud of Daniel's independence and strength of conviction. My own feelings were mixed. I'd grown used to swimming in my older brother's wake, but I'd never resented it, because he'd always let me in on the view ahead: reading me passages from the books he read himself, teaching me words and phrases from the languages he studied, sketching some of the mathematics I was yet to encounter first-hand. We used to lie awake half the night, talking about the cores of stars or the hierarchy of transfinite numbers. But Daniel had told me nothing about the reasons for his conversion, and his ever-increasing piety. I didn't know whether to feel hurt by this exclusion, or simply grateful; I could see that being Transitional was like a pale imitation of being Deep Church, but I wasn't sure that this was such a bad thing if the wages of mediocrity included sleeping until sunrise.

Daniel said, "Why?"

I stared up at the underside of his bunk, unsure whether I was really seeing it or just imagining its solidity against the cabin's ordinary darkness. "Someone must have guided the Angels here from Earth. If Earth's too far away to see from Covenant…how could anyone find Covenant from Earth, without God's help?"

I heard Daniel shift slightly. "Maybe the Angels had better telescopes than us. Or maybe they spread out from Earth in all directions, launching thousands of expeditions without even knowing what they'd find."

I laughed. "But they had to come *here*, to be made flesh again!" Even a less-than-devout ten-year-old knew that much. God prepared Covenant as the place for the Angels to repent their theft of immortality. The Transitionals believed that in a million years we could earn the right to be Angels again; the Deep Church believed that we'd remain flesh until the stars fell from the sky.

Daniel said, "What makes you so sure that there were ever really Angels? Or that God really sent them Her daughter, Beatrice, to lead them back into the flesh?"

I pondered this for a while. The only answers I could think of came straight out of the Scriptures, and Daniel had taught me years ago that appeals to authority counted for nothing. Finally, I had to confess: "I don't know." I felt foolish, but I was grateful that he was willing to discuss these difficult questions with me. I wanted to believe in God for the right reasons, not just because everyone around me did.

He said, "Archaeologists have shown that we must have arrived about twenty thousand years ago. Before that, there's no evidence of humans, or any co-ecological plants and animals. That makes the Crossing older than the Scriptures say, but there are some dates that are open to interpretation, and with a bit of poetic license everything can be made to add up. And most biologists think the native microfauna could have formed by itself over millions of years, starting from simple chemicals, but that doesn't mean God didn't guide the whole process. Everything's compatible, really. Science and the Scriptures can both be true."

I thought I knew where he was headed, now. "So you've worked out a way to use science to prove that God exists?" I felt a surge of pride; my brother was a genius!

"No." Daniel was silent for a moment. "The thing is, it works both ways. Whatever's written in the Scriptures, people can always come up with different explanations for the facts. The ships might have left Earth for some other reason. The Angels might have made bodies for themselves for some other reason. There's no way to convince a non-believer that the Scriptures are the word of God. It's all a matter of faith."

"Oh."

"Faith's the most important thing," Daniel insisted. "If you don't have faith, you can be tempted into believing anything at all."

I made a noise of assent, trying not to sound too disappointed. I'd expected more from Daniel than the kind of bland assertions that sent me dozing off during sermons at the Transitional church.

"Do you know what you have to do to get faith?"

"No."

"Ask for it. That's all. Ask Beatrice to come into your heart and grant you the gift of faith."

I protested, "We do that every time we go to church!" I couldn't believe he'd forgotten the Transitional service already. After the priest placed a drop of seawater on our tongues, to symbolize the blood of Beatrice, we asked for the gifts of faith, hope and love.

"But have you received it?"

I'd never thought about that. "I'm not sure." I believed in God, didn't I? "I might have."

Daniel was amused. "If you had the gift of faith, you'd *know*."

I gazed up into the darkness, troubled. "Do you have to go to the Deep Church, to ask for it properly?"

"No. Even in the Deep Church, not everyone has invited Beatrice into their hearts. You have to do it the way it says in the Scriptures: 'like an unborn child again, naked and helpless.'"

"I was Immersed, wasn't I?"

"In a metal bowl, when you were thirty days old. Infant Immersion is a gesture by the parents, an affirmation of their own good intentions. But it's not enough to save the child."

I was feeling very disoriented now. My father, at least, approved of Daniel's conversion…but now Daniel was trying to tell me that our family's transactions with God had all been grossly deficient, if not actually counterfeit.

Daniel said, "Remember what Beatrice told Her followers, the last time She appeared? 'Unless you are willing to drown in My blood, you will never look upon the face of My Mother.' So they bound each other hand and foot, and weighted themselves down with rocks."

My chest tightened. "And you've done that?"

"Yes."

"*When?*"

"Almost a year ago."

I was more confused than ever. "Did Ma and Fa go?"

Daniel laughed. "No! It's not a public ceremony. Some friends of mine from the Prayer Group helped; someone has to be on deck to haul you up, because it would be arrogant to expect Beatrice to break your bonds and raise you to the surface, like She did with Her followers. But in the water, you're alone with God."

He climbed down from his bunk and crouched by the side of my bed. "Are you ready to give your life to Beatrice, Martin?" His voice sent gray sparks flowing through the darkness.

I hesitated. "What if I just dive in? And stay under for a while?" I'd been swimming off the boat at night plenty of times, there was nothing to fear from that.

"No. You have to be weighted down." His tone made it clear that there could be no compromise on this. "How long can you hold your breath?"

"Two hundred tau." That was an exaggeration; two hundred was what I was aiming for.

"That's long enough."

I didn't reply. Daniel said, "I'll pray with you."

I climbed out of bed, and we knelt together. Daniel murmured, "Please, Holy Beatrice, grant my brother Martin the courage to accept the precious gift of Your blood." Then he started praying in what I took to be a foreign language, uttering a rapid stream of harsh syllables unlike anything I'd heard before. I listened apprehensively; I wasn't sure that I wanted Beatrice to change my mind, and I was afraid that this display of fervor might actually persuade Her.

I said, "What if I don't do it?"

"Then you'll never see the face of God."

I knew what that meant: I'd wander alone in the belly of Death, in darkness, for eternity. And even if the Scriptures weren't meant to be taken literally on this, the reality behind the metaphor could only be worse. Indescribably worse.

"But…what about Ma and Fa?" I was more worried about them, because I knew they'd never climb weighted off the side of the boat at Daniel's behest.

"That will take time," he said softly.

My mind reeled. He was absolutely serious.

I heard him stand and walk over to the ladder. He climbed a few rungs and opened the hatch. Enough starlight came in to give shape to his arms and shoulders, but as he turned to me I still couldn't make out his face. "Come on, Martin!" he whispered. "The longer you put it off, the harder it gets." The hushed urgency of his voice was familiar: generous and conspiratorial, nothing like an adult's impatience. He might almost have been daring me to join him in a midnight raid on the pantry—not because he really needed a collaborator, but because he honestly didn't want me to miss out on the excitement, or the spoils.

I suppose I was more afraid of damnation than drowning, and I'd always trusted Daniel to warn me of the dangers ahead. But this time I wasn't entirely convinced that he was right, so I must have been driven by something more than fear, and blind trust.

Maybe it came down to the fact that he was offering to make me his equal in this. I was ten years old, and I ached to become something more than I was; to reach, not my parents' burdensome adulthood, but the halfway point, full of freedom and secrets, that Daniel had reached. I wanted to be as strong, as fast, as quick-witted and widely-read as he was. Becoming as certain of God would not have been my first choice, but there wasn't much point hoping for divine intervention to grant me anything else.

I followed him up onto the deck.

He took cord, and a knife, and four spare weights of the kind we used on our nets from the toolbox. He threaded the weights onto the cord, then I took off my shorts and sat naked on the deck while he knotted a figure-eight around my ankles. I raised my feet experimentally; the weights didn't seem all that heavy. But in the water, I knew, they'd be more than enough to counteract my body's slight buoyancy.

"Martin? Hold out your hands."

Suddenly I was crying. With my arms free, at least I could swim against the tug of the weights. But if my hands were tied, I'd be helpless.

Daniel crouched down and met my eyes. "Ssh. It's all right."

I hated myself. I could feel my face contorted into the mask of a blubbering infant.

"Are you afraid?"

I nodded.

Daniel smiled reassuringly. "You know why? You know who's doing that? Death doesn't want Beatrice to have you. He wants you for himself. So he's here on this boat, putting fear into your heart, because he *knows* he's almost lost you."

I saw something move in the shadows behind the toolbox, something slithering into the darkness. If we went back down to the cabin now, would Death follow us? To wait for Daniel to fall asleep? If I'd turned my back on Beatrice, who could I ask to send Death away?

I stared at the deck, tears of shame dripping from my cheeks. I held out my arms, wrists together.

When my hands were tied—not palm-to-palm as I'd expected, but in separate loops joined by a short bridge—Daniel unwound a long stretch of rope from the winch at the rear of the boat, and coiled it on the deck. I didn't want to think about how long it was, but I knew I'd never dived to that depth. He took the blunt hook at the end of the rope, slipped it over my arms, then screwed it closed to form an unbroken ring. Then he checked again that the cord around my wrists was neither so tight as to burn me, nor so loose as to let me slip. As he did this, I saw something creep over his face: some kind of doubt or fear of his own. He said, "Hang onto the hook. Just in case. Don't let go, no matter what. Okay?" He whispered something to Beatrice, then looked up at me, confident again.

He helped me to stand and shuffle over to the guard rail, just to one side of the winch. Then he picked me up under the arms and lifted me over, resting my feet on the outer hull. The deck was inert, a mineralized endoshell, but behind the guard rails the hull was palpably alive: slick with protective secretions, glowing softly. My toes curled uselessly against the lubricated skin; I had no purchase at all. The hull was supporting some of my weight, but Daniel's arms would tire eventually. If I wanted to back out, I'd have to do it quickly.

A warm breeze was blowing. I looked around, at the flat horizon, at the blaze of stars, at the faint silver light off the water. Daniel recited: "Holy Beatrice, I am ready to die to this world. Let me drown in Your blood, that I might be redeemed, and look upon the face of Your Mother."

I repeated the words, trying hard to mean them.

"Holy Beatrice, I offer You my life. All I do now, I do for You. Come into my heart, and grant me the gift of faith. Come into my heart, and grant me the gift of hope. Come into my heart, and grant me the gift of love."

"And grant me the gift of love."

Daniel released me. At first, my feet seemed to adhere magically to the hull, and I pivoted backward without actually falling. I clung tightly to the hook, pressing the cold metal against my belly, and willed the rope of the winch to snap taut, leaving me dangling in midair. I even braced myself for the shock. Some part of me really did believe that I could change my mind, even now.

Then my feet slipped and I plunged into the ocean and sank straight down.

It was not like a dive—not even a dive from an untried height, when it took so long for the water to bring you to a halt that it began to grow frightening. I was falling through the water ever faster, as if it was air. The vision I'd had of the rope keeping me above the water now swung to the opposite extreme: my acceleration seemed to prove that the coil on the deck was attached to nothing, that its frayed end was already beneath the surface. *That's what the followers had done, wasn't it? They'd let themselves be thrown in without a lifeline.* So Daniel had cut the rope, and I was on my way to the bottom of the ocean.

Then the hook jerked my hands up over my head, jarring my wrists and shoulders, and I was motionless.

I turned my face toward the surface, but neither starlight nor the hull's faint phosphorescence reached this deep. I let a stream of bubbles escape from my mouth; I felt them slide over my upper lip, but no trace of them registered in the darkness.

I shifted my hands warily over the hook. I could still feel the cord fast around my wrists, but Daniel had warned me not to trust it. I brought my knees up to my chest, gauging the effect of the weights. If the cord broke, at least my hands would be free, but even so I wasn't sure I'd be able to ascend. The thought of trying to unpick the knots around my ankles as I tumbled deeper filled me with horror.

My shoulders ached, but I wasn't injured. It didn't take much effort to pull myself up until my chin was level with the bottom of the hook. Going further was awkward—with my hands so close together I couldn't brace myself properly—but on the third attempt I managed to get my arms locked, pointing straight down.

I'd done this without any real plan, but then it struck me that even with my hands and feet tied, I could try shinning up the rope. It was just a matter of getting started. I'd have to turn upside-down, grab the rope between my knees, then curl up—dragging the hook—and get a grip with my hands at a higher point.

And if I couldn't reach up far enough to right myself?

I'd ascend feet-first.

I couldn't even manage the first step. I thought it would be as simple as keeping my arms rigid and letting myself topple backward, but in the water even two-thirds of my body wasn't sufficient to counterbalance the weights.

I tried a different approach: I dropped down to hang at arm's length, raised my legs as high as I could, then proceeded to pull myself up again. But my grip wasn't tight enough to resist the turning force of the weights; I just pivoted around my center of gravity—which was somewhere near my knees—and ended up, still bent double, but almost horizontal.

I eased myself down again, and tried threading my feet through the circle of my arms. I didn't succeed on the first attempt, and then on reflection it seemed like a bad move anyway. Even if I managed to grip the rope between my bound feet—rather than just tumbling over backward, out of control, and dislocating my shoulders—climbing the rope *upside-down with my hands behind my back* would either be impossible, or so awkward and strenuous that I'd run out of oxygen before I got a tenth of the way.

I let some more air escape from my lungs. I could feel the muscles in my diaphragm reproaching me for keeping them from doing what they wanted to do; not urgently yet, but the knowledge that I had no control over when I'd be able to draw breath again made it harder to stay calm. I knew I could rely on Daniel to bring me to the surface on the count of two hundred. But I'd only ever stayed down for a hundred and sixty. Forty more tau would be an eternity.

I'd almost forgotten what the whole ordeal was meant to be about, but now I started praying. *Please Holy Beatrice, don't let me die. I know You drowned like this to save me, but if I die it won't help anyone. Daniel would end up in the deepest shit…but that's not a threat, it's just an observation.* I felt a stab of anxiety; on top of everything else, had I just offended the Daughter of God? I struggled on, my confidence waning. *I don't want to die. But You already know that. So I don't know what You want me to say.*

I released some more stale air, wishing I'd counted the time I'd been under; you weren't supposed to empty your lungs too quickly—when they were deflated it was even harder not to take a breath—but holding all the carbon dioxide in too long wasn't good either.

Praying only seemed to make me more desperate, so I tried to think other kinds of holy thoughts. I couldn't remember anything from the Scriptures word for word, but the gist of the most important part started running through my mind.

After living in Her body for thirty years, and persuading all the Angels to become mortal again, Beatrice had gone back up to their deserted spaceship and flown it straight into the ocean. When Death saw Her coming, he took the form of a giant serpent, coiled in the water, waiting. And even though She was the Daughter of God, with the power to do anything, She let Death swallow Her.

That's how much She loved us.

Death thought he'd won everything. Beatrice was trapped inside him, in the darkness, alone. The Angels were flesh again, so he wouldn't even have to wait for the stars to fall before he claimed them.

But Beatrice was part of God. Death had swallowed part of God. This was a mistake. After three days, his jaws burst open and Beatrice came flying out, wreathed in fire. Death was broken, shriveled, diminished.

My limbs were numb but my chest was burning. Death was still strong enough to hold down the damned. I started thrashing about blindly, wasting whatever oxygen was left in my blood, but desperate to distract myself from the urge to inhale.

Please Holy Beatrice—

Please Daniel—

Luminous bruises blossomed behind my eyes and drifted out into the water. I watched them curling into a kind of vortex, as if something was drawing them in.

It was the mouth of the serpent, swallowing my soul. I opened my own mouth and made a wretched noise, and Death swam forward to kiss me, to breathe cold water into my lungs.

Suddenly, everything was seared with light. The serpent turned and fled, like a pale timid worm. A wave of contentment washed over me, as if I was an infant again and my mother had wrapped her arms around me tightly. It was like basking in sunlight, listening to laughter, dreaming of music too beautiful to be real. Every muscle in my body was still trying to prise my lungs open to the water, but now I found myself fighting this almost absentmindedly while I marveled at my strange euphoria.

Cold air swept over my hands and down my arms. I raised myself up to take a mouthful, then slumped down again, giddy and spluttering, grateful for every breath but still elated by something else entirely. The light that had filled my eyes was gone, but it left a violet afterimage everywhere I looked. Daniel kept winding until my head was level with the guard rail, then he clamped the winch, bent down, and threw me over his shoulder.

I'd been warm enough in the water, but now my teeth were chattering. Daniel wrapped a towel around me, then set to work cutting the cord. I beamed at him. "I'm so happy!" He gestured to me to be quieter, but then he whispered joyfully, "That's the love of Beatrice. She'll always be with you now, Martin."

I blinked with surprise, then laughed softly at my own stupidity. Until that moment, I hadn't connected what had happened with Beatrice at all. But of course it was Her. I'd asked Her to come into my heart, and She had.

And I could see it in Daniel's face: a year after his own Drowning, he still felt Her presence.

He said, "Everything you do now is for Beatrice. When you look through your telescope, you'll do it to honor Her creation. When you eat, or drink, or swim, you'll do it to give thanks for Her gifts." I nodded enthusiastically.

Daniel tidied everything away, even soaking up the puddles of water I'd left on the deck. Back in the cabin, he recited from the Scriptures, passages that I'd never really understood before, but which now all seemed to be about the Drowning, and the way I was feeling. It was as if I'd opened the book and found myself mentioned by name on every page.

When Daniel fell asleep before me, for the first time in my life I didn't feel the slightest pang of loneliness. The Daughter of God was with me: I could feel Her presence, like a flame inside my skull, radiating warmth through the darkness behind my eyes.

Giving me comfort, giving me strength.

Giving me faith.

2

THE MONASTERY was almost four milliradians northeast of our home grounds. Daniel and I took the launch to a rendezvous point, and met up with three other small vessels before continuing. It had been the same routine every tenth night for almost a year—and Daniel had been going to the Prayer Group himself for a year before that—so the launch didn't need much supervision. Feeding on nutrients in the ocean, propelling itself by pumping water through fine channels in its skin, guided by both sunlight and Covenant's magnetic field, it was a perfect example of the kind of legacy of the Angels that technology would never be able to match.

Bartholomew, Rachel and Agnes were in one launch, and they traveled beside us while the others skimmed ahead. Bartholomew and Rachel were married, though they were only seventeen, scarcely older than Daniel. Agnes, Rachel's sister, was sixteen. Because I was the youngest member of the Prayer Group, Agnes had fussed over me from the day I'd joined. She said, "It's your big night tonight, Martin, isn't it?" I nodded, but declined to pursue the conversation, leaving her free to talk to Daniel.

It was dusk by the time the monastery came into sight, a conical tower built from at least ten thousand hulls, rising up from the water in the stylized form of Beatrice's spaceship. Aimed at the sky, not down into the depths. Though some commentators on the Scriptures insisted that the spaceship itself had sunk forever, and Beatrice had risen from the water unaided, it was still the definitive symbol of Her victory over Death. For the three days of Her separation from God, all such buildings stood in darkness, but that was half a year away, and now the monastery shone from every porthole.

There was a narrow tunnel leading into the base of the tower; the launches detected its scent in the water and filed in one by one. I knew they didn't have souls, but I wondered what it would have been like for them if they'd been aware of their actions. Normally they rested in the dock of a single hull, a pouch of boatskin that secured them but still left them largely exposed. Maybe being drawn instinctively into this vast structure would have felt even safer, even more comforting, than docking with their home boat. When I said something to this effect, Rachel, in the launch behind me, sniggered. Agnes said, "Don't be horrible."

The walls of the tunnel phosphoresced pale green, but the opening ahead was filled with white lamplight, dazzlingly richer and brighter. We emerged into a canal circling a vast atrium, and continued around it until the launches found empty docks.

As we disembarked, every footstep, every splash echoed back at us. I looked up at the ceiling, a dome spliced together from hundreds of curved triangular hull sections, tattooed with scenes from the Scriptures. The original illustrations were more than a thousand years old, but the living boatskin degraded the pigments on a time scale of decades, so the monks had to constantly renew them.

"Beatrice Joining the Angels" was my favorite. Because the Angels weren't flesh, they didn't grow inside their mothers; they just appeared from nowhere in the streets of the Immaterial Cities. In the picture on the ceiling, Beatrice's immaterial body was half-formed, with cherubs still working to clothe the immaterial bones of Her legs and arms in immaterial muscles, veins and skin. A few Angels in luminous robes were glancing sideways at Her, but you could tell they weren't particularly impressed. They'd had no way of knowing, then, who She was.

A corridor with its own smaller illustrations led from the atrium to the meeting room. There were about fifty people in the Prayer Group— including several priests and monks, though they acted just like everyone else. In church you followed the liturgy; the priest slotted-in his or her sermon, but there was no room for the worshippers to do much more than pray or sing in unison and offer rote responses. Here it was much less formal. There were two or three different speakers every night— sometimes guests who were visiting the monastery, sometimes members of the group—and after that anyone could ask the group to pray with them, about whatever they liked.

I'd fallen behind the others, but they'd saved me an aisle seat. Agnes was to my left, then Daniel, Bartholomew and Rachel. Agnes said, "Are you nervous?"

"No."

Daniel laughed, as if this claim was ridiculous.

I said, "I'm not." I'd meant to sound loftily unperturbed, but the words came out sullen and childish.

The first two speakers were both lay theologians, Firmlanders who were visiting the monastery. One gave a talk about people who belonged to false religions, and how they were all—in effect—worshipping Beatrice, but just didn't know it. He said they wouldn't be damned, because they'd had no choice about the cultures they were born into. Beatrice would know they'd meant well, and forgive them.

I wanted this to be true, but it made no sense to me. Either Beatrice *was* the Daughter of God, and everyone who thought otherwise had turned away from Her into the darkness, or...there was no "or." I only had to close my eyes and feel Her presence to know that. Still, everyone applauded when the man finished, and all the questions people asked seemed sympathetic to his views, so perhaps his arguments had simply been too subtle for me to follow.

The second speaker referred to Beatrice as "the Holy Jester", and rebuked us severely for not paying enough attention to Her sense of humor. She cited events in the Scriptures which she said were practical jokes, and then went on at some length about "the healing power of laughter." It was all about as gripping as a lecture on nutrition and hygiene; I struggled to keep my eyes open. At the end, no one could think of any questions.

Then Carol, who was running the meeting, said, "Now Martin is going to give witness to the power of Beatrice in his life."

Everyone applauded encouragingly. As I rose to my feet and stepped into the aisle, Daniel leaned toward Agnes and whispered sarcastically, "This should be good."

I stood at the lectern and gave the talk I'd been rehearsing for days. Beatrice, I said, was beside me now whatever I did: whether I studied or worked, ate or swam, or just sat and watched the stars. When I woke in the morning and looked into my heart, She was there without fail, offering me strength and guidance. When I lay in bed at night, I feared nothing, because I knew She was watching over me. Before my Drowning, I'd been unsure of my faith, but now I'd never again be able to doubt that the Daughter of God had become flesh, and died, and conquered Death, because of Her great love for us.

It was all true, but even as I said these things I couldn't get Daniel's sarcastic words out of my mind. I glanced over at the row where I'd been sitting, at the people I'd traveled with. What did I have in common with them, really? Rachel and Bartholomew were married. Bartholomew and Daniel had studied together, and still played in the same dive-ball team. Daniel and Agnes were probably in love. And Daniel was my brother...

but the only difference that seemed to make was the fact that he could belittle me far more efficiently than any stranger.

In the open prayer that followed, I paid no attention to the problems and blessings people were sharing with the group. I tried silently calling on Beatrice to dissolve the knot of anger in my heart. But I couldn't do it; I'd turned too far away from Her.

When the meeting was over, and people started moving into the adjoining room to talk for a while, I hung back. When the others were out of sight I ducked into the corridor, and headed straight for the launch.

Daniel could get a ride home with his friends; it wasn't far out of their way. I'd wait a short distance from the boat until he caught up; if my parents saw me arrive on my own I'd be in trouble. Daniel would be angry, of course, but he wouldn't betray me.

Once I'd freed the launch from its dock, it knew exactly where to go: around the canal, back to the tunnel, out into the open sea. As I sped across the calm, dark water, I felt the presence of Beatrice returning, which seemed like a sign that She understood that I'd had to get away.

I leaned over and dipped my hand in the water, feeling the current the launch was generating by shuffling ions in and out of the cells of its skin. The outer hull glowed a phosphorescent blue, more to warn other vessels than to light the way. In the time of Beatrice, one of her followers had sat in the Immaterial City and designed this creature from scratch. It gave me a kind of vertigo, just imagining the things the Angels had known. I wasn't sure why so much of it had been lost, but I wanted to rediscover it all. Even the Deep Church taught that there was nothing wrong with that, so long as we didn't use it to try to become immortal again.

The monastery shrank to a blur of light on the horizon, and there was no other beacon visible on the water, but I could read the stars, and sense the field lines, so I knew the launch was heading in the right direction.

When I noticed a blue speck in the distance, it was clear that it wasn't Daniel and the others chasing after me; it was coming from the wrong direction. As I watched the launch drawing nearer I grew anxious; if this was someone I knew, and I couldn't come up with a good reason to be traveling alone, word would get back to my parents.

Before I could make out anyone on board, a voice shouted, "Can you help me? I'm lost!"

I thought for a while before replying. The voice sounded almost matter-of-fact, making light of this blunt admission of helplessness, but it was no joke. If you were sick, your diurnal sense and your field sense could both become scrambled, making the stars much harder to read. It had happened to me a couple of times, and it had been a horrible experience—even standing safely on the deck of our boat. This late at night, a launch with only its field sense to guide it could lose track of its position, especially if you were trying to take it somewhere it hadn't been before.

I shouted back our coordinates, and the time. I was fairly confident that I had them down to the nearest hundred microradians, and few hundred tau.

"That can't be right! Can I approach? Let our launches talk?"

I hesitated. It had been drummed into me for as long as I could remember that if I ever found myself alone on the water, I should give other vessels a wide berth unless I knew the people on board. But Beatrice was with me, and if someone needed help it was wrong to refuse them.

"All right!" I stopped dead, and waited for the stranger to close the gap. As the launch drew up beside me, I was surprised to see that the passenger was a young man. He looked about Bartholomew's age, but he'd sounded much older.

We didn't need to tell the launches what to do; proximity was enough to trigger a chemical exchange of information. The man said, "Out on your own?"

"I'm traveling with my brother and his friends. I just went ahead a bit."

That made him smile. "Sent you on your way, did they? What do you think they're getting up to, back there?" I didn't reply; that was no way to talk about people you didn't even know. The man scanned the horizon, then spread his arms in a gesture of sympathy. "You must be feeling left out."

I shook my head. There was a pair of binoculars on the floor behind him; even before he'd called out for help, he could have seen that I was alone.

He jumped deftly between the launches, landing on the stern bench. I said, "There's nothing to steal." My skin was crawling, more with disbelief than fear. He was standing on the bench in the starlight, pulling a knife from his belt. The details—the pattern carved into the handle, the serrated edge of the blade—only made it seem more like a dream.

He coughed, suddenly nervous. "Just do what I tell you, and you won't get hurt."

I filled my lungs and shouted for help with all the strength I had; I knew there was no one in earshot, but I thought it might still frighten him off. He looked around, more startled than angry, as if he couldn't quite believe I'd waste so much effort. I jumped backward, into the water. A moment later I heard him follow me.

I found the blue glow of the launches above me, then swam hard, down and away from them, without wasting time searching for his shadow. Blood was pounding in my ears, but I knew I was moving almost silently; however fast he was, in the darkness he could swim right past me without knowing it. If he didn't catch me soon he'd probably return to the launch and wait to spot me when I came up for air. I had to surface far enough away to be invisible—even with the binoculars.

I was terrified that I'd feel a hand close around my ankle at any moment, but Beatrice was with me. As I swam, I thought back to my Drowning, and Her presence grew stronger than ever. When my lungs were almost bursting, She helped me to keep going, my limbs moving mechanically, blotches of light floating in front of my eyes. When I finally knew I had to surface, I turned face-up and ascended slowly, then lay on my back with only my mouth and nose above the water, refusing the temptation to stick my head up and look around.

I filled and emptied my lungs a few times, then dived again.

The fifth time I surfaced, I dared to look back. I couldn't see either launch. I raised myself higher, then turned a full circle in case I'd grown disoriented, but nothing came into sight.

I checked the stars, and my field sense. The launches should *not* have been over the horizon. I trod water, riding the swell, and tried not to think about how tired I was. It was at least two milliradians to the nearest boat. Good swimmers—some younger than I was—competed in marathons over distances like that, but I'd never even aspired to such feats of endurance. Unprepared, in the middle of the night, I knew I wouldn't make it.

If the man had given up on me, would he have taken our launch? When they cost so little, and the markings were so hard to change? That would be nothing but an admission of guilt. *So why couldn't I see it?* Either he'd sent it on its way, or it had decided to return home itself.

I knew the path it would have taken; I would have seen it go by, if I'd been looking for it when I'd surfaced before. But I had no hope of catching it now.

I began to pray. I knew I'd been wrong to leave the others, but I asked for forgiveness, and felt it being granted. I watched the horizon almost calmly—smiling at the blue flashes of meteors burning up high above the ocean—certain that Beatrice would not abandon me.

I was still praying—treading water, shivering from the cool of the air—when a blue light appeared in the distance. It disappeared as the swell took me down again, but there was no mistaking it for a shooting star. *Was this Daniel and the others—or the stranger?* I didn't have long to decide; if I wanted to get within earshot as they passed, I'd have to swim hard.

I closed my eyes and prayed for guidance. *Please Holy Beatrice, let me know.* Joy flooded through my mind, instantly: it was them, I was certain of it. I set off as fast as I could.

I started yelling before I could see how many passengers there were, but I knew Beatrice would never allow me to be mistaken. A flare shot up from the launch, revealing four figures standing side by side, scanning the water. I shouted with jubilation, and waved my arms. Someone finally spotted me, and they brought the launch around toward me. By the time I was on board I was so charged up on adrenaline and relief that I almost believed I could have dived back into the water and raced them home.

I thought Daniel would be angry, but when I described what had happened all he said was, "We'd better get moving."

Agnes embraced me. Bartholomew gave me an almost respectful look, but Rachel muttered sourly, "You're an idiot, Martin. You don't know how lucky you are."

I said, "I know."

Our parents were standing on deck. The empty launch had arrived some time ago; they'd been about to set out to look for us. When the others had departed I began recounting everything again, this time trying to play down any element of danger.

Before I'd finished, my mother grabbed Daniel by the front of his shirt and started slapping him. "I trusted you with him! *You maniac!* I trusted you!" Daniel half raised his arm to block her, but then let it drop and just turned his face to the deck.

I burst into tears. "It was my fault!" Our parents never struck us; I couldn't believe what I was seeing.

My father said soothingly, "Look...he's home now. He's safe. No one touched him." He put an arm around my shoulders and asked warily, "That's right, Martin, isn't it?"

I nodded tearfully. This was worse than anything that had happened on the launch, or in the water; I felt a thousand times more helpless, a thousand times more like a child.

I said, "Beatrice was watching over me."

My mother rolled her eyes and laughed wildly, letting go of Daniel's shirt. "Beatrice? *Beatrice?* Don't you know what could have happened to you? You're too young to have given him what he wanted. He would have had to use the knife."

The chill of my wet clothes seemed to penetrate deeper. I swayed unsteadily, but fought to stay upright. Then I whispered stubbornly, "Beatrice was there."

My father said, "Go and get changed, or you're going to freeze to death."

I lay in bed listening to them shout at Daniel. When he finally came down the ladder I was so sick with shame that I wished I'd drowned.

He said, "Are you all right?"

There was nothing I could say. I couldn't ask him to forgive me.

"Martin?" Daniel turned on the lamp. His face was streaked with tears; he laughed softly, wiping them away. "Fuck, you had me worried. Don't ever do anything like that again."

"I won't."

"Okay." That was it; no shouting, no recriminations. "Do you want to pray with me?"

We knelt side by side, praying for our parents to be at peace, praying for the man who'd tried to hurt me. I started trembling; everything was catching up with me. Suddenly, words began gushing from my mouth— words I neither recognized nor understood, though I knew I was praying for everything to be all right with Daniel, praying that our parents would stop blaming him for my stupidity.

The strange words kept flowing out of me, an incomprehensible torrent somehow imbued with everything I was feeling. I knew what was happening: *Beatrice had given me the Angels' tongue.* We'd had to surrender all knowledge of it when we became flesh, but sometimes She granted people the ability to pray this way, because the language of the Angels could express things we could no longer put into words. Daniel had been able to do it ever since his Drowning, but it wasn't something you could teach, or even something you could ask for.

When I finally stopped, my mind was racing. "Maybe Beatrice planned everything that happened tonight? Maybe She arranged it all, to lead up to this moment!"

Daniel shook his head, wincing slightly. "Don't get carried away. You have the gift; just accept it." He nudged me with his shoulder. "Now get into bed, before we're both in more trouble."

I lay awake almost until dawn, overwhelmed with happiness. Daniel had forgiven me. Beatrice had protected and blessed me. I felt no more shame, just humility and amazement. I knew I'd done nothing to deserve it, but my life was wrapped in the love of God.

ACCORDING TO the Scriptures, the oceans of Earth were storm-tossed, and filled with dangerous creatures. But on Covenant, the oceans were calm, and the Angels created nothing in the ecopoiesis that would harm their own mortal incarnations. The four continents and the four oceans were rendered equally hospitable, and just as women and men were made indistinguishable in the sight of God, so were Freelanders and Firmlanders. (Some commentators insisted that this was literally true: God chose to blind Herself to where we lived, and whether or not we'd been born with a penis. I thought that was a beautiful idea, even if I couldn't quite grasp the logistics of it.)

I'd heard that certain obscure sects taught that half the Angels had actually become embodied as a separate people who could live in the water and breathe beneath the surface, but then God destroyed them because they were a mockery of Beatrice's death. No legitimate church took this notion seriously, though, and archaeologists had found no trace of these mythical doomed cousins. Humans were humans, there was only one kind. Freelanders and Firmlanders could even intermarry—if they could agree where to live.

When I was fifteen, Daniel became engaged to Agnes from the Prayer Group. That made sense: they'd be spared the explanations and arguments about the Drowning that they might have faced with partners who weren't so blessed. Agnes was a Freelander, of course, but a large branch of her family, and a smaller branch of ours, were Firmlanders, so after long negotiations it was decided that the wedding would be held in Ferez, a coastal town.

I went with my father to pick a hull to be fitted out as Daniel and Agnes's boat. The breeder, Diana, had a string of six mature hulls in tow, and my father insisted on walking out onto their backs and personally examining each one for imperfections.

By the time we reached the fourth I was losing patience. I muttered, "It's the skin underneath that matters." In fact, you could tell a lot about a hull's general condition from up here, but there wasn't much point worrying about a few tiny flaws high above the waterline.

My father nodded thoughtfully. "That's true. You'd better get in the water and check their undersides."

"I'm not doing that." We couldn't simply trust this woman to sell us a healthy hull for a decent price; that wouldn't have been sufficiently embarrassing.

"Martin! This is for the safety of your brother and sister-in-law."

I glanced at Diana to show her where my sympathies lay, then slipped off my shirt and dived in. I swam down to the last hull in the row, then ducked beneath it. I began the job with perverse thoroughness, running my fingers over every square nanoradian of skin. I was determined to annoy my father by taking even longer than he wanted—and determined to impress Diana by examining all six hulls without coming up for air.

An unfitted hull rode higher in the water than a boat full of furniture and junk, but I was surprised to discover that even in the creature's shadow there was enough light for me to see the skin clearly. After a while I realized that, paradoxically, this was because the water was slightly cloudier than usual, and whatever the fine particles were, they were scattering sunlight into the shadows.

Moving through the warm, bright water, feeling the love of Beatrice more strongly than I had for a long time, it was impossible to remain angry with my father. He wanted the best hull for Daniel and Agnes, and so did I. As for impressing Diana...who was I kidding? She was a grown woman, at least as old as Agnes, and highly unlikely to view me as anything more than a child. By the time I'd finished with the third hull I was feeling short of breath, so I surfaced and reported cheerfully, "No blemishes so far!"

Diana smiled down at me. "You've got strong lungs."

All six hulls were in perfect condition. We ended up taking the one at the end of the row, because it was easiest to detach.

～w

FEREZ WAS built on the mouth of a river, but the docks were some distance upstream. That helped to prepare us; the gradual deadening of the waves was less of a shock than an instant transition from sea to land would have been. When I jumped from the deck to the pier, though, it was like colliding with something massive and unyielding, the rock of the planet itself. I'd been on land twice before, for less than a day on both occasions. The wedding celebrations would last ten days, but at least we'd still be able to sleep on the boat.

As the four of us walked along the crowded streets, heading for the ceremonial hall where everything but the wedding sacrament itself would take place, I stared uncouthly at everyone in sight. Almost no one was barefoot like us, and after a few hundred tau on the paving stones—much rougher than any deck—I could understand why. Our clothes were different, our skin was darker, our accent was unmistakably foreign…but no one stared back. Freelanders were hardly a novelty here. That made me even more selfconscious; the curiosity I felt wasn't mutual.

In the hall, I joined in with the preparations, mainly just lugging furniture around under the directions of one of Agnes's tyrannical uncles. It was a new kind of shock to see so many Freelanders together in this alien environment, and stranger still when I realized that I couldn't necessarily spot the Firmlanders among us; there was no sharp dividing line in physical appearance, or even clothing. I began to feel slightly guilty; if God couldn't tell the difference, what was I doing hunting for the signs?

At noon we all ate outside, in a garden behind the hall. The grass was soft, but it made my feet itch. Daniel had gone off to be fitted for wedding clothes, and my parents were performing some vital task of their own; I only recognized a handful of the people around me. I sat in the shade of a tree, pretending to be oblivious to the plant's enormous size and bizarre anatomy. I wondered if we'd take a siesta; I couldn't imagine falling asleep on the grass.

Someone sat down beside me, and I turned.

"I'm Lena. Agnes's second cousin."

"I'm Daniel's brother, Martin." I hesitated, then offered her my hand; she took it, smiling slightly. I'd awkwardly kissed a dozen strangers that morning, all distant prospective relatives, but this time I didn't dare.

"Brother of the groom, doing grunt work with the rest of us." She shook her head in mocking admiration.

I desperately wanted to say something witty in reply, but an attempt that failed would be even worse than merely being dull. "Do you live in Ferez?"

"No, Mitar. Inland from here. We're staying with my uncle." She pulled a face. "Along with ten other people. No privacy. It's awful."

I said, "It was easy for us. We just brought our home with us." *You idiot. As if she didn't know that.*

Lena smiled. "I haven't been on a boat in years. You'll have to give me a tour sometime."

"Of course. I'd be happy to." I knew she was only making small talk; she'd never take me up on the offer.

She said, "Is it just you and Daniel?"

"Yes."

"You must be close."

I shrugged. "What about you?"

"Two brothers. Both younger. Eight and nine. They're all right, I suppose." She rested her chin on one hand and gazed at me coolly.

I looked away, disconcerted by more than my wishful thinking about what lay behind that gaze. Unless her parents had been awfully young when she was born, it didn't seem likely that more children were planned. So did an odd number in the family mean that one had died, or that the custom of equal numbers carried by each parent wasn't followed where she lived? I'd studied the region less than a year ago, but I had a terrible memory for things like that.

Lena said, "You looked so lonely, off here on your own."

I turned back to her, surprised. "I'm never lonely."

"No?"

She seemed genuinely curious. I opened my mouth to tell her about Beatrice, but then changed my mind. The few times I'd said anything to friends—ordinary friends, not Drowned ones—I'd regretted it. Not everyone had laughed, but they'd all been acutely embarrassed by the revelation.

I said, "Mitar has a million people, doesn't it?"

"Yes."

"An area of ocean the same size would have a population of ten."

Lena frowned. "That's a bit too deep for me, I'm afraid." She rose to her feet. "But maybe you'll think of a way of putting it that even a Firmlander can understand." She raised a hand goodbye and started walking away.

I said, "Maybe I will."

⁓

THE WEDDING took place in Ferez's Deep Church, a spaceship built of stone, glass, and wood. It looked almost like a parody of the churches I was used to, though it probably bore a closer resemblance to the Angels' real ship than anything made of living hulls.

Daniel and Agnes stood before the priest, beneath the apex of the building. Their closest relatives stood behind them in two angled lines on either side. My father—Daniel's mother—was first in our line, followed by my own mother, then me. That put me level with Rachel, who kept shooting disdainful glances my way. After my misadventure, Daniel and I had eventually been allowed to travel to the Prayer Group meetings again, but less than a year later I'd lost interest, and soon after I'd also stopped going to church. Beatrice was with me, constantly, and no gatherings or ceremonies could bring me any closer to Her. I knew Daniel disapproved of this attitude, but he didn't lecture me about it, and my parents had accepted my decision without any fuss. If Rachel thought I was some kind of apostate, that was her problem.

The priest said, "Which of you brings a bridge to this marriage?"

Daniel said, "I do." In the Transitional ceremony they no longer asked this; it was really no one else's business—and in a way the question was almost sacrilegious. Still, Deep Church theologians had explained away greater doctrinal inconsistencies than this, so who was I to argue?

"Do you, Daniel and Agnes, solemnly declare that this bridge will be the bond of your union until death, to be shared with no other person?"

They replied together, "We solemnly declare."

"Do you solemnly declare that as you share this bridge, so shall you share every joy and every burden of marriage—equally?"

"We solemnly declare."

My mind wandered; I thought of Lena's parents. Maybe one of the family's children was adopted. Lena and I had managed to sneak away to the boat three times so far, early in the evenings while my parents were still out. We'd done things I'd never done with anyone else, but I still hadn't had the courage to ask her anything so personal.

Suddenly the priest was saying, "In the eyes of God, you are one now." My father started weeping softly. As Daniel and Agnes kissed, I felt a surge of contradictory emotions. I'd miss Daniel, but I was glad that I'd finally have a chance to live apart from him. And I wanted him to be happy—I was jealous of his happiness already—but at the same time, the thought of marrying someone like Agnes filled me with claustrophobia. She was kind, devout, and generous. She and Daniel would treat each other, and their children, well. But neither of them would present the slightest challenge to the other's most cherished beliefs.

This recipe for harmony terrified me. Not least because I was afraid that Beatrice approved, and wanted me to follow it myself.

~w~

LENA PUT her hand over mine and pushed my fingers deeper into her, gasping. We were sitting on my bunk, face to face, my legs stretched out flat, hers arching over them.

She slid the palm of her other hand over my penis. I bent forward and kissed her, moving my thumb over the place she'd shown me, and her shudder ran through both of us.

"Martin?"

"What?"

She stroked me with one fingertip; somehow it was far better than having her whole hand wrapped around me.

"Do you want to come inside me?"

I shook my head.

"Why not?"

She kept moving her finger, tracing the same line; I could barely think. *Why not?* "You might get pregnant."

She laughed. "Don't be stupid. I can control that. You'll learn, too. It's just a matter of experience."

I said, "I'll use my tongue. You liked that."

"I did. But I want something more now. And you do, too. I can tell." She smiled imploringly. "It'll be nice for both of us, I promise. Nicer than anything you've done in your life."

"Don't bet on it."

Lena made a sound of disbelief, and ran her thumb around the base of my penis. "I can tell you haven't put this inside anyone before. But that's nothing to be ashamed of."

"Who said I was ashamed?"

She nodded gravely. "All right. Frightened."

I pulled my hand free, and banged my head on the bunk above us. Daniel's old bunk.

Lena reached up and put her hand on my cheek.

I said, "I can't. We're not married."

She frowned. "I heard you'd given up on all that."

"All what?"

"Religion."

"Then you were misinformed."

Lena said, "This is what the Angels made our bodies to do. How can there be anything sinful in that?" She ran her hand down my neck, over my chest.

"But the bridge is meant to…" *What?* All the Scriptures said was that it was meant to unite men and women, equally. And the Scriptures said

God couldn't tell women and men apart, but in the Deep Church, in the sight of God, the priest had just made Daniel claim priority. So why should I care what any priest thought?

I said, "All right."

"Are you sure?"

"Yes." I took her face in my hands and started kissing her. After a while, she reached down and guided me in. The shock of pleasure almost made me come, but I stopped myself somehow. When the risk of that had lessened, we wrapped our arms around each other and rocked slowly back and forth.

It wasn't better than my Drowning, but it was so much like it that it had to be blessed by Beatrice. And as we moved in each other's arms, I grew determined to ask Lena to marry me. She was intelligent and strong. She questioned everything. It didn't matter that she was a Firmlander; we could meet halfway, we could live in Ferez.

I felt myself ejaculate. "I'm sorry."

Lena whispered, "That's all right, that's all right. Just keep moving."

I was still hard; that had never happened before. I could feel her muscles clenching and releasing rhythmically, in time with our motion, and her slow exhalations. Then she cried out, and dug her fingers into my back. I tried to slide partly out of her again, but it was impossible, she was holding me too tightly. This was it. There was no going back.

Now I was afraid. "I've never—" Tears were welling up in my eyes; I tried to shake them away.

"I know. And I know it's frightening." She embraced me more tightly. "Just feel it, though. Isn't it wonderful?"

I was hardly aware of my motionless penis anymore, but there was liquid fire flowing through my groin, waves of pleasure spreading deeper. I said, "Yes. Is it like that for you?"

"It's different. But it's just as good. You'll find out for yourself, soon enough."

"I hadn't been thinking that far ahead," I confessed.

Lena giggled. "You've got a whole new life in front of you, Martin. You don't know what you've been missing."

She kissed me, then started pulling away. I cried out in pain, and she stopped. "I'm sorry. I'll take it slowly." I reached down to touch the place where we were joined; there was a trickle of blood escaping from the base of my penis.

Lena said, "You're not going to faint on me, are you?"

"Don't be stupid." I did feel queasy, though. "What if I'm not ready? What if I can't do it?"

"Then I'll lose my hold in a few hundred tau. The Angels weren't completely stupid."

I ignored this blasphemy, though it wasn't just any Angel who'd designed our bodies—it was Beatrice Herself. I said, "Just promise you won't use a knife."

"That's not funny. That really happens to people."

"I know." I kissed her shoulder. "I think—"

Lena straightened her legs slightly, and I felt the core break free inside me. Blood flowed warmly from my groin, but the pain had changed from a threat of damage to mere tenderness; my nervous system no longer spanned the lesion. I asked Lena, "Do you feel it? Is it part of you?"

"Not yet. It takes a while for the connections to form." She ran her fingers over my lips. "Can I stay inside you, until they have?"

I nodded happily. I hardly cared about the sensations anymore; it was just contemplating the miracle of being able to give a part of my body to Lena that was wonderful. I'd studied the physiological details long ago, everything from the exchange of nutrients to the organ's independent immune system—and I knew that Beatrice had used many of the same techniques for the bridge as She'd used with gestating embryos—but to witness Her ingenuity so dramatically at work in my own flesh was both shocking and intensely moving. Only giving birth could bring me closer to Her than this.

When we finally separated, though, I wasn't entirely prepared for the sight of what emerged. "Oh, that is disgusting!"

Lena shook her head, laughing. "New ones always look a bit... encrusted. Most of that stuff will wash away, and the rest will fall off in a few kilotau."

I bunched up the sheet to find a clean spot, then dabbed at my—her—penis. My newly formed vagina had stopped bleeding, but it was finally dawning on me just how much mess we'd made. "I'm going to have to wash this before my parents get back. I can put it out to dry in the morning, after they're gone, but if I don't wash it now they'll smell it."

We cleaned ourselves enough to put on shorts, then Lena helped me carry the sheet up onto the deck and drape it in the water from the laundry hooks. The fibers in the sheet would use nutrients in the water to power the self-cleaning process.

The docks appeared deserted; most of the boats nearby belonged to people who'd come for the wedding. I'd told my parents I was too tired to stay on at the celebrations; tonight they'd continue until dawn, though Daniel and Agnes would probably leave by midnight. To do what Lena and I had just done.

"Martin? Are you shivering?"

There was nothing to be gained by putting it off. Before whatever courage I had could desert me, I said, "Will you marry me?"

"Very funny. Oh—" Lena took my hand. "I'm sorry, I never know when you're joking."

I said, "We've exchanged the bridge. It doesn't matter that we weren't married first, but it would make things easier if we went along with convention."

"Martin—"

"Or we could just live together, if that's what you want. I don't care. We're already married in the eyes of Beatrice."

Lena bit her lip. "I don't want to live with you."

"I could move to Mitar. I could get a job."

Lena shook her head, still holding my hand. She said firmly, "No. You knew, before we did anything, what it would and wouldn't mean. You don't want to marry me, and I don't want to marry you. So snap out of it."

I pulled my hand free, and sat down on the deck. *What had I done?* I'd thought I'd had Beatrice's blessing, I'd thought this was all in Her plan...but I'd just been fooling myself.

Lena sat beside me. "What are you worried about? Your parents finding out?"

"Yes." That was the least of it, but it seemed pointless trying to explain the truth. I turned to her. "When could we—?"

"Not for about ten days. And sometimes it's longer after the first time."

I'd known as much, but I'd hoped her experience might contradict my theoretical knowledge. *Ten days.* We'd both be gone by then.

Lena said, "What do you think, you can never get married now? How many marriages do you imagine involve the bridge one of the partners was born with?"

"Nine out of ten. Unless they're both women."

Lena gave me a look that hovered between tenderness and incredulity. "My estimate is about one in five."

I shook my head. "I don't care. We've exchanged the bridge, we have to be together." Lena's expression hardened, then so did my resolve. "Or I have to get it back."

"Martin, that's ridiculous. You'll find another lover soon enough, and then you won't even know what you were worried about. Or maybe you'll fall in love with a nice Deep Church boy, and then you'll both be glad you've been spared the trouble of getting rid of the extra bridge."

"Yeah? Or maybe he'll just be disgusted that I couldn't wait until I really *was* doing it for him!"

Lena groaned, and stared up at the sky. "Did I say something before about the Angels getting things right? Ten thousand years without bodies, and they thought they were qualified—"

I cut her off angrily. "Don't be so fucking blasphemous! Beatrice knew exactly what She was doing. If we mess it up, that's our fault!"

Lena said, matter-of-factly, "In ten years' time, there'll be a pill you'll be able to take to keep the bridge from being passed, and another pill to make it pass when it otherwise wouldn't. We'll win control of our bodies back from the Angels, and start doing exactly what we like with them."

"That's sick. That really is sick."

I stared at the deck, suffocating in misery. *This was what I'd wanted, wasn't it? A lover who was the very opposite of Daniel's sweet, pious Agnes?*

Except that in my fantasies, we'd always had a lifetime to debate our philosophical differences. Not one night to be torn apart by them.

I had nothing to lose, now. I told Lena about my Drowning. She didn't laugh; she listened in silence.

I said, "Do you believe me?"

"Of course." She hesitated. "But have you ever wondered if there might be another explanation for the way you felt, in the water that night? You were starved of oxygen—"

"People are starved of oxygen all the time. Freelander kids spend half their lives trying to stay underwater longer than the last time."

Lena nodded. "Sure. But that's not quite the same, is it? You were pushed beyond the time you could have stayed under by sheer willpower. And…you were cued, you were told what to expect."

"That's not true. Daniel never told me what it would be like. I was *surprised* when it happened." I gazed back at her calmly, ready to counter any ingenious hypothesis she came up with. I felt chastened, but almost at peace now. This was what Beatrice had expected of me, before we'd exchanged the bridge: not a dead ceremony in a dead building, but the honesty to tell Lena exactly who she'd be making love with.

We argued almost until sunrise; neither of us convinced the other of anything. Lena helped me drag the clean sheet out of the water and hide it below deck. Before she left, she wrote down the address of a friend's house in Mitar, and a place and time we could meet.

Keeping that appointment was the hardest thing I'd ever done in my life. I spent three solid days ingratiating myself with my Mitar-based cousins, to the point where they would have had to be openly hostile to get out of inviting me to stay with them after the wedding. Once I was there, I had to scheme and lie relentlessly to ensure that I was free of them on the predetermined day.

In a stranger's house, in the middle of the afternoon, Lena and I joylessly reversed everything that had happened between us. I'd been afraid that the act itself might rekindle all my stupid illusions, but when we parted on the street outside, I felt as if I hardly knew her.

I ached even more than I had on the boat, and my groin was palpably swollen, but in a couple of days, I knew, nothing less than a lover's touch or a medical examination would reveal what I'd done.

In the train back to the coast, I replayed the entire sequence of events in my mind, again and again. *How could I have been so wrong?* People always talked about the power of sex to confuse and deceive you, but I'd always believed that was just cheap cynicism. Besides, I hadn't blindly surrendered to sex; I'd thought I'd been guided by Beatrice.

If I could be wrong about that—

I'd have to be more careful. Beatrice always spoke clearly, but I'd have to listen to Her with much more patience and humility.

That was it. That was what She'd wanted me to learn. I finally relaxed and looked out the window, at the blur of forest passing by, another triumph of the ecopoiesis. If I needed proof that there was always another chance, it was all around me now. The Angels had traveled as far from God as anyone could travel, and yet God had turned around and given them Covenant.

4

I WAS nineteen when I returned to Mitar, to study at the city's university. Originally, I'd planned to specialize in the ecopoiesis—and to study much closer to home—but in the end I'd had to accept the nearest thing on offer, geographically and intellectually: working with Barat, a Firmlander biologist whose real interest was native microfauna. "Angelic technology is a fascinating subject in its own right," he told me. "But we can't hope to work backward and decipher terrestrial evolution from anything the Angels created. The best we can do is try to understand what Covenant's own biosphere was like, before we arrived and disrupted it."

I managed to persuade him to accept a compromise: my thesis would involve the impact of the ecopoiesis on the native microfauna. That would give me an excuse to study the Angels' inventions, alongside the drab unicellular creatures that had inhabited Covenant for the last billion years.

"The impact of the ecopoiesis" was far too broad a subject, of course; with Barat's help, I narrowed it down to one particular unresolved question. There had long been geological evidence that the surface waters of the ocean had become both more alkaline, and less oxygenated, as new species shifted the balance of dissolved gases. Some native species must have retreated from the wave of change, and perhaps some had been wiped out completely, but there was a thriving population of zooytes in the upper layers at present. So had they been there all along, adapting *in situ*? Or had they migrated from somewhere else?

Mitar's distance from the coast was no real handicap in studying the ocean; the university mounted regular expeditions, and I had plenty of library and lab work to do before embarking on anything so obvious as gathering living samples in their natural habitat. What's more, river water, and even rainwater, was teeming with closely related species, and since it was possible that these were the reservoirs from which the "ravaged" ocean had been re-colonized, I had plenty of subjects worth studying close at hand.

Barat set high standards, but he was no tyrant, and his other students made me feel welcome. I was homesick, but not morbidly so, and I took a kind of giddy pleasure from the vivid dreams and underlying sense of disorientation that living on land induced in me. I wasn't exactly fulfilling my childhood ambition to uncover the secrets of the Angels—and I had fewer opportunities than I'd hoped to get side-tracked on the ecopoiesis itself—but once I started delving into the minutiae of Covenant's original, wholly undesigned biochemistry, it turned out to be complex and elegant enough to hold my attention.

I was only miserable when I let myself think about sex. I didn't want to end up like Daniel, so seeking out another Drowned person to marry was the last thing on my mind. But I couldn't face the prospect of repeating my mistake with Lena; I had no intention of becoming physically intimate with anyone unless we were already close enough for me to tell them about the most important thing in my life. But that wasn't the order in which things happened, here. After a few humiliating attempts to swim against the current, I gave up on the whole idea, and threw myself into my work instead.

Of course, it *was* possible to socialize at Mitar University without actually exchanging bridges with anyone. I joined an informal discussion group on Angelic culture, which met in a small room in the students' building every tenth night—just like the old Prayer Group, though I was under no illusion that this one would be stacked with believers. It hardly needed to be. The Angels' legacy could be analyzed perfectly well without reference to Beatrice's divinity. The Scriptures were written long after the Crossing by people of a simpler age; there was no reason to treat them as infallible. If non-believers could shed some light on any aspect of the past, I had no grounds for rejecting their insights.

"It's obvious that only one faction came to Covenant!" That was Céline, an anthropologist, a woman so much like Lena that I had to make a conscious effort to remind myself, every time I set eyes on her, that nothing could ever happen between us. "*We're* not so homogeneous that we'd all choose to travel to another planet and assume a new physical form, whatever cultural forces might drive one small group to do that. So why should the Angels have been unanimous? The other factions must still be living in the Immaterial Cities, on Earth, and on other planets."

"Then why haven't they contacted us? In twenty thousand years, you'd think they'd drop in and say hello once or twice." David was a mathematician, a Freelander from the southern ocean.

Céline replied, "The attitude of the Angels who came here wouldn't have encouraged visitors. If all we have is a story of the Crossing in which Beatrice persuades every last Angel in existence to give up immortality—a version that simply erases everyone else from history—that doesn't suggest much of a desire to remain in touch."

A woman I didn't know interjected, "It might not have been so clear-cut from the start, though. There's evidence of settler-level technology being deployed for more than three thousand years after the Crossing, long after it was needed for the ecopoiesis. New species continued to be created, engineering projects continued to use advanced materials and energy sources. But then in less than a century, it all stopped. The Scriptures merge three separate decisions into one: renouncing immortality, migrating to Covenant, and abandoning the technology that might have provided an escape route if anyone changed their mind. But we *know* it didn't happen like that. Three thousand years after the Crossing, something changed. The whole experiment suddenly became irreversible."

These speculations would have outraged the average pious Freelander, let alone the average Drowned one, but I listened calmly, even entertaining the possibility that some of them could be true. The love of Beatrice was the only fixed point in my cosmology; everything else was open to debate.

Still, sometimes the debate was hard to take. One night, David joined us straight from a seminar of physicists. What he'd heard from the speaker was unsettling enough, but he'd already moved beyond it to an even less palatable conclusion.

"Why did the Angels choose mortality? After ten thousand years without death, why did they throw away all the glorious possibilities ahead of them, to come and die like animals on this ball of mud?" I had to bite my tongue to keep from replying to his rhetorical question: because God is the only source of eternal life, and Beatrice showed them that all they really had was a cheap parody of that divine gift.

David paused, then offered his own answer—which was itself a kind of awful parody of Beatrice's truth. "Because they discovered that they weren't immortal, after all. They discovered that *no one can be.* We've always known, as they must have, that the universe is finite in space and time. It's destined to collapse eventually: 'the stars will fall from the sky.' But it's easy to *imagine* ways around that." He laughed. "We don't know enough physics yet, ourselves, to rule out anything. I've just heard an extraordinary woman from Tia talk about coding our minds into waves that would orbit the shrinking universe so rapidly that we could think *an infinite number of thoughts* before everything was crushed!" David grinned joyfully at the sheer audacity of this notion. I thought primly: what blasphemous nonsense.

Then he spread his arms and said, "Don't you see, though? If the Angels *had* pinned their hopes on something like that—some ingenious trick that would keep them from sharing the fate of the universe—*but then they finally gained enough knowledge to rule out every last escape route*, it would have had a profound effect on them. Some small faction could then have decided that since they were mortal after all, they might as well embrace the inevitable, and come to terms with it in the way their ancestors had. In the flesh."

Céline said thoughtfully, "And the Beatrice myth puts a religious gloss on the whole thing, but that might be nothing but a *post hoc* reinterpretation of a purely secular revelation."

This was too much; I couldn't remain silent. I said, "If Covenant really was founded by a pack of terminally depressed atheists, what could have changed their minds? Where did the desire to impose a '*post hoc reinterpretation*' *come from?* If the revelation that brought the Angels here was 'secular', why isn't the whole planet still secular today?"

Someone said snidely, "Civilization collapsed. What do you expect?"

I opened my mouth to respond angrily, but Céline got in first. "No, Martin has a point. If David's right, the rise of religion needs to be explained more urgently than ever. And I don't think anyone's in a position to do that yet."

Afterward, I lay awake thinking about all the other things I should have said, all the other objections I should have raised. (And thinking about Céline.) Theology aside, the whole dynamics of the group was starting to get under my skin; maybe I'd be better off spending my time in the lab, impressing Barat with my dedication to his pointless fucking microbes.

Or maybe I'd be better off at home. I could help out on the boat; my parents weren't young anymore, and Daniel had his own family to look after.

I climbed out of bed and started packing, but halfway through I changed my mind. I didn't really want to abandon my studies. And I'd known all along what the antidote was for all the confusion and resentment I was feeling.

I put my rucksack away, switched off the lamp, lay down, closed my eyes, and asked Beatrice to grant me peace.

~~~

I WAS woken by someone banging on the door of my room. It was a fellow boarder, a young man I barely knew. He looked extremely tired and irritable, but something was overriding his irritation.

"There's a message for you."

My mother was sick, with an unidentified virus. The hospital was even further away than our home grounds; the trip would take almost three days.

I spent most of the journey praying, but the longer I prayed, the harder it became. I *knew* that it was possible to save my mother's life with one word in the Angels' tongue to Beatrice, but the number of ways in which I could fail, corrupting the purity of the request with my own doubts, my own selfishness, my own complacency, just kept multiplying.

The Angels created nothing in the ecopoiesis that would harm their own mortal incarnations. The native life showed no interest in parasitizing us. But over the millennia, our own DNA had shed viruses. And since Beatrice Herself chose every last base pair, that must have been what She intended. Aging was not enough. Mortal injury was not enough. Death had to come without warning, silent and invisible.

That's what the Scriptures said.

The hospital was a maze of linked hulls. When I finally found the right passageway, the first person I recognized in the distance was Daniel. He was holding his daughter Sophie high in his outstretched arms, smiling up at her. The image dispelled all my fears in an instant; I almost fell to my knees to give thanks.

Then I saw my father. He was seated outside the room, his head in his hands. I couldn't see his face, but I didn't need to. He wasn't anxious, or exhausted. He was crushed.

I approached in a haze of last-minute prayers, though I knew I was asking for the past to be rewritten. Daniel started to greet me as if nothing was wrong, asking about the trip—probably trying to soften the blow—then he registered my expression and put a hand on my shoulder.

He said, "She's with God now."

I brushed past him and walked into the room. My mother's body was lying on the bed, already neatly arranged: arms straightened, eyes closed. Tears ran down my cheeks, angering me. Where had my love been when it might have prevented this? When Beatrice might have heeded it?

Daniel followed me into the room, alone. I glanced back through the doorway and saw Agnes holding Sophie.

"She's with God, Martin." He was beaming at me as if something wonderful had happened.

I said numbly, "She wasn't Drowned." I was almost certain that she hadn't been a believer at all. She'd remained in the Transitional church all her life—but that had long been the way to stay in touch with your friends when you worked on a boat nine days out of ten.

"I prayed with her, before she lost consciousness. She accepted Beatrice into her heart."

I stared at him. Nine years ago he'd been certain: you were Drowned, or you were damned. It was as simple as that. My own conviction had softened long ago; I couldn't believe that Beatrice really was so arbitrary and cruel. But I knew my mother would not only have refused the full-blown ritual; the whole philosophy would have been as nonsensical to her as the mechanics.

"Did she say that? Did she tell you that?"

Daniel shook his head. "But it was clear." Filled with the love of Beatrice, he couldn't stop smiling.

A wave of revulsion passed through me; I wanted to grind his face into the deck. *He didn't care what my mother had believed.* Whatever eased his own pain, whatever put his own doubts to rest, had to be the case. To accept that she was damned—or even just dead, gone, erased—was unbearable; everything else flowed from that. *There was no truth in anything he said, anything he believed. It was all just an expression of his own needs.*

I walked back into the corridor and crouched beside my father. Without looking at me, he put an arm around me and pressed me against his side. I could feel the blackness washing over him, the helplessness, the loss. When I tried to embrace him he just clutched me more tightly, forcing me to be still. I shuddered a few times, then stopped weeping. I closed my eyes and let him hold me.

I was determined to stay there beside him, facing everything he was facing. But after a while, unbidden, the old flame began to glow in the back of my skull: the old warmth, the old peace, the old certainty. Daniel was right, my mother was with God. *How could I have doubted that?* There was no point asking how it had come about; Beatrice's ways were beyond my comprehension. But the one thing I knew firsthand was the strength of Her love.

I didn't move, I didn't free myself from my father's desolate embrace. But I was an impostor now, merely praying for his comfort, interceding from my state of grace. Beatrice had raised me out of the darkness, and I could no longer share his pain.

5

AFTER MY mother's death, my faith kept ceding ground, without ever really wavering. Most of the doctrinal content fell away, leaving behind a core of belief that was a great deal easier to defend. It didn't matter if the Scriptures were superstitious nonsense or the Church was full of fools and hypocrites; Beatrice was still Beatrice, the way the sky was still blue. Whenever I heard debates between atheists and believers, I found myself increasingly on the atheists' side—not because I accepted their conclusion for a moment, but because they were so much more honest than their opponents. Maybe the priests and theologians arguing against them had the same kind of direct, personal experience of God as I did—or maybe not, maybe they just desperately needed to believe. But they never disclosed the true source of their conviction; instead, they just made laughable attempts to "prove" God's existence from the historical record, or from biology, astronomy, or mathematics. Daniel had been right at the age of fifteen—you couldn't prove any such thing—and listening to these people twist logic as they tried made me squirm.

I felt guilty about leaving my father working with a hired hand, and even guiltier when he moved onto Daniel's boat a year later, but I knew how angry it would have made him if he thought I'd abandoned my career for his sake. At times that was the only thing that kept me in Mitar: even when I honestly wanted nothing more than to throw it all in and go back to hauling nets, I was afraid my decision would be misinterpreted.

It took me three years to complete my thesis on the migration of aquatic zooytes in the wake of the ecopoiesis. My original hypothesis, that freshwater species had replenished the upper ocean, turned out to be false. Zooytes had no genes as such, just families of enzymes that re-synthesized each other after cell division, but comparisons of these heritable molecules showed that, rather than rain bringing new life from above, an ocean-dwelling species from a much greater depth had moved steadily closer to the surface, as the Angels' creations drained oxygen from the water. That wouldn't have been much of a surprise, if the same techniques hadn't also shown that several species found in river water were even closer relatives of the surface-dwellers. But those freshwater species weren't anyone's ancestors; they were the newest migrants. Zooytes that had spent a billion years confined to the depths had suddenly been able to survive (and reproduce, and mutate) closer to the surface than ever before, and when they'd stumbled on a mutation that let them thrive in the presence of oxygen, they'd finally been in a position to make use of it. The ecopoiesis might have driven other native organisms into extinction, but the invasion from Earth had enabled this ancient benthic species to mount a long overdue invasion of its own. Unwittingly or not, the Angels had set in motion the sequence of events that had released it from the ocean to colonize the planet.

So I proved myself wrong, earned my degree, and became famous amongst a circle of peers so small that we were all famous to each other anyway. Vast new territories did not open up before me. Anything to do with native biology was rapidly becoming an academic cul-de-sac; I'd always suspected that was how it would be, but I hadn't fought hard enough to end up anywhere else.

For the next three years, I clung to the path of least resistance: assisting Barat with his own research, taking the teaching jobs no one else wanted. Most of Barat's other students moved on to better things, and I found myself increasingly alone in Mitar. But that didn't matter; I had Beatrice.

At the age of twenty-five, I could see my future clearly. While other people deciphered—and built upon—the Angels' legacy, I'd watch from a distance, still messing about with samples of seawater from which all Angelic contaminants had been scrupulously removed.

Finally, when it was almost too late, I made up my mind to jump ship. Barat had been good to me, but he'd never expected loyalty verging on martyrdom. At the end of the year a bi-ecological (native and Angelic) microbiology conference was being held in Tia, possibly the last event of its kind. I had no new results to present, but it wouldn't be hard to find a plausible excuse to attend, and it would be the ideal place to lobby for a new position. My great zooyte discovery hadn't been entirely lost on the wider community of biologists; I could try to rekindle the memory of it. I doubted there'd be much point offering to sleep with anyone; ethical qualms aside, my bridge had probably rusted into place.

Then again, maybe I'd get lucky. Maybe I'd stumble on a fellow Drowned Freelander who'd ended up in a position of power, and all I'd have to do was promise that my work would be for the greater glory of Beatrice.

~~~

TIA WAS a city of ten million people on the east coast. New towers stood side-by-side with empty structures from the time of the Angels, giant gutted machines that might have played a role in the ecopoiesis. I was too old and proud to gawk like a child, but for all my provincial sophistication I wanted to. These domes and cylinders were twenty times older than the illustrations tattooed into the ceiling of the monastery back home. They bore no images of Beatrice; nothing of the Angels did. But why would they? They predated Her death.

The university, on the outskirts of Tia, was a third the size of Mitar itself. An underground train ringed the campus; the students I rode with eyed my unstylish clothes with disbelief. I left my luggage in the dormitory and headed straight for the conference center. Barat had chosen to stay behind; maybe he hadn't wanted to witness the public burial of his field. That made things easier for me; I'd be free to hunt for a new career without rubbing his face in it.

Late additions to the conference program were listed on a screen by the main entrance. I almost walked straight past the display; I'd already decided which talks I'd be attending. But three steps away, a title I'd glimpsed in passing assembled itself in my mind's eye, and I had to backtrack to be sure I hadn't imagined it.

Carla Reggia: "Euphoric Effects of *Z/12/80* Excretions"

I stood there laughing with disbelief. I recognized the speaker and her co-workers by name, though I'd never had a chance to meet them. If this wasn't a hoax...what had they done? Dried it, smoked it, and tried writing that up as research? *Z/12/80* was one of "my" zooytes, one of the escapees from the ocean; the air and water of Tia were swarming with it. If its excretions were euphoric, the whole city would be in a state of bliss.

I knew, then and there, what they'd discovered. I knew it, long before I admitted it to myself. I went to the talk with my head full of jokes about neglected culture flasks full of psychotropic breakdown products, but for two whole days, I'd been steeling myself for the truth, finding ways in which it didn't have to matter.

Z/12/80, Carla explained, excreted among its waste products an amine that was able to bind to receptors in our Angel-crafted brains. Since it had been shown by other workers (no one recognized me; no one gave me so much as a glance) that *Z/12/80* hadn't existed at the time of the ecopoiesis, this interaction was almost certainly undesigned, and unanticipated. "It's up to the archaeologists and neurochemists to determine what role, if any, the arrival of this substance in the environment might have played in the collapse of early settlement culture. But for the past fifteen to eighteen thousand years, we've been swimming in it. Since we still exhibit such a wide spectrum of moods, we're probably able to compensate for its presence by down-regulating the secretion of the endogenous molecule that was designed to bind to the same receptor. That's just an educated guess, though. Exactly what the effects might be from individual to individual, across the range of doses that might be experienced under a variety of conditions, is clearly going to be a matter of great interest to investigators with appropriate expertise."

I told myself that I felt no disquiet. Beatrice acted on the world through the laws of nature; I'd stopped believing in supernatural miracles long ago. The fact that someone had now identified the way in which She'd acted on *me*, that night in the water, changed nothing.

I pressed ahead with my attempts to get recruited. Everyone at the conference was talking about Carla's discovery, and when people finally made the connection with my own work their eyes stopped glazing over halfway through my spiel. In the next three days, I received seven offers—all involving research into zooyte biochemistry. There was no question, now, of side-stepping the issue, of escaping into the wider world of Angelic biology. One man even came right out and said to me: "You're a Freelander, and you know that the ancestors of *Z/12/80* live in much greater numbers in the ocean. Don't you think *oceanic* exposure is going to be the key to understanding this?" He laughed. "I mean, you swam in the stuff as a child, didn't you? And you seem to have come through unscathed."

"Apparently."

On my last night in Tia, I couldn't sleep. I stared into the blackness of the room, watching the gray sparks dance in front of me. (Contaminants in the aqueous humor? Electrical noise in the retina? I'd heard the explanation once, but I could no longer remember it.)

I prayed to Beatrice in the Angels' tongue; I could still feel Her presence, as strongly as ever. The effect clearly wasn't just a matter of dosage, or trans-cutaneous absorption; merely swimming in the ocean at the right depth wasn't enough to make anyone feel Drowned. But in combination with the stress of oxygen starvation, and all the psychological build-up Daniel had provided, the jolt of zooyte piss must have driven certain neuroendocrine subsystems into new territory—or old territory, by a new path. *Peace, joy, contentment, the feeling of being loved* weren't exactly unknown emotions. But by short-circuiting the brain's usual practice of summoning those feelings only on occasions when there was a reason for them, I'd been "blessed with the love of Beatrice." I'd found happiness on demand.

And I still possessed it. That was the eeriest part. Even as I lay there in the dark, on the verge of reasoning everything I'd been living for out of existence, my ability to work the machinery was so ingrained that I felt as loved, as blessed as ever.

Maybe Beatrice was offering me another chance, making it clear that She'd still forgive this blasphemy and welcome me back. But why did I believe that there was anyone there to "forgive me"? You couldn't reason your way to God; there was only faith. And I knew, now, that the source of my faith was a meaningless accident, an unanticipated side-effect of the ecopoiesis.

I still had a choice. I could, still, decide that the love of Beatrice was immune to all logic, a force beyond understanding, untouched by evidence of any kind.

No, I couldn't. I'd been making exceptions for Her for too long. Everyone lived with double standards—but I'd already pushed mine as far as they'd go.

I started laughing and weeping at the same time. It was almost unimaginable: all the millions of people who'd been misled the same way. All because of the zooytes, and...what? One Freelander, diving for pleasure, who'd stumbled on a strange new experience? Then tens of thousands more repeating it, generation after generation—until one vulnerable man or woman had been driven to invest the novelty with meaning. Someone who'd needed so badly to feel loved and protected that the illusion of a real presence behind the raw emotion had been impossible to resist. Or who'd desperately wanted to believe that—in spite of the Angels' discovery that they, too, were mortal—death could still be defeated.

I was lucky: I'd been born in an era of moderation. I hadn't killed in the name of Beatrice. I hadn't suffered for my faith. I had no doubt that I'd been far happier for the last fifteen years than I would have been if I'd told Daniel to throw his rope and weights overboard without me.

But that didn't change the fact that the heart of it all had been a lie.

~w~

I WOKE at dawn, my head pounding, after just a few kilotau's sleep. I closed my eyes and searched for Her presence, as I had a thousand times before. *When I woke in the morning and looked into my heart, She was there without fail, offering me strength and guidance. When I lay in bed at night, I feared nothing, because I knew She was watching over me.*

There was nothing. She was gone.

I stumbled out of bed, feeling like a murderer, wondering how I'd ever live with what I'd done.

~w~

I TURNED down every offer I'd received at the conference, and stayed on in Mitar. It took Barat and me two years to establish our own research group to examine the effects of the zooamine, and nine more for us to elucidate the full extent of its activity in the brain. Our new recruits all had solid backgrounds in neurochemistry, and they did better work than I did, but when Barat retired I found myself the spokesperson for the group.

The initial discovery had been largely ignored outside the scientific community; for most people, it hardly mattered whether our brain chemistry matched the Angels' original design, or had been altered fifteen thousand years ago by some unexpected contaminant. But when the Mitar zooamine group began publishing detailed accounts of the biochemistry of religious experience, the public at large rediscovered the subject with a vengeance.

The university stepped up security, and despite death threats and a number of unpleasant incidents with stone-throwing protesters, no one was hurt. We were flooded with requests from broadcasters—though most were predicated on the notion that the group was morally obliged to "face its critics", rather than the broadcasters being morally obliged to offer us a chance to explain our work, calmly and clearly, without being shouted down by enraged zealots.

I learned to avoid the zealots, but the obscurantists were harder to dodge. I'd expected opposition from the Churches—defending the faith was their job, after all—but some of the most intellectually bankrupt responses came from academics in other disciplines. In one televised debate, I was confronted by a Deep Church priest, a Transitional theologian, a devotee of the ocean god Marni, and an anthropologist from Tia.

"This discovery has no real bearing on any belief system," the anthropologist explained serenely. "All truth is local. Inside every Deep Church in Ferez, Beatrice *is* the daughter of God, and we're the mortal incarnations of the Angels, who traveled here from Earth. In a coastal village a few milliradians south, Marni is the supreme creator, and it was She who gave birth to us, right here. Going one step further and moving from the spiritual domain to the scientific might appear to 'negate' certain spiritual truths...but equally, moving from the scientific domain to the spiritual demonstrates the same limitations. We are nothing but the stories we tell ourselves, and no one story is greater than another." He smiled beneficently, the expression of a parent only too happy to give all his squabbling children an equal share in some disputed toy.

I said, "How many cultures do you imagine share your definition of 'truth'? How many people do you think would be content to worship a God who consisted of literally nothing but the fact of their belief?" I turned to the Deep Church priest. "Is that enough for you?"

"Absolutely not!" She glowered at the anthropologist. "While I have the greatest respect for my brother here," she gestured at the devotee of

Marni, "you can't draw a line around those people who've been lucky enough to be raised in the true faith, and then suggest that *Beatrice's* infinite power and love is confined to that group of people...like some collection of folk songs!"

The devotee respectfully agreed. Marni had created the most distant stars, along with the oceans of Covenant. Perhaps some people called Her by another name, but if everyone on this planet was to die tomorrow, She would still be Marni: unchanged, undiminished.

The anthropologist responded soothingly, "Of course. But in context, and with a wider perspective—"

"I'm perfectly happy with a God who resides within us," offered the Transitional theologian. "It seems...*immodest* to expect more. And instead of fretting uselessly over these ultimate questions, we should confine ourselves to matters of a suitably human scale."

I turned to him. "So you're actually indifferent as to whether an infinitely powerful and loving being created everything around you, and plans to welcome you into Her arms after death...or the universe is a piece of quantum noise that will eventually vanish and erase us all?"

He sighed heavily, as if I was asking him to perform some arduous physical feat just by responding. "I can summon no enthusiasm for these issues."

Later, the Deep Church priest took me aside and whispered, "Frankly, we're all very grateful that you've debunked that awful cult of the Drowned. They're a bunch of fundamentalist hicks, and the Church will be better off without them. But you mustn't make the mistake of thinking that your work has anything to do with ordinary, civilized believers!"

～w

I stood at the back of the crowd that had gathered on the beach near the rock pool, to listen to the two old men who were standing ankle-deep in the milky water. It had taken me four days to get here from Mitar, but when I'd heard reports of a zooyte bloom washing up on the remote north coast, I'd had to come and see the results for myself. The zooamine group had actually recruited an anthropologist for such occasions—one who could cope with such taxing notions as the existence of objective reality, and a biochemical substrate for human thought—but Céline was only with us for part of the year, and right now she was away doing other research.

"This is an ancient, sacred place!" one man intoned, spreading his arms to take in the pool. "You need only observe the shape of it to understand that. It concentrates the energy of the stars, and the sun, and the ocean."

"The focus of power is there, by the inlet," the other added, gesturing at a point where the water might have come up to his calves. "Once, I wandered too close. I was almost lost in the great dream of the ocean, when my friend here came and rescued me!"

These men weren't devotees of Marni, or members of any other formal religion. As far as I'd been able to tell from old news reports, the blooms occurred every eight or ten years, and the two had set themselves up as "custodians" of the pool more than fifty years ago. Some local villagers treated the whole thing as a joke, but others revered the old men. And for a small fee, tourists and locals alike could be chanted over, then splashed with the potent brew. Evaporation would have concentrated the trapped waters of the bloom; for a few days, before the zooytes ran out of nutrients and died *en masse* in a cloud of hydrogen sulphide, the amine would be present in levels as high as in any of our laboratory cultures back in Mitar.

As I watched people lining up for the ritual, I found myself trying to downplay the possibility that anyone could be seriously affected by it. It was broad daylight, no one feared for their life, and the old men's pantheistic gobbledygook carried all the gravitas of the patter of streetside scam merchants. Their marginal sincerity, and the money changing hands, would be enough to undermine the whole thing. This was a tourist trap, not a life-altering experience.

When the chanting was done, the first customer knelt at the edge of the pool. One of the custodians filled a small metal cup with water and threw it in her face. After a moment, she began weeping with joy. I moved closer, my stomach tightening. *It was what she'd known was expected of her, nothing more. She was playing along, not wanting to spoil the fun—like the good sports who pretended to have their thoughts read by a carnival psychic.*

Next, the custodians chanted over a young man. He began swaying giddily even before they touched him with the water; when they did, he broke into sobs of relief that racked his whole body.

I looked back along the queue. There was a young girl standing third in line now, looking around apprehensively; she could not have been more than nine or ten. Her father (I presumed) was standing behind her, with his hand against her back, as if gently propelling her forward.

I lost all interest in playing anthropologist. I forced my way through the crowd until I reached the edge of the pool, then turned to address the people in the queue. "These men are frauds! There's nothing mysterious going on here. I can tell you exactly what's in the water: it's just a drug, a natural substance given out by creatures that are trapped here when the waves retreat."

I squatted down and prepared to dip my hand in the pool. One of the custodians rushed forward and grabbed my wrist. He was an old man, I could have done what I liked, but some people were already jeering, and I didn't want to scuffle with him and start a riot. I backed away from him, then spoke again.

"I've studied this drug for more than ten years, at Mitar University. It's present in water all over the planet. We drink it, we bathe in it, we swim in it every day. But it's concentrated here, and if you don't understand what you're doing when you use it, that misunderstanding can harm you!"

The custodian who'd grabbed my wrist started laughing. "The dream of the ocean is powerful, yes, but we don't need your advice on that! For fifty years, my friend and I have studied its lore, until we were strong enough to *stand* in the sacred water!" He gestured at his leathery feet; I didn't doubt that his circulation had grown poor enough to limit the dose to a tolerable level.

He stretched out his sinewy arm at me. "So fuck off back to Mitar, Inlander! Fuck off back to your books and your dead machinery! What would you know about the sacred mysteries? *What would you know about the ocean?*"

I said, "I think you're out of your depth."

I stepped into the pool. He started wailing about my unpurified body polluting the water, but I brushed past him. The other custodian came after me, but though my feet were soft after years of wearing shoes, I ignored the sharp edges of the rocks and kept walking toward the inlet. The zooamine helped. I could feel the old joy, the old peace, the old "love"; it made a powerful anesthetic.

I looked back over my shoulder. The second man had stopped pursuing me; it seemed he honestly feared going any further. I pulled off my shirt, bunched it up, and threw it onto a rock at the side of the pool. Then I waded forward, heading straight for the "focus of power."

The water came up to my knees. I could feel my heart pounding, harder than it had since childhood. People were shouting at me from the edge of the pool—some outraged by my sacrilege, some apparently concerned for my safety in the presence of forces beyond my control. Without turning, I called out at the top of my voice, "There is no 'power' here! There's nothing 'sacred'! There's nothing here but a drug—"

Old habits die hard; I almost prayed first. *Please, Holy Beatrice, don't let me regain my faith.*

I lay down in the water and let it cover my face. My vision turned white; I felt like I was leaving my body. The love of Beatrice flooded into me, and nothing had changed: Her presence was as palpable as ever, as undeniable as ever. I *knew* that I was loved, accepted, forgiven.

I waited, staring into the light, almost expecting a voice, a vision, detailed hallucinations. That had happened to some of the Drowned. How did anyone ever claw their way back to sanity, after that?

But for me, there was only the emotion itself, overpowering but unembellished. It didn't grow monotonous; I could have basked in it for days. But I understood, now, that it said no more about my place in the world than the warmth of sunlight on skin. I'd never mistake it for the touch of a real hand again.

I climbed to my feet and opened my eyes. Violet afterimages danced in front of me. It took a few tau for me to catch my breath, and feel steady on my feet again. Then I turned and started wading back toward the shore.

The crowd had fallen silent, though whether it was in disgust or begrudging respect I had no idea.

I said, "It's not just here. It's not just in the water. It's part of us now; it's in our blood." I was still half-blind; I couldn't see whether anyone was listening. "But as long as you know that, you're already free. As long as you're ready to face the possibility that everything that makes your spirits soar, everything that lifts you up and fills your heart with joy, *everything that makes your life worth living*…is a lie, is corruption, is meaningless—then you can never be enslaved."

They let me walk away unharmed. I turned back to watch as the line formed again; the girl wasn't in the queue.

I WOKE with a start, from the same old dream.

I was lowering my mother into the water from the back of the boat. Her hands were tied, her feet weighted. She was afraid, but she'd put her trust in me. "You'll bring me up safely, won't you Martin?"

I nodded reassuringly. But once she'd vanished beneath the waves, I thought: What am I doing? I don't believe in this shit any more.

So I took out a knife and started cutting through the rope—

I brought my knees up to my chest, and crouched on the unfamiliar bed in the darkness. I was in a small town on the railway line, halfway back to Mitar. Halfway between midnight and dawn.

I dressed, and made my way out of the hostel. The center of town was deserted, and the sky was thick with stars. Just like home. In Mitar, everything vanished in a fog of light.

All three of the stars cited by various authorities as the Earth's sun were above the horizon. If they weren't all mistakes, perhaps I'd live to see a telescope's image of the planet itself. But the prospect of seeking contact with the Angels—if there really was a faction still out there, somewhere—left me cold. I shouted silently up at the stars: *Your degenerate offspring don't need your help! Why should we rejoin you? We're going to surpass you!*

I sat down on the steps at the edge of the square and covered my face. Bravado didn't help. Nothing helped. Maybe if I'd grown up facing the truth, I would have been stronger. But when I woke in the night, knowing that my mother was simply dead, that everyone I'd ever loved would follow her, that I'd vanish into the same emptiness myself, it was like being buried alive. It was like being back in the water, bound and weighted, with the certain knowledge that there was no one to haul me up.

Someone put a hand on my shoulder. I looked up, startled. It was a man about my own age. His manner wasn't threatening; if anything, he looked slightly wary of me.

He said, "Do you need a roof? I can let you into the Church if you want." There was a trolley packed with cleaning equipment a short distance behind him.

I shook my head. "It's not that cold." I was too embarrassed to explain that I had a perfectly good room nearby. "Thanks."

As he was walking away, I called after him, "Do you believe in God?"

He stopped and stared at me for a while, as if he was trying to decide if this was a trick question—as if I might have been hired by the local parishioners to vet him for theological soundness. Or maybe he just wanted to be diplomatic with anyone desperate enough to be sitting in the town square in the middle of the night, begging a stranger for reassurance.

He shook his head. "As a child I did. Not anymore. It was a nice idea…but it made no sense." He eyed me skeptically, still unsure of my motives.

I said, "Then isn't life unbearable?"

He laughed. "Not all the time."

He went back to his trolley, and started wheeling it toward the Church.

I stayed on the steps, waiting for dawn.